PEACOCK CRIES

at the Three Gorges

by
Hong Ying

Translated by
Mark Smith and Henry Zhao

MARION BOYARS
LONDON · NEW YORK

First published in Great Britain and in the USA in 2004 by
MARION BOYARS PUBLISHERS LTD
24 Lacy Road, London SW15 1NL
www.marionboyars.co.uk

Distributed in Australia and New Zealand by Peribo Pty Ltd
58 Beaumont Road, Kuring-gai, NSW 2080

Printed in 2004
10 9 8 7 6 5 4 3 2 1
© Hong Ying, 2003, 2004

First published by Unitas Publishing Co Ltd, Taiwan, 2003 as
Kongque de Jiaohan

© This translation from the Chinese by Mark Smith and Henry Zhao 2004
All rights reserved.

A CIP catalogue record for this book is available from the British Library.
A CIP catalog record for this book is available from the Library of Congress

ISBN 0-7145-3100-6

The publishers would like to thank the Arts Council of England
for assistance with the translation of this book.

Set in Sabon 11.5/14pt
Printed in England by Bookmarque Ltd

CONTENTS

Out of the window,
I saw how the planets gathered
Like the leaves themselves
Turning in the wind.
I saw how the night came,
Came striding like the colour of the heavy hemlocks
I felt afraid.
And I remembered the cry of the peacocks.

Wallace Stevens
Domination of Black

Preface

When I was six even dogs wouldn't keep me company. My skin was sallow and my face gaunt. My hair was so thin there wasn't enough of it to make a pony-tail. I was so slow-witted even an old beggar crossing the road could give me a fright. My mother was very disappointed with me. My older sister took advantage of the chaos of the Cultural Revolution and left the rural area of Wushan County in the Three Gorges region in order to stay for a time at our house in the city of Chongqing. Then one day she fell out with my mother about something or other; in a fit of anger she screamed that she was going to go back to the countryside. Sure enough, the next day she started packing her things.

It was a Sunday. My mother sat in the main room in grim silence while all this was going on. Then, suddenly, just as my sister was about to leave, she said: 'If you're really going to go, you might as well take little Six' – that's me – 'along with you. Take her back to my family in Zhong County.'

Later I realized why my mother had done this.

She'd been trying to palm me off on someone for years, but never quite managed it. How lucky for her that my sister was going back to the countryside! She could show me to various relatives and see if any of them would take a liking to me. My mother never hinted at her plan to get rid of me, but I could sense that she didn't want me, so I wasn't entirely opposed to the idea myself.

It was late spring, so it was already quite warm. We had to travel by steamer. It was the first time I'd been a long way from home. My mother went with us to the little quay. She seemed quite indifferent to our departure. I paid her no attention and my sister would do nothing more than scowl at her. When it was time for us to go our separate ways my mother turned her head and walked away as fast as she could, and my sister pulled me by the hand even faster in the other direction. We had to take a ferry across the Yangtze first, and then we got on the big steamer.

I remember us sitting in the bottom compartment, the bilge. The floor was sheet-iron and one could hear the constant rumble of the engine. The over-crowding was made worse by the fact that virtually all the passengers had brought heavily-laden shoulder-poles. It was the middle of the night before we reached Zhong County. My sister said that since it was so late it was hardly worth while finding a cheap boarding house, even if we just paid for one bed and slept in it together. And so, not without a great deal of effort, she managed to talk the people in the harbour into letting us spend the night on one of the benches on the pontoon. We squashed together, making do with my sister's overcoat as a blanket, till dawn. That morning we took a long-distance bus to the place nearest to the village with a road running through it, and completed the rest of the journey through the mountains by foot. As we meandered along the twisting path, I watched the Yangtze appear and disappear beneath us so many times that I became sick to the back teeth of mountain scenery. After what seemed like an age, I heard what sounded like dogs' barking, and my sister said that we'd arrived.

After delivering me to this place in the middle of nowhere, she stayed a couple of nights and then went back to Wushan. I thought that because the village and Wushan were both by the Yangtze they must be near one another, and that my sister would come and visit me. It was only later when I had learned to read a map that I realized how far away Wushan was. It's at the other end of the Three Gorges. So she'd just dumped me there and gone off without a care in the world!

At the entrance to the village I was to live in there was a stone stronghold on the hillock by the stone steps up the slope. It was made of chipped stone. No one really knew when it had been built. Old folk said it went back to the Ming dynasty. They said that the notorious gangster leader Zhang Xianzhong had fought there against the female barbarian general Qin Liangyu in the seventeenth century. The battle was fierce, and so many were massacred that it caused the Yangtze to turn red with blood. The stone stronghold acted as a kind of sentry post for Qin Liangyu's mountain position. It was built entirely of limestone, but over time it had been eroded by the wind. The

stone roof had completely collapsed, and there were
weeds growing in the cracks between the stones in the
front courtyard. The villagers held their open-air
public meetings there and also used it as a place for
drying grain in the sun and things like that. There
were several scarecrows on each of the four walls,
each with a palm-leaf fan in its hand. The fans
moved as soon as wind blew, which would frighten
off the sparrows who had come to peck the grain.
The old stronghold was next to the pond at the
entrance to the village. You could just see it through
the branches of the trees – the necessary credential
for the village's name, Stronghold.

The first person to put me up was my uncle, my
mother's eldest brother. My older sister married his
eldest son, so he was also my cousin. His wife had
died in the great famine and he had never remarried.
He had three sons and one daughter. I slept in the
same bed as his daughter, whom I called 'Little
sister'. My mother's second oldest brother's house
was connected to my younger older brother's house
– both houses having flat tiled roofs and little
thatched pig-sties built onto the side. Next to the
pigsties were the toilets – a few tree stumps nailed
together with basket-woven wheat-stalks filling in
the gaps.

My arrival caused quite a stir. The whole village
crowded outside my uncle's house to have a look at
this oddity, to see what a young lady from the big
city looked like. It was a rare occurrence indeed for
a relative to return to the village – many had left,
like my mother who had fled to escape an arranged
marriage, but once they'd gone they never came

back. People only made a trip to the city when something utterly catastrophic threatened them if they didn't: the only two people there who had ever done it were my two uncles. Before I was born, my grandmother had fallen critically ill so they had carried her on a stretcher to Chongqing and passed her on to my mother, after which they had turned round and gone straight back.

Everyone was very disappointed with this oddity: all they got to see was a puny little girl, with wispy yellowish hair and eyes full of fear, a girl who wouldn't utter a single word and who was wearing clothes almost as ragged as theirs. I hadn't even brought any presents with me; even countryside people will take a few homemade fried dough twists or some brown sugar when they visit relatives. But I had brought nothing at all. My mother had just wanted to get me out of her sight as quickly as possible; she'd given no thought to such details. It wasn't long before the crowd dispersed.

One day my mother's sister came to collect me from the Stronghold. She didn't live far – all she had to do was go over a couple of mountains and three valleys with small brooks. She didn't look like my mother. She had sleepy eyes, and she was short. She didn't have any children and her husband worked in a small coalmine. She was a little better off than my uncles but she lived in constant fear of her husband being blown up: every so often part of the mine would cave in, or there'd be a gas explosion; in fact dead people were budgeted for when managing a small coalmine.

When she began to cry, I began to cry too: I cried

about the fact that my mother had abandoned me, had sent me away to spend the rest of my life in a village in the back of beyond never to return to the city which once I had called home. But as soon as I had started to cry she stopped crying and took me to the stream in the valley to collect crabs.

Once I happened to come across a huge speckled snake. I nearly jumped out of my skin, but my aunt, to my astonishment, stared right into its eyes, picked up a stone and hurled it into the air, muttering something which almost sounded like an incantation as she did so. The snake gyrated high above the ground, but no matter how far it tilted its head back, it still couldn't see where the stone had landed. In the end its whole body tumbled back to the ground and in a flash it was gone. I recovered from my state of panic and asked my aunt what had just happened. She said that if ever I saw that kind of snake again I should work out how long it was and throw a stone so far that even with its head fully twisted round it wouldn't be able to see where the stone had landed, and it would spare me.

I stayed with my aunt for some time. And when my cousin finally arrived to pick me up she said that she'd been delayed – otherwise she'd have come much sooner. Her skin was fair and clear, not like a weather-beaten sun-tanned country woman at all, and her hair was coiled up neatly behind her head. Her clothes were clean as well. In fact, all in all, I was astonished by her appearance and stared at her in admiration. My aunt was reluctant to part with me, but my cousin was resolute; she said that when my mother had lived in the village they had been best friends, and now that she had sent her daughter here, how could she possibly not take an interest in her? But after a day's discussion they finally came to an agreement: I would leave my aunt to stay with my cousin.

My cousin's place was a long way off, along the Yangtze near Fengdu County Town. We walked for a whole day along the mountain paths to get there. She walked slowly because, she said, when she was small her feet had been bound as her family had had high hopes that she might make a good marriage. She hadn't been able to stand it so she'd stealthily unbound her feet, until her family found out. They beat her mercilessly and re-bound her feet, but she unbound them again. And so it went on a few times more, meaning that her feet never quite made the grade. We talked the whole way, arriving at her home when it was pitch black. My cousin was the first person to encourage me to talk; she liked asking me questions and I liked replying. Of all the people I had come across she was the only one who asked me what life was like in the big city.

She said she wished she had run off to Chongqing with my mother. She'd probably only have got herself a job as a textile worker, but it would still have been better than being in the countryside.

I asked her why she hadn't.

She said there were certain things she hadn't been prepare to lose.

I asked her what things. She laughed and said that I was only a baby and didn't understand; she'd tell me when I was old enough to understand.

My cousin's husband had some rice and sweet

corn porridge waiting for us when we walked in the door. Her house was very much a house, compared with those of my other relatives, made of stone, high roofed, in fact it was an old blockhouse. After the Liberation when all land was being divided up, a lot of Guomindang rank-and-file 'reactionary' soldiers had been blown up in that stone house – there was so much bad *qi* there that no one had wanted it when houses were being allocated, so her family had ended up getting it. And when she met her future husband who had come to the village to work as a stone mason he was invited to become a 'live-in' son-in-law.

When she told me this story she explained that she could withstand the bad *qi* because she had a good horoscope. What she said made sense.

In front of the house there was a plum tree. I was still there when it began to blossom. I remember I used to climb the tree every day and look into the distance trying to spot my cousin's husband walking home along the mountain path which led to the entrance to the village.

Everyday I would go with the local children into the mountains to collect firewood and cut some hogweed. We would always eat our evening meal very early – every family did the same – to save the kerosene in the lamps. When we were really busy in the fields, and ended up eating late, we would rely on the light from the fire in the stove, in which we burnt straw stalks and withered grass, as we washed and prepared the food.

In my second year there, just before Qingming Festival, we – the whole extended family – went to the mountain beyond the pass to visit the grave of my maternal grandmother. There were weed dumplings thrown all over the road to distract the attention of the evil spirit dogs. Everyone had a strip of white cloth tied over their heads to symbolize filial piety. Ancestors protected us: whenever adversity was imminent a spirit would leap into action to come to the aid of their descendants. They had cut out quite a few paper people, paper horses and paper cows and sheep, as well has some paper houses and paper beds, which they burnt in front of the graves, the idea being that their ancestors would then be able to enjoy these things in the netherworld.

As we were coming back my second oldest uncle said he wanted to take me to a big stone stronghold. I thought he meant the one in the village, so I said I'd already been. My oldest uncle then said that the one in the village was the small stone stronghold, the one by the river was the big stone stronghold – famous all over Sichuan Province – right on the edge of a cliff, twelve storeys high, so high the top of it was hidden in the clouds. But my second oldest uncle fell ill during the spring ploughing so his wife made one of my cousins take me back to my cousin's house. My cousin said it was right not to have gone – the place had long since been closed up by the Red Guards who were 'supporting the revolution by casting away the four olds'; the Bodhisattva statue inside had been smashed to smithereens.

At the end of the summer my cousin gathered together all the old bits of cloth she could find in the house and used flour to make a paste which she smeared over them, giving them a hard shell, then she would cut them out, and make them into the shape of shoe uppers. Every evening before supper she would take advantage of the remaining daylight to sow a few stitches.

One hot sunny August day my oldest uncle received a letter from my mother (written by my second oldest sister), with some money enclosed for the journey back to Chongqing. My mother wanted my youngest aunt to take me back to Chongqing to go to school. I visited all the villages, and in end, clutching my cousin to me, I began to cry. My cousin said: 'You're a good girl... and you said you're mother didn't want you! I never believed it for a minute.' Then she began to cry too, telling me how much she'd miss me. But she was pleased for me that I had the opportunity to go back to the big city.

They took me back to the pass, and my youngest aunt joined us at dusk. My youngest aunt and my cousin both gave me a red cloth shoe, sewn with strong stitches, and the right foot, made by my youngest aunt had two little pea blossoms embroidered on it. They made me stick out my feet, one after the other, and try them on. They were a little bit big, but they both said that this was a good thing since my feet were growing so fast – I'd still be able to wear them in my second year of school. I asked them how they'd managed to make me a pair of shoes without telling me.

They said they had had a premonition that I would be leaving soon. They'd gone to the ancestral shrine for a blessing so that the one who wore the shoes would have a safe journey. Red also meant good fortune – I would be able to walk to the ends of the earth in safety. The further one travelled, the better the fortune, they added, so that my fate would at the very least be better than theirs.

When no one was looking my second oldest uncle slipped me 10 yuan. I knew it was a lot of money, moreover, I had never held money in my hand before, so I said I didn't want it. But, my uncle, who was normally as meek as a rice ball, said, 'If you don't take it I'll tie you up in the house and not let you go.'

When I got back to Chongqing I gave the money to my mother. She took it and tears began to gush down her cheeks.

My youngest aunt found life in Chongqing very difficult – everything was strange to her and she couldn't stop worrying about her husband, so she went back after just a couple of days. About a week after she'd gone I still had a needle with a thread on, so I sewed on one of my father's buttons when it dropped off. My older brothers and sisters thought this hilarious, saying only a country bumpkin would carry a needle and thread on their sleeve, and they took it away from me. I wore the red cloth shoes, which I had worn all the way to Chongqing, and to my first day at primary school. Everyone crowded round me laughing at them, and even though the shoes had been so skillfully made, my classmates seemed to find them the funniest things they had ever seen. But I didn't care. In any case my feet grew quickly and before the end of the first year they were already too small for me, so I cut off the back and used them as a pair of slippers. When I was in the third year, one day my older sister and I went down to the Yangtze to wash our clothes and shoes and they

PREFACE

were washed away in the current – I tried to chase
after them but they got swallowed up by a whirlpool.

It was years before I realized how much of a
burden I must have been to my mother's relatives in
the countryside. All of them were extremely poor,
and it can't have been easy having an extra mouth to
feed, so they had come to an agreement to, as it
were, spread the load.

My big-mouth older sister hadn't wasted any time
telling them all that I was illegitimate, but it didn't
make any difference, if anything they treated me
better than they treated their own children.
Whenever there was only one crude wheat pie left,
they would always insist on letting me have it and
going hungry themselves.

If my mother hadn't suddenly hadn't that change
of heart, hadn't suddenly taken pity on me and asked
her sister to bring me back to the big city to learn to
read and write, I'd probably have ended up a
farmer's wife, not that that would have been any
great tragedy – there is no shortage of poets and
novelists in the world, if anything there are far too
many. But it made a huge difference to me on a
personal level: that one decision changed the entire
course of my life. My relatives in the Three Gorges
are third-class citizens in China. If my mother had
left me there, I would be moving higher up the
mountain just like they are now, I would have to
work in the fields every day just like they do; I'd
probably already be making shoes for my
grandchildren.

Even writing these words down now terrifies me.
Since the National People's Congress gave the

Three Gorges Dam Project the go ahead in 1992, I have been beside myself with worry. I am a daughter of the Three Gorges. I had one great wish, and that was to write a book about the region. This book has been written from the heart. I've written it bit by bit over many years. In 2002, I went back to the Three Gorges and paid a visit to my mother's village. Everything was just as it had been – the only major difference was that most of people I had known there had passed on – life in the countryside is short and bitter. They are buried next to my maternal grandfather's grave in the cemetery on the mountain beyond the pass. I didn't really know any of my younger relatives there, but I chatted to them and found that some of them were depressed and anxious, while others seemed to be excited: they were looking forward to making a fresh start.

Life in the village was still almost as hard as it had been all those years ago. So much of China has changed so dramatically, but there are still many places where nothing seems to have changed at all. Before the reservoir is finished, everyone in the region must either move somewhere nearby above the water level or leave the province. People in the village said that it's not just their area that is going to be wholly or partially submerged; 110 towns are going to be underwater by 2009 – not to mention the countless number of villages.

The official version is that houses built above the water level will have 'a road at the front and fields at the back', and everyone will be able to start a new, better life. But the people in the village told me that the mountain is utterly unsuitable for agriculture, and any 'fields' there would be useless.

As I stood on the mountain I recalled a story I had heard when I was little. During a time of turmoil and disaster there was a family who received the help of their ancestors and hid under a blanket at the bottom of a lake. One day a former neighbour of theirs wanted to borrow a plough from them, so he went to the lake and called out the family's names three times, and in no time at all a plough emerged on the surface of the lake.

If the spirits of our ancestors really do exist, then one day I am going to stand on the shores of that colossal new lake and call out the names of my relatives three times, in the hope that that pair of beautifully crafted red cloth shoes might rise to the surface. The world I experienced when I was six is a ray of light in a dark childhood. Will that rise to the surface too?

But if ever again I go through the Yangtze's waters – on a boat – I shall scatter some flowers in the water, pea blossoms, just like the ones on my red shoes, so that the petals may sink down into the hands of my Three Gorges' relatives.

Hong Ying

For my Mother's home village

Chapter One

It is hard to imagine such a thing. It is even harder to imagine that something like that could happen to you. But when a woman is thrown in jail, tied to a man she doesn't even know, she has to deal with more than just her own anger and grievances.

After the door has been slammed shut and the cell is plunged into complete darkness, they can see absolutely nothing at all. The floor and walls feel like silky smooth moss, the air is stale and there is a strange smell: a rank whiff of blood mixed with the overwhelming stench of urine.

She props herself up on her arms, trying to raise her body off the ground, but the man's weight pulls her down and they both fall back where they started. The man tries his utmost to keep a polite distance from her, but the embarrassing thing is that the harder they try to avoid contact, the more likely they are to bump into one another. Every touch makes them feel more awkward. The last thing either of them wants is to substantiate the terrible charge made against them.

She tries as best she can not to move the hand that is tied up with his, moves her body backwards a little and feels her way to a corner of the room where there is a cold mat, with frayed edges, covering some damp straw. Who knows how many prisoners have sat here awaiting their fate?

The very thought of it makes her panic; she realizes she is in a predicament she can't face alone. She desperately wants to hold hands with the man who is to share her fate, to speak to him, to open up to him, but the guard who is standing on the other side of the cell door shouts at them to shut up every time they start to speak.

She can feel the man's even breathing and quiet heart beating, which calms her down a little. They are like two halves of a talisman, and because of the unreasonableness of the world they have been united and thus realize that all was one in the beginning.

Coming to the Three Gorges had turned out to be her journey to prison, but had she known that it would lead her to understand something which had been a mystery to her for several lives, she would not have regretted it for a single second.

After all, how many people find themselves in the world before their birth? Though, as yet she could see nothing; the reflection of the mountain cliff-tops was blurred by the speed of the surging river.

Chapter Two

She never expected the hovercraft to be so quick; it had hardly taken any time at all to reach Liang County.

A luxury cruiser was going downstream; it must have just left Liang's little harbour. She pressed her face against the glass to get a better look at the place, a place which twenty-four hours earlier she'd never even heard of.

The town was neither large nor small and like every other city in the Three Gorges region it was divided into two very distinct halves. Everywhere in the area – be it on the mountain slopes or the walls of buildings – a red line had been painted marking 175 metres above sea level. Above this line was Liang's New City – all fresh paint, new tiles, and blindingly clean glass. Below it was Liang's Old City – a strip of grey – messy, dirty and dilapidated.

This strangely incongruous combination was like a very unusual sort of cake: the sponge long since covered in mould but the decorative icing on top was exquisitely designed and perfectly fresh.

Liu watched as the greyish little harbour grew closer. The engine stopped, and the huge cloud of spray created by the hovercraft suddenly disappeared.

When she got out she noticed something different about this particular town: it was built on a stretch of red sandstone, spread out, flat and somehow sloppy-looking. In stark contrast, on the slopes of the majestic mountain ridge which towered behind it, stood the New City. It was incredible; her eyes lit up as soon as she saw it. The spring sun shone on both of these two layers, brilliantly reflected by the upper but absorbed by the lower, making its greyish mass even more of an amorphous eye-sore.

When the reservoir was completed, people here would wake up one morning to a completely new world and everything that wasn't new enough would be submerged in the great all-cleansing waters of the Yangtze.

Liu was a little confused. Her mother had arrived in Liang County more than forty years ago, so she could only have seen the Old City. Had those grey-black ramshackle buildings ever looked better than they did now?

There was only one thing she was sure of: when her mother saw that mountain ridge for the first time, she was definitely feeling a lot better than Liu now felt.

The day before she had still been in her laboratory at this time.

She had made a rule that no laboratory staff were allowed to talk on the phone during working hours, not even on their mobiles. To set an example, Liu didn't even have a mobile phone; she thought them unnecessary. All calls would be taken by the office and could be dealt with during official breaks. The main reason for this was that every time someone took a telephone call they had to wash their hands and change their gloves, otherwise their work could get contaminated.

It came as quite a surprise when one of the office girls had run in especially to get her. The person on the phone had said it was urgent.

She had no option but to put down the glass plates in her hand. Her eyes needed a rest anyway; looking through a microscope all day could be so tiring. She pushed through two doors and entered the administration office.

'Ah, Professor Liu!' said the voice on the phone. It was a woman's voice. She introduced herself as Miss So-and-so, 'secretary of the Great Lake Development Company', and went on to say: 'Director Li said that I absolutely had to get hold of you; he's got a present he wants to give you.'

Liu frowned; it was all very strange. Li Lusheng, her husband, called home at least once every other day, but he would never send someone to deliver a present. He hadn't mentioned anything the day before and he hardly ever phoned her at the laboratory for fear of disturbing her while she was working. He always called her at home in the evening or at the weekend. Why would he give her work number to a woman she'd never heard of?

'What present?' she asked tersely, trying her best not to sound annoyed.

'I have no way of knowing.' Her voice was young

and a little coquettish. 'I'm on a business trip to the Ministry of Water and Electricity. I have just arrived in Beijing. Director Li said I had to give you the gift in person and that it must be today.'

'Give it to me in person!?' She said, unable to hide her surprise. She glanced over at the girl who had come into the laboratory to call her. She was sitting quite nearby and had turned her head to see what was going on. She must have noticed the surprise in Liu's voice. What was Li up to? In all the ten years they'd been married, he had hardly ever done anything romantic like giving surprise presents.

'Why does it have to be given to me in person?'

Since returning to China, Liu had never worked anywhere but the Institute of Genetic Engineering at the Academia Sinica. She had never been to the headquarters of the Three Gorges Dam Project, despite the fact that Li was always asking her to go and visit him there. It just didn't seem worth it since he came to Beijing on business so often, sometimes twice a month; in fact, he spent as much if not more time in Beijing than at the Three Gorges. Besides, she did not want her work to suffer just so she could go and visit her husband. In any case, he was always so busy when he came to Beijing that he hardly had any time to spend at home relaxing; goodness knows how hectic his life must be at the Dam Site. But she had no complaints. In the ten years they'd been married it had always been the same. However, there was no point in her going to the Three Gorges since there would hardly be any time for them to spend together anyway.

'Director Li has instructed me to give it to you in

person.' The woman on the phone could tell that Liu wasn't in the mood for all this. Her tone became more resolute: 'I am sorry to have disturbed you – it's just a little package.'

Liu realized she had overreacted. It wasn't worth getting worked up about a thing like this. Suddenly she had a brilliant idea: she told the woman her mother's telephone number and said she could deliver it in person to her, then she'd go to her mother's place to pick it up as soon as she had time.

The woman on the phone didn't have much choice, though Liu could tell from her intonation that she wasn't best pleased. Still, Liu was adamant. If she was going to be roped into playing this silly game, she wanted to win.

It wasn't until Liu put the phone down that she noticed something different about the windows. The glass was as old and dirty as ever, but you couldn't even tell whether the trees outside were green anymore; they looked as if they were covered in dirty old rags. She usually only paid attention to the laboratory itself – it had to be spotless, strictly conforming to the required standards for genetic experimentation. The room was completely sealed with the air-conditioning set at a constant temperature. She noticed tiny grains of yellowish sand creeping in through the crack in one of the windows. She touched it with her fingers and saw how fine the particles were. She looked round but no one was looking at her – everyone was busy with paperwork or typing away at their computers. The girl who had just called her to the telephone was the only person who noticed the puzzled expression on her face: 'Sandstorm,' she said.

'I know. I've lived in Beijing for years, but it's almost June. We've already had three sandstorms this year.'

The office, hitherto apparently oblivious to what Liu was doing, suddenly broke into animated discussion. They had been talking about the problem of worsening sandstorms just before she came in. They only stopped because she was there. Some people thought it was because too much of Inner Mongolia's wasteland had been reclaimed and turned into pasture, some thought it was something to do with overgrazing, and others thought it was because traditional Chinese medicine shops were buying too much bramble seed, so that the protective vegetation had been destroyed.

Liu didn't find the topic nearly as interesting as the experiment she was in the middle of, so she went back to the lab.

When Liu left the building at the end of the day she had to cover her face with a silk scarf, as did all the other women who worked there. The scarves had bright floral patterns on them which made the women appear incongruously cheerful. Liu was used to sandstorms but she was amazed when, standing on the stone steps leading to the main entrance of the Research Institute, she looked at the street in front of her. The whole city was painted an earthy yellow and the air smelled of dust. The visibility was perhaps less than a hundred metres; every one of the huge skyscrapers had disappeared in the grey mists. Even the willow trees were suffering under the weight, their long branches sweeping the road as the wind blew. Cars had to put their headlights on and drive extremely slowly. Pedestrians appeared suddenly from nowhere like ghosts, covered in dust from head to toe, walking sideways in the sand-filled winds. The setting sun was a dark yellow colour – a bit like a dawn moon.

Thinking back to the discussion among the office staff she realized that the sandstorm couldn't only be affecting Beijing – it must be sweeping from North to South. Half of China must be witnessing something the ancients only saw during a solar eclipse.

She felt sand squeezing through every seam of her clothing. It even seemed as though sand was getting through her skin, making her feel heavier. The man next to her had a cold and had to breathe through his mouth. He had to stop and spit the sand out. Just as she was leaving the Institute one of the girls in the office had told her that her mother had called saying that she must go to her house that very day without fail.

Her mother must be taking Li's mysterious present too seriously. Liu thought it best to go straight home; she could go to her mother's another day. Besides, the weather was so bad and it was getting colder by the second.

At last a taxi came. It charged her twice the normal rate, but she didn't care. As the taxi drove submarine-like into the sea of sand, she worked out that, if every square metre of China were covered by one kilo of sand, it would be impossible to take it all back to where it came from: the transport infrastructure just would not be up to it.

'Where to?' the driver asked.

She opened her mouth to tell him her address but for some reason she found herself saying: 'Summer Palace back street, please,' – her mother's address.

Chapter Three

She couldn't remember ever having heeded her mother's advice. Even as a little girl she had never done as she was told. Why should she start now?

Her mother said a lot that evening, talking quickly and excitedly. She tried hard to persuade her to go south, and if she hadn't got time, then to make time. 'Go on! Go to Liang County! After all, it is where you were born.'

She thought she had been born in Chongqing, the huge city near the Three Gorges. However, that evening her mother told her that she had been born on a boat going from Liang County to Chongqing, and at the moment of her birth they had still been in Liang.

Her father had died young during the Cultural Revolution. She was only a girl of fifteen at the time. She'd squeezed onto a train full of Red Guards and made her way from Chengdu, the provincial capital, to Beijing. She soon lost her Sichuanese accent. She was seen as a bit of a tomboy by the youngsters in the military compound. Liu had always thought that her mother must have eaten something unclean when pregnant with her – why else was she so different from other girls who grew up among the green hills and clear waters of the beautiful South?

She'd asked her mother about this once. 'Eaten 'something unclean'! During pregnancy! How ever did you think that one up?'

Now however, standing on the dust that had been blown from Liang County, and recalling the look of surprise on her mother's face when she had asked this question, she couldn't help laughing; no one could possibly describe this place as anything but 'unclean'.

Chapter Four

Liu's mother lived out in the suburbs just north of the Summer Palace. She refused to live in the city; she said the hustle and bustle made her nervous. After the posthumous rehabilitation of Liu's father, she had been transferred to Beijing and worked as one of the countless deputy heads of the Publishing Bureau until her retirement. A publishing house paid her a full salary for reading manuscripts which they weren't sure whether to publish.

The taxi drove into the compound. The gate was guarded by soldiers. The blocks were only six storeys high. Each flat had its own lift, there were two flats per floor and although it looked a bit tatty on the outside, inside it was all beautifully maintained. The garden wasn't bad either, with pretty flowerbeds, an attractive lawn and even some evergreen pine trees.

Liu got in the lift and went up to the fourth floor. As soon as she stepped out the corridor lights came on automatically.

She rang the bell and her mother shouted

'Coming!', but it took her quite a while to open the door. As soon as she saw Liu she said: 'Get all that dust off! You can't come in until you're clean!'

She laughed. Her mother had always been obsessed with cleanliness; her cleaners were made to scrub the floor on their hands and knees. As she got older – particularly after becoming a widow – she only got worse. She was dressed neatly but informally with her feet tucked into a little pair of soft-soled slippers, a world away from the ravages of the sandstorm outside.

She didn't utter a word of complaint about the sandstorm everyone was moaning about. She just went straight to the wardrobe and got out a pair of slippers for her daughter. She hardly had any wrinkles – she looked after herself extremely well. Liu often felt that she looked more like a younger sister than a daughter, and a less impressive one at that. Her mother was also more intelligent looking and more perceptive than she was, but at least they both had the same figure and they were both 1.67 metres tall.

Liu took her coat off and tried to get as much of the dust off as she could, beating it vigorously before going in and hanging it up on the hook behind the door.

The flat was spacious: there were two sitting rooms and three bedrooms and it even had two balconies. The waxed floorboards had a slight springiness to them.

The sandstorm was raging as fiercely as ever, howling madly against the window panes. It was wonderful to be indoors in such a beautifully clean flat. Liu's mother asked if she would like her to turn on the electric heater. Liu shook her head but took the towel she was offered and went straight into the bathroom to have a shower. There were some Chinese rose petals floating in a porcelain basin on the floor, releasing a wonderful fragrance. She washed thoroughly and noticed that her skin seemed damaged by the sand, so she applied some of her mother's body lotion.

Sitting herself down on the L-shaped sofa she pulled over a cushion and noticed that there was an orchid on the tea table, a branchless stem with nine flowers that were pink and green like butterflies. She couldn't help exclaiming, 'Mother! That's so beautiful!'

Her mother infused two cups of her favourite 'Princess Lan of Yunnan' tea, put them neatly on a Japanese lacquered tray with a teapot, a small plate of almonds and a dish of dried fish slices. Then she put the tray down on the tea table and said, 'There are orchids everywhere in the South, but there are even more beautiful things as well: in the Three Gorges part of the Yangtze there is a type of peach blossom fish.'

'Peach blossom fish?'

'Haven't you ever seen one?' Her mother went on to explain that one used to be able to see translucent peach blossom fish in the clear emerald green waters of the Yangtze. They probably came from the mountain tributaries. There were hordes of them! All different colours: jade-white, creamy pale yellow, light pink – complementing the colours of the peach trees on the mountains.

'It must have been some kind of freshwater jellyfish,' said Liu, considering the matter carefully.

'I don't think it can have been an ordinary fish,' she added tentatively.

'Well, I saw them nevertheless.'

'Why didn't you tell me – seeing an incredible thing like that?'

'You've never shown much interest in what I have and haven't seen. When was the last time we had a chance to chat like this? You're always so busy!'

She switched on the mock antique table lamp and took a well wrapped gift-box off the bookshelf which she passed to Liu. 'This is it,' she said.

Liu tore open the gold wrapping paper – there was no question it had been wrapped in the shop – revealing a black lacquered box with an exquisite Chinese landscape engraving on it. Inside the box, however, there was a bottle of French perfume – 'Opium' by Yves Saint-Laurent. Such a strange name.

She realized it must have been what that strange woman on the phone had brought over. She took the bottle out of the box and looked carefully before spraying some of it on the back of her hand. She smelt it but didn't really know what to make of it, so she stretched her hand over to her mother to see what she thought of it.

'What does it all mean? It's not like him to go to the trouble of sending a secretary over to deliver it...'

She deliberately used the word 'secretary'. She wanted to stay calm and thought that saying the word 'woman' might be more difficult.

Her mother replied in a serious voice: 'Are you just pretending to be stupid?'

If the present had some kind of symbolic meaning, Liu's mother was far more likely to work out what it was than Liu herself was; she was very perceptive. Her mother crumpled up the gold wrapping paper and threw it in the black wicker waste paper basket. Liu did not doubt that there was some obscure rationale behind the present, but she hadn't a clue what it was.

'The secretary was very attractive — beautifully made-up, very trendy hairstyle and dressed in the latest fashions. She said that she was carrying out your order since you had no time, so you gave her my number and since you had entrusted the task of receiving the present to me, I asked her over.' She smiled disdainfully. 'But of course it's not her. I am not praising your husband's taste. If it were her, she wouldn't have come and seen me.'

'Does your intuition tell you that there is someone else?' Liu said straightforwardly, without a trace of panic.

Her mother drank a sip of tea and said, 'I'm afraid so.' She stopped. Seeing no reaction on Liu's face, she continued: 'It also tells me that Lusheng still hasn't decided what to do, in other words, he doesn't know whether or not he wants to get a divorce.'

'So this present is a warning?'

'I think he's trying to remind you of something. He's asking whether or not you're still a woman.'

Liu forced a laugh: 'That's what you've been wondering.'

'You always were a tomboy, and now you're not like a woman at all,' she sighed. 'I gave up talking to you about all this a long time ago, but Lusheng has asked you down there so many times and you never go. You can hardly say his request is unreasonable.'

41

'It's not that I don't want to go. It's just that I really can't leave my work, and he comes to Beijing so often.' She was getting upset. There was about to be an incredible breakthrough in genetic engineering, opening up a whole new world to the scientific community. She was leading the most important genetic research project in the country and they were at a crucial stage. How could she up and leave to play the 'little woman' and go and see her husband?

'So, do you understand his work? Do you care about what he's doing?' Her mother asked.

'You mean the construction work at the Three Gorges?' asked Liu. 'I've read some articles discussing the pros and cons. I haven't really any grasp of the technical side of it – the generation of electricity, flood prevention and all that. However, as far as the fundamental question is concerned – should we or shouldn't we interfere with nature – I have absolutely no doubt: I think that the people against it are naive. Mankind has always interfered with nature, and will continue to do so. After all, my own job is interfering with nature.'

'You seem to understand his work very well.' Her mother's eyes drifted over to the two large goldfish with spectacular tails swimming around in the tank. 'You two should get along fine – both 'changing the world'. How could there be any trouble between you? You should get together now and have a nice long chat.'

'I don't know. We're both so busy, there's no point making a special journey all that way. There's nothing to chat about.' Liu became thoughtful and paused for a while before continuing somewhat unwillingly: 'I suppose things have changed a bit. Ever since he became General Director of the company, he hasn't shown any interest in what I do....but then neither have I shown much interest in what he does. We've nothing in common to talk about.'

Her mother suddenly raised her head, looking at Liu with a very serious expression on her face. 'It's not perhaps that you're not interested in men?'

Liu thought that was a question her mother should not have asked. She had been living on her own ever since Liu's father had died. Liu had often thought that her mother was lonely, and the thought passed through her head that perhaps she should remarry, but it wasn't her place to say so. Besides, since her father had been a veteran Communist cadre of the War of Resistance against Japan, his widow was well taken care of.

She threw the question back at her mother: 'Didn't you always tell me I should be a bit guarded with men, never too accommodating?'

'You shouldn't be too accommodating before you get married,' her mother replied patiently, 'but you have to be accommodating after you've got married. You should understand, power is the only aphrodisiac for the modern man.' Her mother smiled. She had a smug expression on her face every time she came up with one of these pearls of wisdom. Although she too counted as a veteran cadre, having been a member of the party for all these years, Liu thought that her mother was actually a bit of a hedonist.

Liu hated this kind of talk; as far as she was concerned, the conversation was going downhill. She

43

put down her tea cup and stood up.

'Well then, mother, have you got anything else to say? It's time I was going.'

Her mother stopped smiling but didn't want to argue with her; she didn't want them to part on bad terms. Instead she grabbed Liu's arm and said with utmost sincerity, 'Darling! Come now, don't take my little joke so seriously. Why don't you stay the night? What's the point of going back in a sandstorm like this? If you're really tired you can sleep by yourself, but the best thing would be for you to sleep with me in my bed. We've not been together for far too long. I really do think you should take a trip down South. It's completely up to you of course, but there's another reason why I'd like you to stay here tonight. It's something to do with when you were born. I should have told you years ago, just never seemed to get the chance.'

Without waiting for any reply she got up and went into the kitchen. 'The new maid's a great cook. I've already asked her to start making a good dinner. I'm sure you've been eating junk food. Well anyway, it looks like this storm has enabled me to have a distinguished guest stay the night!'

Chapter Five

Liu often found her mother's advice irritating, but she was always proved right in the end. Liu woke up early the following morning and went straight home to pick up a few things and make three phone calls – one to book a plane ticket, one to the Research Institute to request leave and one to tell her husband, Li, she was coming. Then she closed her suitcase and set off for the airport.

The sun was shining, and everyone had completely forgotten the sandstorm which had been raging the whole of the previous day and all through the night. The flight went smoothly and she arrived on time at Yichang airport. There was an Audi saloon waiting for her outside, but no sign of Li. The man who had come to meet her was the company's head of staff, Mr Han. He said Li Lusheng had been called away to Beijing; there was an important meeting which he had simply had to attend. There had been no way to call and let her know because he had left just as her plane was taking off.

So they had passed each other in mid-air. Maybe,

as she was gazing out of the window, she'd spotted his company's little jet plane fly past in the blue sky. Mr Han said that Director Li had asked him to stay behind at the airport to pass on his apologies to his wife. Mr Han looked no more than thirty. He was thorough in his work and concise in his speech. He gave off the impression of being extremely capable and efficient. He was short and had good skin. He was wearing a pair of frameless glasses and a silver-grey suit which made him look like a successful Hong Kong financier.

The motorway from Yichang airport to the Dam Site was lined with leafy green trees. One would never have guessed that they had been planted only five years previously. Just as Liu was about to ask him how they could have grown so quickly, Mr Han said, 'We chose a fast-growing type, nice and big in just three years.'

The road through the area where the dam was to be built was lined with peach trees in full blossom and the ground was covered with pink petals which had fallen from the trees. It looked beautiful.

Mr Han explained everything: 'Right from the very beginning Director Li insisted that creating things of beauty should be the top priority. If the construction site itself is beautiful, people will believe the project is environmentally friendly. We all thought it was a waste of time, but Director Li argued fiercely for investment in 'environmentally friendly beautification'; he even put his case to the Central Committee. Now he's been proved absolutely right.'

'Really?' Liu did not know Li had come up with such a brilliant idea. He had never talked to her about it.

Mr Han sighed with admiration: 'How far-sighted he is. How clever!'

'You see,' he continued, 'of the millions of visitors who come to the Three Gorges, most also come to have a look at the Dam Construction Site. However, the most important thing is not the revenue from tourism, but rather the image of construction. Sooner or later you have to try to make the whole area look good; leaving it until the last minute, putting up with all those shacks and all the other mess, that's not the way things should be done.'

After a short pause he began again: 'In our post-modern society, image is more important than reality. And Director Li realized that before anyone else.'

Even as they drove along the north bank of the Yangtze they could see the towering building of the construction headquarters and the twenty-five storey hotel far off in the distance. They sped over the specially constructed bridge and reached the five star Dam Hotel. Liu was impressed, but she was beginning to find Mr Han's tireless enthusiasm a little wearying. She had hardly been able to stop herself from bursting out laughing at his use of 'post-modern'.

He took her up to the penthouse suite and said, 'The room next to yours is the President's Suite. It's very hard to get. Li asked me to convey his apologies.' She detected no irony in his explanation.

Liu couldn't think of anything to say – the suite she was in was luxurious enough and might have been the Foreign Minister's. The sitting room had two three-seater sofas and one long coffee table against the wall. The suite looked as smart as in the best hotels in Hong Kong.

When she opened the curtains, which were so long that they touched the carpet, she could see the entire construction site. She was speechless. Machines were cutting through mountains and lorries were moving about on top of the dam but, except for the occasional flash of someone using a welding torch, you could hardly see any human activity at all There was an eye-catching slogan on top of the gigantic six-gate lock: 'See yesterday as backward, regard the best as standard!' The whole site looked like a chess-board. Two-thirds of the vast Yangtze had already been blocked up.

Seeing her amazement, Mr Han went over to the window. 'In the papers,' he began proudly, 'they say this will be the biggest construction project in human history, but Mr Li says we shouldn't say that because future construction projects will be even bigger, and then people will laugh at our boastfulness.'

Liu turned round. This man's adoration of Li seemed quite genuine. She had never imagined that Li had a calculating side to his personality, never imagined that he would become proficient in propaganda as well. He had studied project management in America; weren't propaganda slogans beneath him?

Mr Han didn't notice the expression on Liu's face and continued with his interminable praise of her husband.

'Director Li insisted that, wherever possible, there should be a line drawn at 145 metres above sea level marking the level of the water after the initial flooding, and at 175 metres above sea level marking the level of the water after the final flooding. At first many people were against the idea – they said it would be ammunition for the opponents of the dam because they would be able to see exactly how much of the beautiful scenery would be disappearing – but Director Li said that not marking the water levels would make people even more suspicious. Now the two lines have become a tourist attraction. People respect the fact that we're not trying to hide anything. It stops them from fearing the unknown.'

Liu was growing impatient and wanted Mr Han to stop talking. She was just about to ask him for a local map when the phone began to ring.

He walked over to the table by the wall. As soon as he picked up the phone his smile vanished. 'No,' he said quietly. Then after a while: 'Absolutely not.' He put down the receiver, took out his mobile phone, opened the door and walked out into the corridor, closing the door behind him.

The phone rang again. Liu had no choice but to answer it. She heard a woman's voice. 'Mr Han,' the woman began gently but firmly, 'you are loyal. Like a dog is loyal. That's your best quality. But there's someone I want to talk to. I have the right. You can't keep me quiet forever.'

Liu was startled.

She realized immediately what was going on. Her heart began to beat frantically and her face turned deathly pale. Her mother had warned her of this. Liu realized that the woman's insult hadn't been meant for her. However, the calmness of the woman's voice made Liu determined not to be so undignified as to argue with her.

'Hold on, I'll get Mr Han for you.'

For a few seconds the woman on the phone was silent with shock, but regained her composure almost immediately: 'You must be Director Li's wife.' Without waiting for a response she continued, 'May I speak with you?'

Liu had no choice but to match the woman's composure: 'I'm not interested in anything you have to say. You should speak to the person you were looking for.' At that moment she saw Mr Han push the door open and rush back into the room. 'Don't call me here again. I have urgent business elsewhere. I must leave this place immediately,' she said, raising her voice so Mr Han could hear exactly what she was saying.

Mr Han tried to grab the receiver before she put it down, but he was too slow. His outstretched hand froze in mid-air.

Liu controlled her anger and said coldly, 'If Director Li is not here, there's not much point in my staying.'

'But you have only just arrived! Would you at least tell me where you are going?'

Twice Mr Han tried to push his glasses into position and twice they slipped back down. He was stuttering as though he had a fishbone in his throat: 'Please tell me where you're going! Please!'

'Ambitious little sycophant, doing Li's dirty work for him!' Liu cursed silently. Then, picking up her unopened suitcase, she stormed out of the room. 'I don't think it's any of your business where I'm going!'

Mr Han caught up with her at the lift landing, his face horribly pale. He realized that the very thing he had been instructed to prevent at all costs had already happened. 'Would you like me to arrange a car?'

He reached over to take her suitcase, but she pushed his hand away gracelessly. 'You have done quite enough, thank you. Now I have something private to attend to. Please don't bother to see me out.'

The lift door opened and she walked in. She pressed the button, staring coldly at Mr Han. He wanted to join her in the lift but, seeing the expression on her face, he lost his nerve.

The lift descended without interruption.

Alone in the claustrophobic confines of this tightly sealed metal box, the accumulating pressure of Liu's anger became almost uncontrollable. She couldn't believe her husband could behave so shamelessly, and that the woman was so brazen as to call her the minute she arrived. But the worst thing about her husband's betrayal was the blow to her self-esteem: if he could have an affair with this woman then possibly, no, probably, he had had affairs with other women as well. Maybe their 'perfect marriage' had been nothing but a sham from the very beginning.

Under no circumstances would she try to compete with this other woman. She wouldn't allow herself to fall that low. She had never been in a situation like this before, but she realized that first and foremost she had to maintain her self-respect; without it she was nothing.

Chapter Six

That was how she ended up in Liang County.

Liu walked up the stone steps above the quay. On the dock workmen were busy unloading, and amid loud thuds, the air filled with dust swirling up off the ground. There was rubbish everywhere – by the roadside, on the shore, even on the tops of some of the one-storey houses. A foul stench was rising in the hot sun. It seemed as though no one had done anything about the rubbish in the town for years; some of it even seemed to be fermenting. Maybe they were waiting for the final flooding to wash it all into the new reservoir.

In fact, the river itself was already full of rubbish – floating bits of plastic and chunks of foam, even an old mattress. Whirlpools that could make sailing boats disappear were apparently unable to push them underwater. Liu could well imagine how much rubbish there would be when the reservoir was finished, and how long it would be stuck there before it was flushed out into the sea. So much for Li's 'environmentally friendly beautification' – surely he should have done something about the rubbish before attempting the much vaunted 'beautification'.

The pathway at the top of the long flight of stone steps was lined on either side with small stalls covered by large umbrellas which acted as sunshades. The stallholders were arranging their produce on little wooden tables – dried bean curd, slices of pig's head meat, pot-stewed duck – all shining with grease. They were using plastic fly-swatters to try to drive away the flies. Huge square cleavers lay on blackish tree stumps which were used as chopping boards. Liu tried her utmost not to look – she couldn't believe that people could actually eat those things. But if there are people selling, there must be people buying...

'Buy it hot, love! Jiang family traditional stewed duck!'

They had the effrontery to call her 'love'! Only one person had ever called her 'love', and that was her nanny when she was a child. She could understand Sichuanese dialect; she had picked it up from her nanny, until her parents had found out and had sacked her on the spot. When the stallholder called her 'love' the second time, Liu realized she actually rather liked it.

A motorcyclist rode up to her and said he could take her to a hotel that was only 15 yuan a night.

'How far is it?' She asked.

'Not far.'

She had known the answer already. The Old City was not big, everything was within walking distance. It hardly mattered anyway. She knew the New City was a much more suitable place to look for a hotel,

54

but then she didn't want to go back to her usual lifestyle quite yet. So she decided it would be better to stay in the Old City after all. The motorcyclist had already found another willing passenger – a young girl. She was holding on to his waist. When he started up the bike it sounded like someone firing a machine-gun, leaving the pungent smell of exhaust fumes as they rode up a long winding road leading to the busy streets in the centre of town.

Most of the roads didn't have names or numbers. Maybe they had done once. Maybe the sign-posts had been in the way of the lorries carrying building materials and had got knocked down. They passed row upon row of run-down, ramshackle huts, with shutters that banged and squeaked in the wind. Seeing such a maze of a place, Liu decided the best thing to do was, in fact, to find a hotel in the New City. The Dam Hotel had been a bit too luxurious, but here things were so basic she just did not think she would be able to endure it. At that very moment she happened to spot a taxi dropping someone off. She walked over to it, sat down in the back, and said to the driver, 'Take me to the best hotel in town.' She was apprehensive; the 'best' in a place like this was unlikely to be more than mediocre.

'The Golden Pleasure Hotel. Four Stars,' the driver said proudly.

'Then go there.'

The Golden Pleasure Hotel turned out to be grander than expected. It had been built in the highest part of the New City and had spectacular views. In the main lobby there were huge hanging baskets filled with beautiful flowers arranged with exquisite taste. The marble floor was so immaculately clean that it reflected the light from the chandeliers hanging down from the high ceiling. It looked like the Imperial Dynasty Hotel in Beijing. Liu wondered what kind of person came to stay in a place like this, here in the middle of nowhere.

By the time she had settled into her room it was already a quarter past four. She called room service for something to eat – a bowl of beef noodles for lunch. When the waiter had cleared everything away and closed the door behind him, she lay down on the bed and tried to make sense of everything that had happened, but it was impossible. She decided to call her mother – not to ask her advice (she never asked anyone for advice) – just to tell her where she was.

However, she could not get an outside line from her room. She called the reception desk and they told her the deposit she had paid did not cover long-distance phone calls. She would have to pay a separate deposit for that.

She had not brought much cash with her, but she had no choice. She went down to the ground floor and paid the deposit. As she made her way back up to her room she felt a little better, a little more like her old self, and so she decided to get on with what she had to do. It would not matter if she did not call her mother until she got back.

Just as she was about to leave the hotel she realized she had forgotten to bring her address book with her. She would have to fetch it from her room. She was not usually this disoriented. When she nipped into the bathroom to wash her hands, she looked in the mirror and saw a woman in a smart suit. She looked like one of those immaculately dressed female cadres from the big cities. She opened her suitcase and looked for something a bit plainer to wear. She found a casual jacket and some cotton trousers. Then she took off her high-heels and changed them for something more comfortable to walk in.

She thought she must look like a teacher. But when she caught a glimpse of herself in the wardrobe mirror she saw a college student. It was her short hair that made her look so much younger, as long as you did not look too closely. Yet recently her periods had become more and more irregular and she was having trouble sleeping. She felt a sudden onrush of self-pity: a woman on the verge of menopause and she had fallen victim to a man's betrayal. She had never expected it to happen to her. She felt angry. In order to make herself feel better she decided to have a long, hot shower.

Compared to the filth of the Old City, the bathroom seemed like heaven. It contained a huge mirror, lights that could be dimmed, a spotless black and white marble floor, and on the wall two tiles inlaid with rustic patterns. It was all very fashionable. Next to the washbasin there was a reproduction antique lacquered box filled with silky white tissues, and toiletries were laid out on a big lacquered tray. The large pile of white towels had a delicate lemon fragrance.

Liu stepped into the bathtub and drew the curtain. She wanted to give her hair a thorough wash.

She heard the telephone ring above the sound of

running water. But no one knew she was there. She turned the water down to a trickle. She could clearly hear that the phone really was ringing. It must be reception calling. The ringing stopped. She carried on rinsing the shampoo out of her hair and turned the water back up. The ringing started again. She stepped out of the bathtub and picked up the receiver hanging on the wall just above the lavatory.

To her great surprise it was Li: 'You got to Liang then...is everything alright? I'm still in Beijing.' He wasn't in the slightest surprised that she had moved hotels.

'How did you find me?' Liu asked, trying to sound as calm and composed as possible. She looked in the mirror and saw her own pained expression. She knew the answer: someone must have followed her to the hotel from the Dam Site where she had boarded the boat. Mr Han wasn't the only one; Li must have an army of running dogs. Wherever she went he would immediately know how to find her.

Li ignored her question and said, 'Be careful.'

Liu's anger finally erupted: 'You are the only thing I need to be careful of! I'll ask you again: How did you find me here?' She was gritting her teeth, desperately trying to control herself.

'The area is still dangerous.'

'Don't threaten me!'

'Haven't you seen the anti-dam posters that have been stuck up in the Old City – and the New City – on doors, on walls – they're everywhere.'

'I didn't see any.'

'They must all have been removed then. You should leave Liang as soon as possible. Do you want me to send someone to pick you up?'

Li had gone too far. She had come to Liang County on personal business; she wasn't sightseeing. Yes, there were a few shanty-towns along the river, full of people who had been forced to leave their homes and were still waiting for relocation. And there were those people who had refused to leave, but there was nothing remarkable in that. Even the taxi driver had said that reluctance to leave home was quite normal. And even if the tensions were as bad as Li had said, was that any reason for her to leave? After all, Liang was her birthplace, and there was something she wanted to do there, something that had nothing to do with her husband.

'It would be best if you went back to the Dam Site.'

'In future, would you mind not sending any more of your sycophantic minions to spy on me?'

'Don't...'

Liu raised her voice, barking into the receiver: 'There's no point spying on me!'

'I really don't want to do anything but help you.'

That was the last straw. She screamed down the phone, 'You only want to help me? You disgust me! That perfume you sent me, it stinks. It sickened me to death!'

Li ignored her outburst and went on, 'We've never let one another down!'

'Hypocrite!' She would have liked to throw the word at him, but contented herself with slamming the phone down as violently as she could. She was still naked and felt as if he had been watching her all the time. The thought made her uneasy.

She stepped back into the bathtub and turned the shower back on, but she turned it the wrong way and was hit by a stream of ice-cold water. She quickly turned it the other way as far as she could, sending the water thudding into her body. Why am I so upset? I've never lost control like this, never. But why should I try to calm down?

Why had that woman wanted to talk to her? What did she want? A showdown? She had obviously been very involved with Li. It could not just have been a fling. Maybe she was worried. Maybe Li was giving her the cold shoulder – otherwise why on earth would she make such a stupid move and risk ruining everything? Though her voice was not that of a young woman, she was probably attractive and capable. Her words, while controlled, were nonetheless aggressive, disdainful of Mr Han. She knew where she stood.

Well then, Liu thought, I'm not going to fight you over this adulterer.

The fact that Li had betrayed her was beyond question. His deliberate avoidance of the subject was a silent confession of guilt. She knew him too well. He used to say: 'The one who keeps calmest is always the winner.'

The question now was whether or not they should get divorced. Liu knew she was not the perfect wife. In fact, they had been leading separate lives for some time. Divorce wouldn't make much difference; it would be a formality.

Thinking along these lines, Liu realized that she had been used all along. Their marriage was convenient in that it enabled Li to indulge his weakness for womanising whilst at the same time giving his superiors the impression that he was the perfect family man.

She was tormented by the necessity of maintaining her self-respect. She did not want to ask the woman what was going on between her and Li. She would rather not know. That way at least she would be spared the painful details. Knowing the whole story is always much worse than just knowing the broad outline. And, after all, the marriage had also provided her with an effortless family life.

Suddenly she felt troubled by the thought that there must be something wrong with her. A normal woman would be raging with jealousy by now – screaming and shouting, hurling plates onto the floor and saucepans out of the window. But she hadn't done any of that. So why did she care so little for their perfect marriage? Maybe that was it – maybe it was because everything was so 'perfect' on the outside that they had so little interest in one another.

When she was in America writing her thesis there was a period of time when, perhaps hallucinating due to exhaustion, whenever she was looking at something under a microscope she would always see a desert. She never understood the symbolic meaning of the desert. There was only one person in it – a woman who was trudging alone through the sand. She thought the woman must be herself. Once she saw a bazaar in the desert. She rushed over to it as fast as she could. Her father was there. The lamps were bright and there were crowds of people singing and dancing. Her father was leading a camel. He said to her, 'I can't bear to see you so unhappy. I will come and see you again – but only if you are happy.' And with these words her father vanished into the crowd.

She hadn't seen her father under a microscope since. She hadn't even dreamt about him at night.

She remembered that a few days later Li had come to America on business and had stopped off to see her. Early in the morning, just before he left, she told him what she had seen. He said that he regarded her father as a hero, since it was he who had carried his own wounded father off the battlefield and saved his life. 'Our families are linked through life and death; you are more important to me than anything.'

At the time his words had comforted her, but now she felt that they implied something more sinister. Although Li had benefited greatly from being the son of a war veteran, he never thought highly of what the older revolutionaries had achieved. On the contrary, he thought much more highly of the present generation. That being the case, why should he be faithful to her because of the gratitude owed by his father to hers?

Chapter Seven

This so-called 'city' didn't seem to have any kind of bus service; it wasn't big enough. There were taxis everywhere, and they were certainly cheap enough: the minimum fare was 5 yuan, a fraction of the price of a taxi in Beijing. But it was a fair price, considering how close everything was to the hotel. The high street in the centre of town had the elegant name of 'Rinsing Silk Road'. The houses that fronted the street were exquisite. Quite a few shops and businesses had just opened; there were flowers outside and red and gold characters displayed on the posters just inside the doors to welcome new customers.

There were some policemen standing in the middle of the road directing traffic – and doing a good job too. The huge electronic screen had an advert for *Wahaha* mineral water on it one minute, then the latest stock market news the next. But as the taxi went down into the Old City the view became very different; the streets were crowded with people, there were stalls on both sides of the road, there was black smoked meat hanging in people's doorways, and fresh vegetables (some of which were clean and some of which weren't) lay in heaps on the ground.

The people too looked different – anxious – as if waiting for something to happen. Even though it would be some time before the flooding – in fact the reservoir would not reach the 175m mark until after 2009 – many of the houses had been demolished and people were already being evacuated. It almost looked like a war zone. The Dam Project had become the centre of everyone's life; people didn't see any point hanging about. 'Best get on with it and embrace the future!' seemed to be the prevalent attitude.

The taxi suddenly came to a stop. The driver announced, somewhat irritably: 'You'd better walk. It only gets worse from here on. The streets are all baskets and stalls.'

He was right. The Old City was no place for cars. 'How far is it to Herring Lane?' Liu asked, trying out her Sichuanese dialect.

'It's very near here, now.' The driver stuffed the bills she handed him in the glove compartment. Liu got out and walked over to the side of the road. She had to find someone she could ask for directions. People in Sichuan did not speak normally; they shouted, and their dialect was higher pitched. They seemed incapable of talking quietly, but they were equally incapable of being anything other than helpful. Liu had no trouble finding the mountainside residential area.

The place was quiet, perhaps a little too quiet. There was no sign of the noisy exodus, perhaps because it was higher than the 175m mark. There was rubbish everywhere, just like in the rest of the city: rotten vegetables, smashed glass and the inevitable chunks of synthetic foam. Whereas most of the Old City was preparing for the future, the areas above the flood line didn't have to bother.

There were no tall buildings; most of the houses only had one storey, though some people had built a second storey on top. The roofs were rotten and some of the walls had cracks in them. But there was one good thing about the place; dotted among the houses there were palm trees and black rafter trees, and there were sweet-scented oleanders growing on the slope, and in the courtyards old wooden buckets, and even old chamber pots and spittoons, were used for growing flowers and plants.

She carefully made her way down some steps. Opposite an electricity pylon there were a few houses attached to a factory wall. This was the place she was looking for: Number 78a Herring Lane.

Liu's mother had said, 'Please go and visit Auntie Chen.' She had then proceeded to find her address book and wrote down the address. She said she'd got it from a letter she'd had from Auntie Chen years before, and that she hoped she hadn't moved.

Liu had asked curiously, 'What is Auntie Chen, by profession?'

'Same as me,' her mother had said, pointing to herself, 'a housewife.'

'That's not what I meant.' Liu didn't always appreciate her mother's sense of humour. 'I meant before she retired. She must be about your age. You were at the Bureau Directorial level. What was she?'

Liu's mother had become pensive and waited a little while before replying. 'Her life hasn't been easy. In fact, it's been pretty awful. Her husband was a veteran of the People's Liberation Army, but he made political mistakes and that was it – he lost his job. She complained on his behalf and she lost hers too. After that I think she was a factory worker and then she retired.'

Liu was rather taken aback. Her mother had continued:

'We haven't been in touch for decades. I only ever got one letter from her, saying that her husband had passed away. She wanted his old superior – your father – to help clear his name. She didn't know that your father was dead too.' She sighed. 'Of course I never wrote back.'

'Why not?'

'Oh, lots of reasons. I think we've got a lot to talk about tonight. Auntie Chen thought that her husband's name could be cleared by no one but your father.'

'Was it to do with something that happened when you were all in Liang County?' Liu asked, eager to know more. 'Why do you want me to visit her?' She wondered what she could do about something which had happened long ago between two old widows.

'When I was pregnant with you she was my best friend,' her mother began, 'if you want to know what happened when you were born, I'm afraid I can't tell you. She's the person you should ask. You're a smart girl. You know how to deal with this kind of thing. And, of course, you weren't involved like I was. You're the next generation. You will go, won't you? For me?'

At the time Liu hadn't been able to see any reason to refuse her mother's request, so she had agreed immediately. Only now did she feel uneasy as she thought back to what was said that day.

She was now standing on the threshold of an unfamiliar world, and she suddenly felt very afraid.

The black door was half open. Most doors were left open during the day, because the windows were so small. She tried to look in but couldn't see much; all she could make out was that the floor was slightly lower than the ground outside. There was a pungent smell of Chinese herbal medicine coming from inside.

'Is Auntie Chen at home?' she shouted.

No reply. She shouted again. Her heart was pounding. She was getting nervous.

She summoned up the courage to go in, venturing slowly down the steps. Before she had even had time to examine her surroundings a woman popped up out of nowhere right in front of her. Liu almost jumped out of her skin and immediately took a couple of steps back.

The woman looked icily at her uninvited visitor. Liu announced, 'I'm looking for Auntie Chen.'

The young woman remained silent as though Liu hadn't said anything. A medicine pot was bubbling away on the earthen stove. The woman squatted down to air the fire with a palm fan, filling the whole place with the smell of burning coal.

Liu took the hint and walked back up the steps. A crowd of children had gathered outside the door to see what was going on. She turned and looked back. The woman was watching her leave, an unpleasant smile revealing her white teeth gleaming in the darkness.

Obviously there was no Auntie Chen to be found at that address. She felt embarrassed.

In the dark doorway of the neighbouring courtyard there were some men and women playing Mah-jong. There were some underpants and children's clothes hanging out to dry above their heads. They were sitting round a black table, all deep in concentration. No one wanted to be interrupted. At any one time half of China must be playing this game, thought Liu to herself. The poor bet enough money for a small bowl of noodles and the rich bet enough to buy a car or even a house.

Liu asked them about Auntie Chen. There was no reply. Eventually a young girl who was watching turned round and told her that Auntie Chen did in fact live at the house, but her husband was in hospital and she might be out visiting him.

Liu breathed a sigh of relief. The person her mother wanted her to find still lived there. 'Excuse me, when might she be coming back?' she asked.

The girl didn't say any more.

Their game came to an abrupt halt. A woman with hair dyed dark red let out a piercing scream as a rat ran up one of the table-legs. It was almost bald, which made it look particularly ugly. Liu couldn't help letting out a little scream herself as she saw it scuttle about among the Mah-jong pieces. It then jumped off the table and tried its best to scurry through the many pairs of feet.

People were shouting: 'Kill it! Kill it! It's a king rat that's not afraid of anything!' Everyone ran off looking for something to kill it with. There was chaos. Somebody knocked over a jar of pickles which made everyone jump up and down swearing and cursing. The sour smell was awful. Eventually somebody hit the rat with a shovel – it had probably eaten poison and was about to die anyway.

'It's only been a few days since we killed them all off with that poison. Surely they can't be back already.'

Someone shouted: 'Whoever it was who didn't put poison down in their house has caused this. I'm warning you – next time the inspector comes it's you who'll be paying, you cheap bastard!'

'Are you accusing me? If you are you'll have to prove it!' A man in flip-flops pulled the table out of the way and walked up to the man who was shouting.

Liu was not impressed. Auntie Chen wasn't in and hanging around waiting for her was not an attractive alternative. She decided to go back to the hotel and relax for a while.

As she was leaving she saw, stuck up on the grey wall, a glossy poster advertising 'Eminent Residences on Cloud Lake', complete with an artist's impression of a beautiful garden villa.

Enjoy Euro-American style!
Boost your business confidence!
Show off your high social status!
Be more patriotic!

High-class residential area in the North
Mountain Region. Designed to your
specifications and tailored to your tastes.

Elegant and imposing. World class. Stunning
scenery. Only for the rich and successful.
Each home will have its own swimming pool,
tennis court, yachting harbour and view of the
new Three Gorges Lake.

Liu was shocked.

There were a few sketches of plans: 'Two
reception rooms, five bedrooms and four bathrooms
totalling somewhere in the region of 1000 square
feet. Two entrances: main entrance and servant's.
Staff dining room. Skylights. Rockery and
ornamental waterfall at the back, swimming pool at
the front. Spacious two-car garage. Garden area in
excess of 1,200 square feet.'

She looked closely. As expected, the yachting
harbour had not been left out of the sketch. A
Western-style yacht was moored at the dock and the
lake was dotted with multi-coloured sails.

This was a surprise. How could there be enough
people in the area who were rich enough to make it
worth turning this dilapidated old village into a
millionaire's playground?

Liu needed to go to the toilet. Luckily she found a
public toilet on the other side of the road – it was
one of those ones made of brick which you only ever
see in the countryside. She went in but rushed out
almost immediately in shock. There was someone in
the men's toilet next door who, from the sound of it,
was suffering from an acute attack of diarrhoea. Liu
hadn't been to a toilet like that, shared by a whole
neighbourhood, in over twenty years.

Chapter Eight

Next morning she woke up early. Her window was covered in little droplets of condensation and the river was shrouded in mist. She went out into the street, walking carefully on the wet cobblestones, and made her way down some stone steps from the upper street to the lower street. It was easy, really. The day before Liang had seemed like a maze, but now she felt she had a rough idea of what was where.

She craved some soya milk and fried fritters but changed her mind when she smelled the freshly baked wheat cake that came wrapped in leaves. As she was walking she noticed a woman sitting on the pavement on the other side of the road. She looked familiar. Yes – of course – it was that young woman at Auntie Chen's address who'd refused to speak to her. She seemed to be waiting for someone. Her face was covered in sweat; it looked as if she'd just finished some hard physical work.

After a while the young woman got up and started walking down the slope. Liu was curious and decided to follow her. Almost all the houses in the area were being knocked down and the ubiquitous rubble made trailing her difficult. There were some women clearing plaster from old bricks to make them reusable. Others, bodies bent under the weight of the baskets of bricks they were carrying on their backs, were making their way slowly up the slope to the new construction sites. They were all twenty to thirty-year-old women who were used to hard work – their bodies strong, their faces sunburnt and covered in dust. Their skin had not yet started to develop wrinkles, but living like this it wouldn't be long before the ravages of age took their toll.

Liu reached the bottom of the slope which led to the great Yangtze River itself. However, the woman she was following had disappeared without trace.

There was someone holding up a placard. He was trying with great enthusiasm to recruit labourers to go to the little island near the opposite shore to help slice potatoes and put them out to dry. '5 yuan a day! 5 yuan a day!' he kept shouting. '5 yuan a day! Liu was shocked. That was no more than the price of three newspapers. How could the wages be so low? The loads on those women's backs must have weighed at least 75 kilos. How much were they earning? She didn't dare ask.

As she walked along by the river she realized she was heading in the direction of Herring Lane. She decided to see whether Auntie Chen had returned.

She was actually already in Herring Lane – at the other end – and it was as gloomy as ever. On the pavement the residents were making briquettes from crumbs of coal, but nobody seemed to mind if they got broken by the careless feet of passers-by. The continuous crashing noise was the sound of the nearby pig-bristles processing factory emitting filthy, frothy water into an open ditch beside by the roadside.

Liu saw an old woman with a tattered straw hat on her head and a towel on her shoulder, bent over a bucket and busily washing radishes under a tap. Every so often she had to straighten up to catch her breath.

Liu was walking over when the woman spotted her. She looked her up and down and her cold stare turned into a surprised smile. She waited for Liu to reach her, and straightaway said:

'You're the spitting image of your mother. No mistake about it.' She straightened up. 'You were looking for me yesterday weren't you?'

Liu had tried to prepare herself but she was nevertheless taken aback. So this was the Auntie Chen her mother had asked her to go and see – a fat, dark and saggy-skinned old woman. She was dressed in a patched blouse and worn-out shoes. It was almost impossible to believe that such a person had ever been good friends with Liu's mother – a woman who was so fair-skinned and sophisticated. They appeared to have come from different worlds.

Liu immediately said that she had been sent by her mother who had given her a few presents to pass on to her. Her mother had in fact done no such thing, but Liu suddenly realized that she should have done.

'So she's remembered me at last!' croaked Auntie Chen, almost in tears.

She wiped her hands with a rag and looked closely

at Liu: 'Yes, you are your mother's daughter alright. Just as slender, and just as shapely. In fact, you're even prettier than she was back then.'

Liu felt a little embarrassed, but at the same time Auntie Chen's informal manner and direct approach put her very much at ease.

'I left your presents in my hotel room,' she said, thinking of a way to make her well-intentioned lie more convincing.

'The golden lark at the window would not stop chirping this morning; I knew it meant a guest would be coming to see me and here you are!' said Auntie Chen, disregarding the remark about the presents. She picked up her bucket and asked Liu to follow her down the stone steps. In no time at all they were at her front door.

Auntie Chen invited her in and asked her to sit down. The place still stank of herbal medicine. She opened the door to let some light in. The only thing that distinguished this house from all the thousands of almost identical grey-tiled little houses in Liang County was the lack of clutter. There was no statue of the god of wealth, or of Guanyin, goddess of mercy. The furniture consisted of nothing more than one small wooden table, two stools and a bed in the bedroom. There wasn't even a black and white television.

Liu sat down and said, 'My mother misses you. She wants to know how life is treating her old friend.'

Auntie Chen laughed. 'See for yourself. There's nothing left. Everything's had to be sold. Even the rats have gone, which is quite something.'

She said her husband was in hospital waiting for

an operation. He had stomach cancer. He had been laid off and was no longer entitled to take advantage of his health insurance. That meant they had to pay for everything – the medication, the healthcare and even the bed. It cost them more than 200 yuan a day. And the surgery would require 5,000 yuan up front. Without that money all they could do was wait for the cancer to spread to other parts of his body.

She poured a cup of hot water explaining that ever since her husband had become ill she hadn't even been able to afford tea leaves. She took off her hat revealing a head of short unkempt hair, some grey and some white.

Liu picked up her cup and said, 'Don't worry Auntie Chen, hot water is fine.'

'People don't call me Auntie Chen anymore.'

She explained that her first husband, Old Chen, had died back in 1973. He had been kicked out of the party in the fifties for 'opposing the leadership'. During the early days of the Cultural Revolution he was accused of being a 'black hand' – someone behind the scenes who instigated armed conflicts between Red Guard factions – and he was sent to prison, where he eventually died. Even when things started getting better his name was never cleared – he still remained on 'the list of shame'. Auntie Chen had been so distraught that she decided to write to Liu's mother for help, something she had later regretted. Auntie Chen spoke quickly but without any trace of bitterness. Liu would never have guessed from her tone of voice how much suffering and injustice she had endured. However, once she had started there was no stopping her.

'I was nearly fifty but what could I do? I had to get married again. So I did. I married Old Wang, a neighbour. He was only a factory worker but he was a kind man and very good to me. Nowadays everyone in the lane calls me Mother Wang, hardly anyone round here knows I used to be Mrs Chen.'

At that moment a young woman entered the house and walked down the stone steps. The room was so dingy that Liu couldn't make out who the person was; all she could see was how filthy she was.

'Come over here my girl, we have a visitor. She's come a long way!' shouted Auntie Chen.

The girl filled a washbasin with water, picked up a rag and walked into the other room. It was the same girl that Liu had seen the day before.

'Is she your daughter?' asked Liu.

'Yes. Well, she's my adopted daughter. Her name is Diegu. You must have seen her yesterday. She's not well... It's her chest. But we can't afford proper medicine, so I'm trying to cure her with herbal remedies.'

'I thought I'd come to the wrong place,' said Liu.

'She has a little problem up here,' explained Auntie Chen, tapping her head. 'She's never really learnt how to deal with other people. Twenty years ago there was a famine in Henan; some of the survivors fled and passed through Liang. She was one of them. Old Chen – bless his soul – found her at the end of the lane. She was having an epileptic fit and was foaming at the mouth and shaking like you wouldn't believe. The others had gone on and left her there, so he brought her home. We managed to make her come round but she's always been a bit slow. She works as a street sweeper – has to get up at dawn every day. The wages are so low – it's just not right, but what's worse is that they're thinking of phasing the job out altogether.'

Liu didn't mention that she'd seen her earlier that morning. She obviously had a brick carrying job to which she went after she'd finished the sweeping. How could she ever hope to get better if she had two jobs? Auntie Chen poured the dark red infusion into a bowl, carried it into the bedroom and told her to drink it up quickly, while it was still hot.

'Mother, have you had lunch? How are things at the hospital?' she asked.

'They're fine. I woke you up yesterday, didn't I, when I came back late? So why don't you go and have a rest.'

Liu could see how much they loved each other. Auntie Chen came back into the outer room and suddenly clapped her hands: 'Your mother must have told you about Yueming! She has, hasn't she? Yueming – my son – was born on the same day as you were – same day, same month, same year.'

But Liu's mother had never once mentioned that Auntie Chen had a son. All she'd ever said was that Auntie Chen was pregnant at the same time as her. They'd been quite famous at the time in Liang; they were known as 'the two big-bellied female cadres'. When Liu and her parents left Liang, the Chens had stayed behind. Old Chen was a straightforward sort of man; he had been in charge of 'the department of armed forces'.

'Oh yes, of course she has,' lied Liu. 'Where is he now?'

'I was just about to go and see him. He's at Water Moon Temple.'

Liu had read about Water Moon Temple in a tourist pamphlet in the hotel. It was Liang's only tourist site. Perched on Nanhua Mountain, it was said to have been built six hundred years ago, during the Ming Dynasty. But what could Auntie Chen's son be doing there?

'He's not a monk,' explained Auntie Chen. 'He used to be a primary school teacher in a nearby village.'

Auntie Chen looked old but her mind was quick. She guessed immediately what was on Liu's mind.

'After the Resettlement the school was closed down and now he paints pictures for the temple gift shop. I don't know why he doesn't just become a monk. He's too old to be single...and it doesn't matter what I say to him. There are girls who like him, but he never shows any interest.' She sneaked a glance at Liu and sighed.

Liu wanted to go and have a look at the temple anyway so she asked Auntie Chen if she might accompany her.

Auntie Chen looked hesitantly at Liu as though she wanted to say something, then suddenly her face burst into a smile and she agreed.

Chapter Nine

They turned out of the lane and headed west through the streets of the Old City. Strings of bright red peppers, garlic and even long strips of smoked black meat had been hung in front of many shops, as if to ward off evil spirits. There was a barber's stall at almost every other crossroads, where the barbers stood, staring at people's hair as they walked past. Haircuts were very cheap: eight jiao for a short back and sides, 3 yuan for a 'style'.

Liu was intimidated by the barbers. She didn't like being stared at by men wielding big pairs of scissors. Each stall had a big iron nail hammered into the nearest wall or telegraph pole from which would hang the entire selection of the stall's hair-cutting equipment. The colour of the towels left something to be desired and the mirror, propped up against a stone, caught the distorted reflection of everyone who walked by.

Auntie Chen stopped in front of a little shop which sold chilli paste. She explained that there were two ways up the mountain. There had once been a road which went along the mountain ridge, but it had been turned into a cable car route. You weren't allowed to walk up it anymore. Instead you had to buy a ticket which cost 50 yuan. 'And who can afford that, apart from the tourists?' asked Auntie Chen. The other way up was a long meandering road which would take them a considerable distance out of their way.

Liu understood Auntie Chen's embarrassment. She knew that this was not a good time to reveal how wealthy she was, so she said, 'You choose; I really don't mind.'

Auntie Chen thought about it and replied, 'Why don't we take a motorbike taxi?'

They turned into the main street. In front of them was a large ornamental archway designed to mark the beginning of the road up to the Temple. It was clumsily built because it was below the flood line; there were several brand new, more impressive versions higher up the mountain which would face the reservoir.

Auntie Chen agreed to pay 5 yuan per person for a motorbike taxi. She put on a helmet and passed one to Liu who hesitated for a moment while she wondered whether to look inside to see if it was clean. In the end she decided just to put it straight on her head. When she was ready Auntie Chen said to Liu's driver: 'Go slow and keep your distance. Be careful.'

The motorbikes drove out of the city up the twisting road with the mountain on one side and the river on the other. Liu felt a bit awkward wrapping her arms around the waist of a man she had never met before, but one glance at how steep the cliffs were was enough to make her lose her inhibitions.

Her driver started off at a reasonable speed but soon sped up. Taking no notice of Auntie Chen's words of caution, he drove right up behind the vehicle in front before dodging the oncoming traffic as he overtook. But he knew what he was doing and Liu only felt nervous for the first couple of minutes. Once they'd left the city the views were spectacular. The air was fresh and a fine spray from the jade-green river brushed her cheeks.

The driver tried to make conversation: 'So what do you do then? You're not from around here...have you come to see relatives? Or just here on holiday? You've not picked a very good time – we're still trying to kill all these bloody rats. At night there are thousands of them dying in the streets and when you wake up they're all floating in the river. It's not a pretty sight, not pretty at all.'

Liu listened patiently. 'Problem is, they're cleverer than us. It's no easy task trying to kill a horde of rats you know. They've started moving up into the New City already – and we're still stuck down here! But they manage to stop most of them. Every night they put a line of poison round the whole area and most just die there and then – piles of them lying dead in the streets each morning.'

Liu realized he was getting a bit carried away. He went on to say that the only place the rats didn't dare go to was the Temple on the mountain, since it was a place watched over by the Boddhisattva.

At that moment sunlight streamed through the gaps between the pillars of rock up ahead and in no time at all the mist over the river had completely disappeared, revealing the water itself – a mosaic of rippling waves and swirling whirlpools that blurred the reflection of the green mountains above. There was one solitary raft floating downstream. Peak upon peak as far as the eye could see – tall, majestic and inspiring – disappeared into the mists beyond. And the higher they went, the more they could see and the smaller the green line of the river became.

When the motorbike stopped Liu got off and passed her helmet to the driver. His head was dripping with sweat. She tried to pay him but Auntie Chen was having none of it: 'Whatever would you think of me if I let you pay?' Liu backed off reluctantly.

When the drivers asked if they should wait, Auntie Chen waved them off, saying that only a fool would pay to go downhill.

They were at the back wall of the Temple courtyard. The main hall was on the very top of the mountain. From up here the city looked like a melon which had been sliced through: one half of the melon was resting on either side of the river. The river also looked different, more like a long yellow road weaving its way through the mountains.

The cluster of Temple buildings was encircled by walls. Auntie Chen pushed open one of the small side doors and they walked into an outer courtyard. There seemed to be some kind of building work going on – there was a lot of banging and what sounded like the clanking of tools. There were many workmen around, but Liu couldn't see what part of the Temple was being worked on. It seemed as if even the ancient

Temple was preparing to embrace modernity.

They walked into one of the quieter courtyards and Auntie Chen called out, 'Yueming!'

A door opened and out walked a middle-aged man wearing an old ink-spattered jacket. He had a crew-cut, making him look just like all the other men in the Old City. There was nothing remarkable in his appearance; he looked like an ordinary village primary school teacher.

He was obviously surprised to see his mother with a young woman he didn't know, but he made the effort not to let it show.

'This is Liu,' said Auntie Chen, 'The Liu I'm always taking about.'

Yueming extended his hand and said, 'It's an honour to meet you.'

Auntie Chen slapped the back of his hand. 'Stop behaving like a fool! Liu was born on the same day as you. What's this about "honour"?'

Yueming ignored her and shook hands with Liu.

'Hello. Your mother invited me along, I hope I'm not disturbing you,' Liu said politely.

'Not at all, please, come in and sit down.'

They went inside and Liu wandered around looking at his pictures. He waited till she was at the far end of the room and seized the opportunity to pull his mother to one side, whispering: 'My boss came round yesterday and said the most he could lend me was a thousand. He said business at the gift shop wasn't too good, and even with the monks blessing the pictures in front of the customers they can't put the prices up more than 20 yuan. But I kept on asking and in the end he agreed to lend me one thousand five hundred.'

Auntie Chen collapsed into a bamboo chair, almost knocking the ink pot off the table. She sighed: 'The operation can't wait. Somehow or another you have just got to get another three thousand. I'll try asking in the Lane again, but you know as well as I do that that won't bring in more than a thousand – if that. We need four thousand at the very least, and they say if we want it done well it'll be five thousand. What are we going to do?'

Yueming looked embarrassed; he did not know what to say. Liu deliberately moved a little further away. She knew when to mind her own business. They spoke softly, in the local dialect; Liu had already recovered her childhood comprehension of it to a surprising extent. Three thousand meant very little to her, but was this really the right time for her to display her generosity?

The room was quite large and seemed to be a kind of a Temple storehouse room. On either side of the doors and windows hung the paintings Yueming had made for the gift shop; they were all traditional water-colour landscapes and each one was accompanied by a famous classical poem about the Three Gorges. The poems were quoted in all the tourist guide-books about the Three Gorges. As far as Liu was concerned, water-colour landscapes were all much the same – always had been and always would be – and Yueming's were certainly nothing special. In fact, the unnecessary addition of dots of red peach blossom and green willow leaves in the corners made them look rather tasteless. Yueming was churning them out like a machine to supply the shop; he was, at best, a hack painter.

At the other end of the room there was a long old wooden table with a small bucket of glue, a broad-brush and rolls of paper on it. There was also a ceramic jar holding several brushes – all of different sizes. Underneath there was a bucket full of inky water, murky after being used to wash brushes.

It seemed Yueming had to mount the pictures as well as paint them. They couldn't be sold unless they were mounted properly. He was probably paid more for the mounting than for the painting.

A few bits of paper had been thrown onto the floor, one of which caught her eye; it was lying upside down but the paper was so thin you could see that something had been painted on the other side. She turned it over. It was not at all what she was expecting – it looked like a painting but only consisted of a few coarse, broad strokes, a few swishes of the brush and ink of a very uneven texture. In the middle there was one small dot of dazzling red and a few splashes of black. She looked more carefully at it. There was something truly unique about it.

She turned over one of the others. This one was even more intriguing. Torrents of water had run down the paper in a slight curve; they seemed to have been moving quickly, as though nothing could have stopped them from cascading off the bottom of the paper. In the end, however, something had stopped them and the ink had been absorbed by the dark yellow grain of the paper. The resulting image resembled the hazy outline of distant mountain ridges – floating clouds shrouding layered rock formations – and yet not one single thing had technically been 'painted'.

Liu was no expert on art and she had certainly never had any understanding of modern abstract art. As far as she was concerned, Western art galleries were full of pictures by arrogant people who had nothing better to do than compete in their audacity to con gullible patrons. But these two paintings entranced her with their distinctive composition and forcefulness. She could clearly make out the texture of the rocks along the Gorges and yet, somehow, she could see that no rocks had been painted. The picture encouraged the viewer's imagination to transcend everyday reality. The apparently random brush-strokes and the uncontrolled splashes of ink captured something rare and beautiful about this world and yet, at the same time, they resonated with something beyond our world.

The more she looked, the more the paintings seemed to come alive; they were full of a sense of movement, flowing with the vigour of the Great River itself. Liu was transfixed – how could these two remarkable paintings ever have ended up discarded on the floor?

Mother and son were still at the other end of the room, heads together, talking quietly but animatedly. Yueming looked the more worried of the two. Liu walked over and asked: 'How much do sell your pictures for?'

He looked up. His Mandarin was not perfect but he spoke more clearly than most people she had heard. He must have grown accustomed to speaking correctly as he was a teacher.

'I only copy other people's paintings. The shop sells them for between one and two hundred each, and I get ten per cent.'

'What!' exclaimed Liu involuntarily, 'You only get 10 or 20 yuan per picture?'

'It's not bad you know – the paint and the brushes aren't mine, the studio isn't mine, and the gift shop certainly isn't mine,' Yueming replied calmly. 'But then, of course, I can't bless them as the monks do.'

'Well,' began Liu, pointing to the two on the floor under the table, 'how much are those two?'

He took a few steps in the direction of the table and realized which ones she was talking about: 'They're just paintings that have gone wrong, waste paper.' He looked straight into Liu's eyes in a way that was almost rude.

It was the first time Liu had had a good look at his eyes. They were heavy and cold. Perhaps it was because he'd spent too much time looking at the mountains. He was polite, but his eyes were remote and inscrutable. It was as though a wide river was flowing between him and whoever he looked at.

'Waste paper?' Liu asked, unconvinced. They couldn't possibly be, but even if they were, she still liked them. 'I want to buy them – two thousand for each one.' Seeing the astonished reaction on both their faces she added, just to show that she was serious, 'But you'll have to mount them, and I want your seal and signature on them as well.'

'I can't sell them.'

Liu thought she must have misheard, but he repeated: 'They're just pictures which have gone wrong, of course I can't take any money for them.' His tone was forceful, as though deliberately to refute Liu.

Liu blushed. She wanted to explain that those two paintings really were worth that much, that she really felt that strongly about them, but she could see from Yueming's eyes that there was no point. He knew exactly what was going on. He was not as docile as he seemed.

Auntie Chen, still sitting in the bamboo chair, didn't utter a single word.

Yueming turned round: 'Mother, go home. I'll think of something. I'll find the money and give it to you in a couple of days.'

Liu and Auntie Chen walked outside. The view was breathtaking. In the middle of the great panorama was Liang County, vast and sprawling. Even the Old City looked impressive from this distance. Liu had always imagined she would be disappointed when she finally saw the Three Gorges, but she wasn't disappointed in the slightest. On the contrary, they were more beautiful than she had ever believed possible. Often the weight of expectation crushes the enjoyment of the moment. Films and photos can make a place look more spectacular than it really is and also destroy its mystery. Even the Grand Canyon had fallen short of her expectations. It was like meeting a film star in the flesh: they are never as interesting nor as beautiful as when they're on the big screen.

The Three Gorges, despite centuries of praise from poets, looked as pure and fresh as the day Nature had first created them. According to the boatmen May was the best time to visit – after the humidity had been washed away by the cleansing rain of

April, and before the summer storms had brought the floods which would turn the Yangtze into a yellow torrent of liquid mud.

If you took the time to stand still and watch the river you could see that it didn't just flow; it was permanently in a state of flux, swirling in endless permutations. Under the emerald-blue sky a hovercraft was making its way upstream, cutting a long white line in the water as if making a slow tear in a sheet of silk. Behind the lake the green mountains stretched away into the distance. Further down it was possible to make out the pair of red granite cliffs known as the Gorge Gateway; they had been sculpted over thousands of years by the might of the surging river which was forced between narrow rocks at this point and became a fierce torrent of whirlpools and rapids.

Liu had seen the Three Gorges from the boat and from her hotel window. She didn't know why she should feel so moved by the view right now. Why should she be so overawed by the vastness and beauty of what lay before her?

Chapter Ten

Later, when she came to think about it, it struck Liu as very strange that her mother had never mentioned the fact that Auntie Chen had a child. Perhaps it had just never occurred to her that her friend's pregnancy would almost certainly result in the birth of a child. Or maybe she just didn't care.

The evening of the sandstorm, when Liu and her mother had talked late into the night, Liu had heard, for the first time, the story of her birth way back in 1951.

Her mother freely admitted that she should have said something sooner. She'd been waiting for the right moment, and with Liu always being so busy, that moment had never come, or so she said.

The candles had nearly burnt themselves out. She always lit a few candles after dinner when she was on her own, saying that it made the place feel more homely. Liu knew perfectly well why she hadn't told her before – and it had nothing to do with either of them being busy – she had been waiting for a time that suited her, that was the truth of the matter. She had no trouble whatsoever in keeping something to herself. She was the kind of person who would willingly take her secrets to the grave.

'Prefect Liu, my husband...' she began.

Liu could still remember the calm tone of her mother's voice as she told the story. And thinking back to what her mother had said, she realized that it made no difference to her. Her image of her father would never change.

Her father, the man who had been called 'Prefect Liu' forty years earlier, had been the political commissar of a regiment in the People's Liberation Army. By the time Sichuan Province was liberated, he had already been a revolutionary for more than ten years.

He joined the army when he was a student. His parents were wealthy peasants. Liu's mother came from Southern Jiangsu. She joined the army in the winter of 1949, following which she was sent to work in Chongqing, where she met her future husband and got married.

Her father already had a wife back home in the countryside, but divorce was common at the time. Young cadres would find a new wife from among the female students who joined the revolutionary cause. Liu had always known that her mother was a 'revolutionary wife', but she'd never given it much thought.

In the spring of 1951 her father was appointed Prefect of the Liang Region. There were quite a few counties in the area which were still full of counter-revolutionary bandits hiding in the mountains. Getting rid of them was going to be a difficult job, and trying to arouse enthusiasm in the revolution was going to be even harder. Almost all the important positions were given to ex-soldiers from the north. He brought a few cadres from his regiment along with him, including Battalion Commander Chen who married a local girl, to show how committed he was to supporting the revolution in that part of China.

Liu's father did not allow his wife to come to Liang County. He said it was too dangerous there, and insisted that she should stay in the huge nearby city of Chongqing. But she missed him dreadfully and, besides, she wanted to get more involved in the revolution. China was burning with revolutionary zeal and Liu's mother wanted to be a part of it. Liu's father was pleased she was so keen, but still thought it better for her to stay where she was, for the sake of their unborn child more than anything. Life was easier there and there was an excellent gynaecological hospital run by foreign nuns.

Liang was an important port on the Yangtze. Sailors and boatmen enjoyed spending the night there since it was dangerous to travel downstream in the Gorges because of the many hidden rocks. The men in the boats coming upstream liked to relax in Liang before going on to Chongqing and unloading.

Prostitution was considered every bit as necessary a part of the shipping industry as adequate warehouses and docks. Every evening, as soon as it was dark, hordes of sailors would swarm into the bars and brothels. It was big business.

By 1951 most of the bandits had been suppressed and the local government was firmly in control. It was time to start 'cleaning up the filth of the past'.

On arrival Liu's mother reported immediately to the relevant authorities. She was assigned to the Women's Association, which was just what she had hoped for. The Association was very different back then; it didn't use to hand out sinecures as it began to do later. Working for the Women's Association was tough. They desperately needed people like Liu's mother to help in the critical early stages of the project to educate prostitutes. And, of course, everyone was delighted to see the wife of a Prefect doing her bit – despite being pregnant. It was just what was needed to boost morale.

She was happy in her work, not least because she became such good friends with Auntie Chen, the wife of her husband's old comrade, Commander Chen. He was a war veteran who had been in the field everywhere from Manchuria to Sichuan. He was an uncompromising old soldier who made up in bravery for what he lacked in education. When Communist troops had had to retreat from the battlefield of Siping, it was thanks to the self-discipline of men like him that the army did not fall apart altogether.

Auntie Chen had grown up in the nearby county of Fengdu. She'd run away from home to escape an arranged marriage and stumbled across a group of Communist guerrillas in the mountains who had persuaded her to join their cause. When Commander Chen and his troops arrived in Liang they were ordered to find themselves suitable girls and get married. He wasn't interested in city girls, so he picked a strong country girl who knew the meaning of hard work.

Liu's mother and Auntie Chen used to tease each other saying that their pregnancies were a 'peace sickness'. Most of the battles had already been fought; the only thing left to do was to flush the last few remaining bandits out of the mountains. It was the right time to have children. Their only worry was that children born at such a peaceful time would turn out to be too gentle and quiet, that they would lack revolutionary spirit.

Auntie Chen a strong young woman, built for bearing children; she had no trouble at all remaining active throughout the pregnancy. Liu's mother called her 'big sister'. Later she found out that Auntie Chen was actually six months younger than her, but it was too late: the name stuck. Auntie Chen looked out for her, and she found she could talk to her about anything. They were both very enthusiastic about their work. They wanted to reform as many prostitutes as possible and turn them into new women, into new revolutionaries, just like themselves.

The prefectural administration office, in the same place as it had been under the nationalists, was an old building with a fishpond and rockery in the courtyard. Of course, during the war the goldfish were not fed, and died, so it had become nothing more than a stagnant pool. The various departments were situated along the long winding corridor, and the kitchen was at the back of the courtyard, near where Liu's parents and the guards lived.

The rural economy still hadn't recovered – there was only one market every ten days and food was scarce – so Prefect Liu asked his guards to go up into the mountains in search of sustenance. They had no difficulty in finding things – be it growing in the ground, running through the forest or swimming in the rivers – all they had to do was take it.

For some unknown reason she found it very difficult to relax during her pregnancy. She felt so exhausted she could hardly keep her eyes open, but when it came to actually going to sleep she felt wide awake. Nobody seemed to know why but the atmosphere in the compound seemed quite tense at that time. Her husband and Auntie Chen tried to get her to rest more, saying that all she should be worrying about was the health of the baby, but she didn't take much notice.

One night Prefect Liu didn't get back until after midnight. Liu's mother had just managed to get to sleep, but woke up as soon as he came in. The weather was sultry and airless. Her husband had managed to get them a double bed, but he hadn't been able to find a double mosquito net so they had to get another one. He hadn't found a big enough bed-mat either, so they had to make do with two small ones. She stretched out her arm from under the mosquito net wanting to hold her husband's hand, but he drew it back slowly. He needed sleep.

At daybreak the local militia captain asked the guard to go and knock on the door and wake Prefect Liu up. The guard hesitated, but did as he was told. Prefect Liu got up, got dressed and went out, closing the door behind him.

His wife, still half asleep, heard voices outside. She quickly got out of bed and put some clothes on.

There was a man outside who looked like a soldier although his uniform was torn and he appeared rather dishevelled. He looked as if he had just rolled down a cliff, but he bore no scars. He kept waving his pistol about and ranting incomprehensibly. Prefect Liu ordered his guards to disarm him immediately, but they said they had already checked the gun and it was empty. The captain said that his militiamen had found him while out on patrol. He'd been walking on the slope leading to the Temple, not far from the city. They had asked him what he was doing, but he had answered incoherently. He seemed to have been just wandering around.

Prefect Liu was worried. It wasn't the first time something like this had happened. Soldiers who could keep perfectly calm in battle seemed to be falling under some kind of evil spell. He ordered the captain to take the man back to the barracks and said to the soldiers, 'He's ill, he must have caught something. He'll be alright after a few days rest.' Looking round, he added, 'It's nothing out of the ordinary, and I forbid you from spreading silly rumours to the contrary.'

He went back inside and said to his wife, 'It's strange... why didn't we hear any gunshots? When I arrived here there were still some snipers left up in the mountains, and whenever anyone fired a gun, you could hear it for miles around.'

'Are there no bandits there now?' His wife asked.

'No, there's only a Temple up there, on the peak.' He thought for a moment and added, 'Bandits? Hmmm...'

'What was that?'

'Nothing. It'll be morning soon. Go back to bed for a while.' He sat at the table. 'Am I just worrying about nothing…?'

Chapter Eleven

That morning there was a cadres' meeting, chaired by Prefect Liu. The first item on the agenda was to check the progress of the Programme to Reform Prostitutes. All the female cadres attended. Liu's mother hadn't had the opportunity to attend many meetings since she'd arrived in Liang so she was excited. Despite having hardly slept a wink, she still managed to arrive on time.

However, she wasn't in a position to contribute very much. It was Auntie Chen who read out the report, saying what difficulties they had encountered in their work. One problem had been that the prostitutes were resentful of the rough treatment they had been subjected to when arrested by the militia. Some of the more timid ones had become even shyer, and some of the more headstrong ones had become even more difficult. Some of them wouldn't sit still during class, and, when it was their turn to speak, they would just act the fool or start swearing. When they were doing mat-weaving quite a few of them refused to concentrate and made fun of anyone who did. And recently things had got even worse: they had started having fights in the dorms – biting and clawing at one another and rolling around on the floor. It was very difficult to separate them; the supervising cadres could hardly tear them apart. In the end the guards had to separate them using their rifle butts.

Liu's mother found it all very interesting, but her husband banged the table disapprovingly, saying that the report was full of too much insignificant detail. He wanted it to focus on 'serious enemy activity'. It seemed that Auntie Chen had failed to mention certain incidents which he considered to be highly important.

The criticism prompted Auntie Chen to announce that one of the prostitutes had resisted reform and hanged herself.

The whole meeting started to buzz.

She said that things had got a bit tense because the first class was about to be disbanded and, when it was, the prostitutes were to be married off to factory workers and peasants who had no other way of finding a wife. There had been a terrible uproar; some had taken to crying for hours on end, some had refused to eat, some had pretended to be ill. There had been no way of keeping them in order.

One of them, a girl named Red Lotus, was finding it harder than the others to come to terms with giving up her former life-style. When prostitutes hit twenty they usually start wanting to change their ways and get married; they find someone from another village who doesn't know much about them and settle down. But Red Lotus was different. She had become a 'big sister' among them.

Prefect Liu interrupted her: 'Comrades, it is essential to examine a situation such as this in terms of class struggle. This Red Lotus is obviously the proprietor of a brothel, a Madame, and as such, she is a local despot.'

Auntie Chen blushed a little, 'Of course, yes, a local despot... a female local despot.'

She continued by saying that at first she had thought that it was just a case of a few prostitutes having got together and elected her their leader. Now she could see that the matter wasn't that simple. Red Lotus hadn't spoken a word out of turn all this time, nor put a foot out of line, but it was all just an act. And now this had been proved, she and three others had run away.

Prefect Liu was very serious: 'We must stop this kind of thing from happening at all costs!'

Auntie Chen replied, 'At first we didn't worry about it too much because, in our new society, they'll just be arrested again if they try to go back to their old ways, wherever they are. But now we understand: this is the battleground on which we must continue to fight!' Her voice was flat; she was obviously just repeating something her leader had told her. 'Letting them escape is letting reactionaries escape. This is a struggle in which leniency has no place.'

Prefect Liu now took over: 'They will have split up by now. There is no point trying to catch them all. We must focus all our energies on re-capturing the counter-revolutionary rebel, Red Lotus.' He looked at the militia captain, who hurriedly reported that he had already sent a detachment to find her. Prefect Liu nodded, his face stern. 'Cleaning up the filth of the Old Society is an important duty. Treachery from within is much more dangerous than an enemy soldier with a gun in his hands. We must be constantly on our guard!'

He pulled a document out of his file and began to read it aloud. It had been sent by the Provincial Party Committee.

It was short, but no one understood much of it. After he'd finished he gave his own explanation of what was meant by 'suppressing counter-revolutionaries'. His Mandarin had a Henan accent which sounded strange and wasn't always very easy for Sichuanese people to understand. But it didn't matter; if anything, it gave his voice an air of authority.

'Our prefecture is lagging behind,' he said, raising his voice, 'if we keep on being as sloppy as this we will be failing in our duty to the Party and our superiors will lose confidence in us. Many comrades seem to believe that the battle is over. Far from it. The roots of feudalism go deep! We must, for example, be more diligent in the 'Campaign against Reactionary Cults'. Right now that is our top priority in the suppression of counter-revolutionaries.'

All that could be heard was the sound of pens scribbling away; everyone was busily taking notes. Prefect Liu had deliberately spoken slowly so everyone would have enough time to write down what he said. The long pauses between words and sentences made the speech inspiring in its solemnity.

He lit a cigarette, sitting comfortably in his rattan chair. Commander Chen, who was chairing the meeting, added a few words stressing the importance of passing on what they had just heard and saying it was imperative that everyone should understand.

Liu's mother felt that her husband had changed dramatically since he had left the army. His political speeches had been so dull and direct back then; there had been no political theory. How inspiring he had now become! 'Indeed, Liang has made him!' She looked around. No one was talking. Everyone seemed to have been silenced by the force of her husband's words.

Old Chen was the first to speak: 'If any comrade has a question, please seize this opportunity to ask!'

Most people still seemed lost in thought, but one young cadre had finished taking notes and decided to ask:

'Would our leader please tell us how to distinguish between 'Destroying Reactionary Cults' and protecting 'Legitimate Religious Activities'?'

Prefect Liu exhaled a small puff of smoke. Clearly, this was the question he had been waiting for.

'It is Party policy to permit legitimate religious activities. But permitting something is not the same as encouraging it. As you all know, "Religion is the opium of the people". We want to educate the masses to spurn this reactionary opiate. Comrades responsible for our culture and education will have to work especially hard to achieve this.'

Everyone breathed a sigh of relief. Culture and education had never been matters of great urgency. But the young cadre asked another question:

'So what should we do if some religious leaders start trying to compete with us for the support of the masses?'

Prefect Liu smiled. This young comrade had an inquisitive mind, which he liked. Most of the cadres looked completely blank whenever politics was discussed at meetings. What could you expect? They had been brought up to be nothing more than peasants or factory workers. He replied: 'We can only tolerate their religious activities; we cannot tolerate their political activities. We can tolerate those who are in agreement with Party policy, but we cannot tolerate anyone who resists the revolution. Any religious organisation which does not accept Party leadership should be treated as a counter-revolutionary cult!'

His speech reached such a crescendo that no one dared make the slightest sound even when he had finished. He changed the subject, asking an apparently unrelated question:

'Is there a Buddhist Temple here?'

Old Chen replied: 'Yes. On Nanhua Mountain, about five miles out of town. It's called Water Moon Temple. It's a well-known scenic spot.'

Prefect Liu asked: 'The Abbot of the Temple, he's called Master Yutong, isn't he?'

Old Chen replied: 'Yes, that's right. And there are a few young monks there too.'

'Have you investigated the Abbot?'

The militia captain took it upon himself to answer the question: 'We have. The former county administration did not keep any records on monks. The Temple is said to be over seven hundred years old, but it's been completely renovated several times.'

'How do we know that this person has not committed any anti-revolutionary crimes?'

Old Chen and the militia captain exchanged glances. After a few seconds Old Chen said: 'It would appear that this person has never taken any part in local politics. People don't even recall ever having seen him anywhere but on the mountain.'

Prefect Liu's expression changed. Old Chen obviously had no understanding of politics.

'A month ago I invited all local VIPs to attend a conference. The Abbot was the only person who had the effrontery to decline. He refused to leave the mountain. Such insubordination will not be tolerated. Maybe he treated the warlords in the same way, but that doesn't excuse his behaviour. This is not a question of bowing to the Communist Party, and it certainly isn't a question of bowing to me. The Communist Party represents the people. If he doesn't want us to represent him, then he's not one of the people!'

Old Chen did not know how to reply. In the end he just asked, 'So... what then?'

'The revolution is the future; the time has come to make all opposition to our cause a thing of the past!'

'So the Abbot is a counter-revolutionary?' blurted out Old Chen clumsily.

How long was Old Chen going to last if he carried on like this?

Prefect Liu surveyed the faces in the room: 'In this prefecture we tread the path of revolution. Or would you all rather pay homage to some Buddha? Can we knowingly allow such behaviour to continue without making any effort to control it, without even asking any questions? Our track record in suppressing counter-revolutionaries here is not impressive. And the reason for that is that not even our own ranks understand what we are trying to achieve.'

'So... what should we do?' asked Old Chen.

Prefect Liu stood up. He had had enough. He was irritated by his comrades' inability to grasp the simplest aspects of Party policy. This wasn't the first time they had proven themselves so useless.

'That's all for this morning. This afternoon each department will discuss the Directive of the provincial Party committee.'

Old Chen declared the meeting officially closed and everyone stood up and filed out. It was only when everyone else had left that Prefect Liu noticed his wife – her face deadly pale – sitting alone in the corner. He walked over to her and said; 'That was a long meeting... you shouldn't have come.'

'The meeting was very interesting,' she replied. 'It's just a bit stuffy in here. I'll feel better when I get some air.'

'Those chain smokers! Sorry – I had a couple myself this morning – just to wake me up a bit,' he said. He hardly ever smoked or drank, but he'd slept badly the night before. He helped her out of her round-backed armchair and they walked back to the back courtyard. On her way she noticed that the camellias had begun to wilt. Petals and leaves covered the ground. The sky was overcast.

Prefect Liu thought his wife would be better after a rest, but when he got back after the afternoon meeting she was still in bed, white-faced and gasping for breath. She was in a great deal of discomfort. He dashed out immediately to call for Dr Qi.

They didn't have to wait long before a guard escorted Dr Qi, a handsome man with delicate features, into the compound. He examined the patient carefully but couldn't find anything wrong. He said it might be the baby kicking in the womb, 'But the position of the foetus is perfect,' he added reassuringly.

Prefect Liu asked the doctor to step outside with him.

'Honestly, is there any kind of problem?' He asked quietly, knowing the doctor wouldn't have wanted to tell whole truth in front of his wife.

'She has a fragile constitution – always has had by the looks of it,' he replied, 'To be honest, she should never have come here with the baby due in less than a month. It wouldn't have been a bad idea for her to have stayed where she was until after the birth.'

Dr Qi had originally been a medical officer in a warlord's army; he had only started working for the People's Liberation Army when Communist troops had entered Sichuan. He was good at his job, so Prefect Liu had asked him to come with him to Liang to look after the cadres.

He whispered hesitantly: 'There have always been a lot of diseases in the air round here. The people here are too sanguine.'

Old Liu smiled and patted his shoulder: 'You're a revolutionary cadre now! You shouldn't say things like that! You should keep your ideas in line with Marxist science.'

The doctor laughed nervously: 'Quite right. Thank you for the criticism. I must study harder.'

Prefect Liu saw the doctor out and turned to look at the mountains. The clouds were moving quickly – the peaks had long since been shrouded in white – and as he stood there the whole range disappeared in the wispy swirling mists. Within seconds it became so overcast that it felt like dusk. He turned the other way and looked at the smoky haze above the Yangtze; it was like a giant carpet pressing down on the water's surface. Even the sound of the towmen singing on the shore seemed to have lost its usual liveliness, drowned out by the roar of the crashing waves.

'Nothing's easy in these damn Gorges,' he thought to himself. 'In this Campaign... I've got to think of way...a way to get myself noticed...a way to get promoted...sent somewhere better – I can't spend the rest of my life here.'

Chapter Twelve

Having said goodbye to Yueming by the gates of the Temple, Liu and Auntie Chen set off back down the mountain. Liu found the journey hard going. Her companion, however, appeared invigorated by every step she took: 'I'm used to it, you see... I've been climbing hills since childhood.' It seemed odd that someone who looked so old could be in such good shape.

She had to go to the hospital in the afternoon to take over from Diegu, so she suggested meeting after supper in order to continue talking about the old days. As they said goodbye she clasped one of Liu's hands tightly in both of hers and smiled at her with genuine affection.

Auntie Chen suggested meeting after supper, which was just what Liu had been hoping for. She was longing to hear more of Auntie Chen's story but she knew that there was no way they could chat over supper. Auntie Chen couldn't possibly afford to invite Liu, and Liu did not think that Auntie Chen would want to come to the Golden Pleasure Hotel restaurant – she would not feel comfortable there.

Besides, meeting later in the evening would give Liu a chance to have a rest. She was tired after the long walk and found the humidity of the air, so typical of late spring and early summer in the south, particularly soporific.

She stood for a while by the river, watching the bustle of people busy working, surrounded by all that rubbish. She felt different, but she couldn't quite put her finger on how or why. She'd seen the poorer areas of big cities in other countries, but she had not seen anywhere like this in over twenty years. It wasn't like London's East End or New York's Bronx. Those places had been properly built and then neglected. This was different, more like a giant campsite. There was no reason to look after anything. Everyone was just waiting until it was time to leave.

In the distance she could see the Liang Government Building – an imperious jade-white structure, built on high ground, taller than anything else around. She almost mistook it for the American Congress Building on Capitol Hill. Could there really be enough government officials to fill all those rooms? Opposite the impressively wide flight of stone steps leading to the main entrance was Rinsing Silk Lane, the main street. On one side was a large and well-designed new park that was full of greenery. One the other side was a series of tall shiny buildings, probably all occupied by banks and corporate offices. By far the most ostentatious building housed the Construction Bank – an lavish structure with a black marble floor and a large glass revolving door.

Liu inserted her 'Million Gold' credit card into the cash machine. She hadn't brought much cash with her and she needed 1,000 yuan. She tapped in her personal number but the machine spat out her card.

When her card had been rejected for the third time, Liu realized she would have to queue inside. The service counter was brand new and had bullet-proof glass; it was one of the longest she'd ever seen, but only two of the twenty or so windows were open. She took her place in the queue.

When she finally spoke to one of the bank clerks she showed her card and explained what had happened: 'I don't think your cash machine is working and I need to get some money out, urgently.'

The clerk was a young girl who seemed inexperienced. She turned round and asked the people working behind her what she should do. Another girl who seemed slightly older approached the counter and told Liu that the bank had only just opened which meant that only a limited service was available. The new cash machine had arrived but wasn't yet fully operational.

'Well, could you give me some cash over the counter?'

The girl examined Liu's card: 'We can't accept any cards which are from outside Sichuan or which have been issued by any bank but the Construction Bank.'

'Why's that?'

'That's the regulation. Maybe head office would change its policy if more people complained. I think the nearest bank which accepts cards like yours is in the city of Chongqing – you can go there and back in a day if you go by hovercraft.'

Liu's eyes widened in angry disbelief: 'Only a day!' She was about to launch into a speech asking why the whole area was still living in the dark ages, but thought better of it. What right did she have? She was only a visitor. Besides, it was a miracle that a place like Liang had a bank at all. It would have been a bit unfair to judge one's own country by Western standards.

Auntie Chen's plight was desperate. If going to Chongqing was the only way to get hold of some money then maybe she'd just have to go. It was only a day there and back after all.

Chapter Thirteen

She went back to the Golden Pleasure Hotel. When she opened the door to her room she saw an envelope on the carpet. She opened it and saw that it was a message from her husband asking her to call him. She threw it in the bin and went into the bathroom to wash her face. She was tired, so she fluffed her pillows, took off her shoes and lay down on the bed. As she lay there, just beginning to relax, she suddenly remembered she still hadn't phoned her mother. She sat up and dialled the number. There was no reply, just an answer phone. She left a message saying she'd arrived safely in Liang County and read out the hotel telephone number from the information pamphlet and also left her room number. How surprised her mother would be that she should have arrived in Liang the same day she had left Beijing!

For some unknown reason she found herself thinking back to one of her mother's birthdays. It had been just the two of them. They'd had a couple of glasses of cheap wine and were chatting away to each other when her mother had asked her – quite out of the blue – 'What made you pick a subject as new as genetic engineering?'

'I've already told you,' she had replied, a little annoyed. 'I was a so-called "Workers, Peasants and Soldiers" student. I was assigned to the biology department to research agricultural production. I never chose it; nobody ever asked me.'

'Alright! Alright! I know all that! What I meant was, isn't it funny that you ended up researching how human beings are created.'

Liu laughed: 'That's more something for the Gynaecology Department, or even the Theology Faculty.'

'No, I mean, how is it that it's your decisions which make a person 'This One'.

Liu hadn't been expecting her mother to be so philosophical: 'It's not just genes. Other factors play a much bigger role.'

'Yes, yes,' her mother replied impatiently; she hated clichés. 'Social conditions make someone who they are. Don't fob me off with all that. What I'm trying to say is that genes determine the aspects of one's life which can never be changed.'

'You've got that right...my being so ugly is all your fault!'

'Don't you be so spoilt... Everyone told me you were "Miss University".'

'How could I have been "Miss University" during the Cultural Revolution?' No one would have dared say such a thing, not even in private!'

'Well, "Miss University" was the girl Li was chasing.'

Li was a strange man. He was as tall as his father – almost 180cm. He was not typically handsome, but there was something about him that girls liked. He was one year older than Liu's mother. He thought of her as a sister. It didn't occur to him to ask her out on a romantic date until he saw how hard all the other boys were trying. One of Li's classmates had asked her out to go and see a film, and when he found out he was furious. The night of the date Li ambushed her on Nameless Lake, which was always frozen solid in winter, and told her everything.

It was a cold winter's day and the sun had long since disappeared beneath the horizon. That was the moment when they formally became 'in love'. Now she came to think of it, she'd never really made the choice to end up with Li; it had just seemed inevitable. She had never really liked her fellow-students. They were all a bit parochial, rather short-sighted and irritatingly indecisive.

'The son of a cadre marrying the daughter of another cadre is the most natural thing in the world. Other people just don't feel comfortable around you,' said her mother, adding: 'I'm just a little concerned that this kind of intermarriage might increase the chances of genetic defects if you ever have children.'

Liu burst out laughing. Her mother had always been quick-witted, and she admired her for it. She felt that her own conversation lacked colour; she wasn't very good with words.

Her mother continued: 'As Chairman Mao said, "There are good people who come in the back door and bad people who come in the front door" So the descendants of cadres must have both good and bad genes.' She chuckled.

Liu could imagine how hard it must have been for her father to woo her mother. They first saw each other when a troupe of university students came to perform for the Liberation Army troops. He fell in love with her at first sight. The head of the troupe tried to act as a go-between, but her mother was hesitant. In the end he said to her: 'Getting married to a revolutionary cadre wouldn't just be good for you, it would be good for your future children.' And that did the trick.

'If only the door had been open, I know I'd have got in on merit,' said Liu. 'But now even my PhD mortarboard won't hide the ugly cap of a "Workers, Peasants and Soldiers" student under-graduate degree.'

Liu was well aware that she and Li had taken full advantage of all kinds of new opportunities long before most people. China had changed a great deal since the seventies and they had always been the first to take advantage of the latest developments. They hadn't gone out of their way to find out what the next development was going to be, but they would overhear things because they were well connected. Even before the Cultural Revolution had ended the two of them put everything else aside and concentrated on learning English. Then, after a couple of years, the Minister of Water Resources had sent Li to America to study, and not long after that Liu had gone too. That had been at a time when university entrance exams were re-introduced after a ten year hiatus and most young people were fighting to get a place at a university in

China. Competition was fierce as there was only one place for every hundred applicants. Liu did another undergraduate degree in biology in the US and then embarked upon her postgraduate studies in genetic engineering. Li studied project management and returned to China after getting his MBA. When he returned the idea of studying abroad was just beginning to gain popularity.

Long before there was any serious debate about the Three Gorges Project, Li had already become the deputy head of the planning commission of the Ministry of Water and Power. Not long after that he began working on designs for the dam itself.

When, after ten years of study, Liu finally returned to China, she discovered that her husband had become the key figure in the greatest project in human history. And within months of her return he was promoted to the position of 'Deputy Head of the Yangtze Hydraulic Bureau and Director of Peace Lake Development Company'.

Suddenly the telephone rang. Liu turned and reached behind her for the receiver. 'Hello,' she answered.

'Hello.' She raised her eyebrows in disbelief. Li had the nerve to phone her again.

True, he was still her husband, but not even a not-yet-divorced husband has the right to continually harass his future ex-wife. Why should she go back to that wretched 'beautified' Dam Site of his? Why couldn't he just leave her where she actually wanted to be?

She was on the verge of giving him a piece of her mind when he said, 'Liu, I was afraid you had left

Liang. I'm so glad you haven't. I left you a written message and a message on your answer phone. You never got back to me.'

'What?' She was surprised. She looked at the answer-machine. Yes, she must have a message – the red light was flashing.

'I left a message asking you not to leave. I'll do my best to come round this evening, otherwise I'll be with you tomorrow morning at the latest.' He said this gently, just as though nothing had happened. There was no mention of the abrupt end to their last conversation.

She glanced at the huge bed in her room. Her response was straightforward: 'Why?' she asked.

This was her place of birth; her being here had nothing to do with him.

Li replied, 'I have a meeting there – two business consortiums, one from Hong Kong and one from Taiwan, are arriving in Liang tomorrow. They will have sightseeing in the morning, negotiations in the afternoon and a big dinner in the evening.'

'And what's that got to do with me?'

'Nothing, I'd just like to see you. We missed each other when you went to the Dam Site. It was my fault. So, now you're in Liang and I'm going to be in Liang, I don't want to make the same mistake again.'

Liu began to feel her anger boiling up again. If he had something to say why couldn't he say it over the telephone? Why did he have to see her in Liang? As far as she was concerned there was nothing to discuss – she'd just start shouting at him like she had the day before on the phone. It would simply be a waste of time.

Suddenly she remembered Auntie Chen and blurted out: 'Bring me 5,000 yuan...there's something I want to buy – a picture, an antique.'

'Of course I'll bring it for you.' He put the phone down, apparently anxious not to give her the opportunity to change her mind.

Liu replaced the handset in a daze. What did she think she was playing at? Whatever had possessed her to agree to Li's totally unreasonable request? What possible reason was there to give in so easily to a man so shameless?

She knew her own mind. She wasn't one of those women who are always in thrall to the desires of men. She was angry with herself for conforming to the stereotype of the submissive woman.

She casually picked up the tourist guide. The printing was poor and the language florid to the point of being almost unreadable. Would the problems which existed between them be solved like this? Or should they be solved at all? She really had no idea what she should do. Maybe that was why she had behaved so foolishly.

Then again, taking money from him wouldn't be the same as talking things over with him. She could go as soon as she had the money. She still had the choice to leave.

She sighed and put her hands in her pockets. In one of her pockets she could feel a folded piece of paper. She took it out. It was a flier advertising a song and dance group which had come to Liang from another province: 'Pretty girls and handsome boys, great songs and wild dancing, spectacular staging: all in celebration of the Dam Project!' The words were accompanied by a few pictures of scantily clad young women.

Of course, now she remembered. She had been given the flier by someone standing at the crossroads – they had been handing them out to anyone who'd take one. Most of the people she'd seen looking at it had laughed and made some kind of lewd comment. She couldn't understand exactly what they'd said because they were speaking too quickly, but it had been along the lines of, 'I wonder how much it would cost to give her one?'

She threw it in the waste paper basket. In a strange way she envied the ordinary people she'd seen in Liang. She envied them their lack of restraint, their love of life. They worked hard all day, then they got together to play *mah-jong* before going to bed and indulging in one of the simplest yet most satisfying pleasures of which man is capable. Whereas she...she had nothing enjoyable in life other than her work. She had neither cats nor hobbies. She couldn't remember the last time she had been out to see a film or hear a concert. Every day was the same: she would come back from work, eat, go to bed, read for a while and then, at ten o'clock, she would switch the news on, but she could never watch it right through. Her eyes would grow heavy and she'd drift off to sleep. It was a good way to live. She didn't need a man.

She walked along the muddy shore of the Great River – avoiding the dock – away from the hustle and bustle of barges, tugboats and tourist cruisers.

It was the first time she had had a close look at the Yangtze; she had never realized how filthy the water was. Just like she had never really had a good look at her husband...

The little island near the opposite bank was nothing more than a small strip of land a couple of inches above the water level. Something or other seemed to be cultivated on it and there were a few shacks. Of course it would disappear when the flooding started. Nothing had been built in the whole area for fifty years or so, except the temporary buildings for agricultural purposes; although the project hadn't been formally approved by the People's Congress until 1992, everyone had known it would happen sooner or later. Obviously there was no point in investing in something that was going to end up at the bottom of a lake. While everyone else in China had been debating the pros and cons, as far as local cadres were concerned it wasn't a matter of if; it was simply a matter of when. They had devoted their lives to the Dam. To question whether or not it would go ahead would have been like questioning whether or not their lives had any purpose.

Two workers carrying heavy oxygen cylinders were walking towards her: 'Make way! Make way!' Liu moved to a steeper part of the sloping bank.

The cruisers were all waiting for business. A group of tourists boarded one which had already started its motor. Within seconds it had driven off and disappeared behind the steep cliffs of the mighty Gorge.

All those years ago her mother had come to Liang

County to be with her father. And now her husband was coming to Liang to spend time with her. How the world had changed.

Or had it?

Chapter Fourteen

When her mother had first sailed down the Yangtze the translucent peach blossom fish had been swimming over moss-covered pebbles in clear emerald green water. Those days were long gone; the water was now so muddy that no freshwater jellyfish could survive.

However, perhaps not everything had changed. She thought she would try to find the old prefectural compound. Surely that was still there. After all, her mother had asked her to go and have a look if she were passing.

She asked passers-by. Apparently even that had gone. It had been wishful thinking on her mother's part.

The single-storey buildings and veranda had long since been replaced by large concrete offices. The local cadres had been so excited about the Resettlement Programme that they had made sure that their offices were among the first to be relocated to the New City, into that magnificent new building. The final flooding of 2009 was just a pretext for all their grand designs. The only part of the compound left was a small concrete building with a sign outside saying: 'Rat Extermination Office'. In the back courtyard there were boxes and boxes of extra-strength rat poison, and in the front yard there were hordes of people queuing up to buy it, though 'buy' is hardly the right word: the price was negligible, a purely symbolic token of payment.

Liu kept her distance. It was hard to imagine what it must have been like back then – the winding corridors, the exquisite woodwork, the trees and plants in the courtyard, fresh flowers all the year round, the morning dew, the bright sun.

Liu imagined how gentle and loving her mother must have been every time she put her hands over her womb and her unborn child. Liu's mother had once also been a young woman, hair cut short, going by boat from Chongqing to Liang County all by herself, gazing from afar at the patch of dusty grey on the mountainside. And as the boat drew closer she would have made out the black roof tiles and the little buildings – some made of mouldy old stones, some of wooden boards, and the spire of the French missionary church sticking up in the middle. And as she lifted her head she would have been able to see the green mountains stretching away into the distance.

The prefectural compound would have been very impressive, not unlike the kind of house she would have grown up in. There used to be vines and brightly-coloured peonies growing in the courtyard, adding an air of civilisation to the place. Liang was altogether much better than Liu's mother had been expecting – it had a long history and all modern conveniences, including a post office from which it was possible to send telegrams and make long-distance calls. There were four mixed schools and one Catholic girls' school. It was not such a remote place after all.

On one occasion Liu's mother had inadvertently walked into a street outside the walls of the Old City. It was paved with flagstones. The sun had already set behind the western mountains and the streets were lit by oil lamps. People had started coming out of their houses; everyone was wearing bright green and bright red and the women wore their hair bound up in coloured cloth. Everyone was unusually lively. Some of the young men had been wearing a kind of turban. It was a so-called 'Dancing Funeral'. Men and women were walking and waving their hands around with their fingers in 'the lotus posture'. The trumpeters were dripping with sweat and the bystanders were alternately laughing and crying.

Liu's mother had started to feel tired and so she had gone into a teahouse. There were lots of people already there, all dressed rather exotically. An old woman had approached her and said: 'Hello love, it's your first time here, isn't it? I see you're expecting – why don't I get you some Jianr tea?'

The teacup arrived almost immediately; strangely it had a lid. A young man poured the tea from an iron teapot with an extremely long spout from almost half a metre away. It tasted a bit like herbal medicine – rather bitter but with a sweet aftertaste. Looking out of the window she could see jasmine hanging from the city wall.

Suddenly a shower broke, and she was left trapped

in the teahouse; she could not move on for the time being. Nearby she could hear shrieking. She looked around to see where the noise was coming from and saw a monkey which seemed to belong to the old lady. The light was beginning to fade. Listening carefully she could also hear the shrill calls of animals in the mountain forest; they sounded rather sad.

After a while she went home. Her husband had been out of his mind with worry. When she told him where she'd been he told her that street was one of the few remaining 'Old Dynasty' streets and he made her promise never to go there again, particularly in her condition. 'It's where the Miao and Tujia people go for festivals. Completely uncivilised – they're little more than savages.'

Liu's mother didn't mind listening to this well-meant reprimand; on the contrary, she rather enjoyed the fact that he cared so much.

The courtyard was full of bamboo. She often used to potter about there having a look at all the plants and flowers. Sometimes she would even sit down and read a good revolutionary novel while waiting for her husband to come home.

Most of what her mother had told her the night before she had left Beijing was about what had happened the day before she was born. Her mother had been in extreme discomfort for a few days. Her feet had become so swollen she could hardly walk, and she had to wear her husband's shoes. Loathe as she had been to do it, she had had to request leave from her work at the Women's Association.

At midnight someone started knocking on the

main gate of the compound. Prefect Liu was still reading reports in the dim light of his kerosene lamp, tapping his fingers agitatedly. The knocking grew louder and more urgent. Reluctantly he stood up; the expression on his face was sombre. His wife felt a little better, and she had even managed to fall asleep, but of course the knocking had woken her up immediately. He reached for his pistol. The person knocking on the door had already been let in – Prefect Liu could hear him talking to the guards.

He opened the door and walked out. It was the captain of the Liang detachment. He had come to report that Red Lotus had been arrested; she had been captured on Nanhua Mountain by the guards lying in ambush at the pass.

At that moment Old Chen came running in. He seemed as excited as the captain; they had both thought it was going to be much harder to find Red Lotus.

Prefect Liu was less impressed. He was about to criticise both of them for making so much fuss about something so insignificant. After all, there was nothing very remarkable in having managed to catch a prostitute.

However, the name 'Nanhua Mountain', caught his attention.

'Nanhua Mountain?' He asked. 'How far was she from Water Moon Temple?'

Old Chen replied: 'Not far – she was caught on the road that pilgrims take.'

'So she was caught at the Temple!'

Old Chen corrected him: 'No, not in the Temple, on the road outside the Temple.'

'So she must have just left the Temple.'

'I really couldn't say.' replied Old Chen, glancing at the detachment captain. But the excited captain had no more idea what the conversation was about than he did.

Prefect Liu paused in thought before asking: 'Where is she now?'

'She's still on the mountain. I told my men to bring her over tomorrow morning.'

'Right, pick a group of my best guards here in the compound.' He turned to Old Chen: 'Make sure they're all war veterans, and all Party members. I'll go with you.'

Old Chen and the captain were rather taken aback. They couldn't understand why Prefect Liu was so worried about this prostitute.

'It's too dark,' Old Chen protested mildly. 'Only local soldiers can handle the mountain paths, our old soldiers won't manage it; there aren't any local soldiers who have joined the Party yet.'

'Do what I tell you!' shouted Prefect Liu. 'Come on! Get on with it! We set off in ten minutes.'

He turned round and went back to his living quarters to find his wife sitting up in bed, evidently distressed by all the commotion. 'Don't worry,' he said to her, 'it's nothing much – nothing compared to what we went through during the war. I'll be back soon. You try to get some sleep.'

He got changed and left.

But she didn't get much sleep. She lay there waiting anxiously the whole night. Occasionally she drifted into a light doze, but she would wake at the slightest sound.

Prefect Liu didn't get back until dawn. He was covered in mud from head to toe. The first thing he did was take off the leather belt which held his pistol. His wife quickly got dressed and made him a cup of hot tea. While the tea was being made she helped him out of his filthy sodden clothes, and found him something clean to put on. He told her he could manage by himself and urged her to go back to bed.

A guard brought him some hot water. He washed and put on his clean clothes. He told the guard to stand at the main gate and ordered him not to let anyone disturb him. He wanted to get some sleep, but was to be woken up at exactly eight o'clock.

He started snoring as soon as his head touched the pillow. His wife hadn't gone back to bed; she was too concerned about how exhausted Prefect Liu was. She kept watch at the door while he slept. She listened as the day gradually grew noisier – it seemed to be getting noisy earlier than usual. Then she remembered: it must be market day. City businessmen still hadn't recovered sufficiently from the war to invest in any large-scale trade, which meant that markets like these really prospered. She went into the outer room to brush her hair. The guard was talking to some people in the yard, apparently trying to dissuade them form coming in. She went to see what was going on.

The guard filled her in: 'There have been quite a few people wanting to come in, but, don't you worry, I sent them away. We don't want to have to interrupt Prefect Liu. He needs his rest.'

'They say Red Lotus has been caught, and that monk Yutong!' he informed her, unable to keep the thrilling news to himself, 'They are now in the custody of our comrades outside the city – but the news has already spread all over town. The streets are packed – everyone's waiting to see the two of them: a thief and a whore, immoral reactionaries.'

Now she knew what her husband had been doing all night. The birds were chirping under the low cloudy sky. She suddenly felt nauseous, her stomach churning uncontrollably; she wanted to be sick. She moved over to lean against the doorframe.

The guard didn't appear to notice her reaction and carried on talking. A few seconds later someone started knocking on the gate again.

She looked at him and said: 'Be a bit quieter when you're sending people away. I don't want my husband to be disturbed.' Her mouth felt unbearably dry, so she went back to her room to drink some water.

She made her way slowly to the table in her room, but stumbled and knocked the mirror off the wall; it slid first onto the chair and then crashed onto the ground. The noise woke Prefect Liu. He put his hand over his eyes to block the bright sunlight streaming through the windows. He looked like a young boy in need of being looked after, like the good-natured army officer who had fallen for her when they had first met. Secretly he'd always been a bit nervous of pretty girls, and he told her later that it had taken him a long time to pluck up the courage to speak to her. When they were first introduced he had blushed even more than she had. She found such bashfulness very touching – how could a Red Hero, who'd fought long and hard risking his life, be so shy in the company of a young girl?

She picked up the mirror. It hadn't broken, but it was cracked. She sat down. 'Sorry to have woken you,' she said. Her apology was superfluous. By this time it had become so noisy outside he would almost certainly have woken up anyway.

The noise appeared to remind him of something, and his infantile expression of helplessness disappeared almost immediately: he was, once again, Prefect Liu. He reached out for his watch, took one look at the time and leapt out of bed.

His wife opened her mouth as though about to say something, but remained silent. Prefect Liu knew what she wanted to ask; it was written all over her face. He looked at her coldly, his expression austere. He'd never looked at her like that before. Now she felt even more tongue-tied; she didn't know where to begin.

She brought him a bowl of rice porridge, which he drank down in one gulp, without even waiting for her to give him any pickles to go with it. She brought him another bowl. The atmosphere in the room was uncomfortable; not a single word had been exchanged.

The detachment captain was outside shouting to Prefect Liu that everything was ready. He put down his second bowl and went out.

She watched from the open door as her husband and the detachment captain walked along the veranda into the other courtyard. She stood up, hesitated for a while, then decided to follow them. She couldn't walk very fast, and even needed to stop for a little rest when she reached the fishpond.

The cadres were already assembled in the main hall of the compound – the meeting room. They were talking to one another in groups of three or four. They couldn't go out onto the streets – there were too many people. Any cadre who was spotted was sure to be surrounded and bombarded with questions, to which they wouldn't know the answers. That's why they were having the meeting: when the mood of the crowd was as volatile as it was that day, all the cadres felt they needed their leader to brief them on what to do and say.

Prefect Liu looked at the cadres and said resolutely: 'Everyone who is neither involved in the suppression of counter-revolutionaries nor in the reform of prostitutes should get back to their posts and carry on with their duties as normal. Everything is under control – there is no cause for excitement or alarm.'

When the other cadres had left he gave a brief outline of what the situation was and proceeded to give instructions on how to go about arranging the appropriate propaganda, how to organise the public trial, and how to draft a report to present to the provincial government.

His wife never made it to the meeting; she was feeling too unwell. In the short time she had been sitting by the fishpond the sky had turned a pasty white, like the eyes of a dead fish. She went back to the empty courtyard where their living quarters were. The clamour from the streets was getting louder all the time. It made her uneasy. Suddenly the gate was pushed open and hordes of people came running into the compound. They were saying that Red Lotus was about to be brought through. She wanted to see for herself, but there were so many people that she didn't dare push forward for fear of hurting her unborn child; she made her way onto the veranda.

She heard her husband shouting angrily, roaring at the top of his voice: 'Untie them! Cover them! Have some decency!'

More and more people crowded into the courtyard, knocking over the flowerpots and trampling on the budding chrysanthemums. She'd never seen people look so excited – their eyes bright, their voices hoarse with shouting. Prefect Liu commanded everyone to be quiet, saying: 'We must uphold our Party's policy never to maltreat prisoners – even counter-revolutionaries. Guards – take care of the compound. Commander Chen, you go and make the appropriate arrangements in the meeting area. The criminals should be locked up in the Department of Military Affairs.'

She could hardly breathe; it was as though something was stuck in her chest. She went back to her room – it was probably nothing more than the result of having had too little sleep. She still couldn't work out exactly what was going on; she wanted one of the guards to go and get Auntie Chen to keep her company, but there were no guards to be seen. Besides, Auntie Chen must be up to her neck in work – rousing the masses and sorting out the meeting area. She sat down by the dining table, her stomach aching with hunger. She tried to eat some of the left-over porridge but somehow couldn't get it down. She went out and made her way to the compound kitchens in the hope of finding some vegetable soup. There was nobody there; they must all have gone out to see what the commotion was, so she hobbled back to her room and lay down on the bed.

Prefect Liu popped in for a minute. They spoke, briefly, but nothing much was said. He'd come to get his pistol; he said he wanted to go to the meeting area in person to check that everything was as it should be; he didn't want there to be the slightest hitch in an event of this magnitude. He had just been on the phone to the Provincial Party Committee who had told him to go ahead with his chosen course of action. His wife was just about to ask him what this was when he hurried out without even shutting the door.

She called after him saying she didn't feel well and asking him to come home as soon as he could.

He turned round, somewhat angrily, and said, trying to retain his composure: 'This is a key moment for the revolution; you'd do well to cooperate!'

She watched as he walked off. She had a premonition that something terrible was about to happen. Something definitely wasn't right.

The public trial meeting area was in the centre of town, quite a way from the compound. She could hear shouting in the distance – like muffled thunder. She had never been to a public trial before and could scarcely imagine what it would be like. She could feel the sharp pains in her belly getting worse and worse; the child had always kicked a bit but she'd never felt anything like this. It was as though the baby was angry, fed up with being confined in its watery prison, and wanting to break free. Her groaning became screams of agony, but the more she shouted the worse it seemed to get. A guard was passing and looked in to see what was going on. She turned round instantly, grateful for the opportunity to send for help, and begged him to go and tell Prefect Liu and the doctor immediately.

After a while the guard came running back to the compound. Breathlessly he informed her that he had found the doctor who would be arriving any minute. He had found Prefect Liu as well, but he was busy presiding over the public trial. Public feeling was very strong and he was about to sum up and pronounce judgement. He had told the guard to tell his wife that he would be along as soon as the 'meeting' was over – she'd just have to do her best to hold on.

'So when will the meeting end?' she asked, lying on the bed.

The guard, evidently used to such happenings, replied nonchalantly: 'Well, I expect it'll end when the criminals have been shot.'

She couldn't help utter a cry of despair: 'Won't end till the criminals have been shot!?' By this stage she was in so much pain – physically and emotionally – that her whole face was drenched with tears: 'And when will that happen?'

'Any moment!' replied the guard, excited by all the questioning, 'Any moment!'

So that was why Prefect Liu had been so keen to check the meeting area in person. Of course – it was all clear now. She became a little more clear-headed and stopped crying. 'Who are they going to shoot?'

'The counter-revolutionaries.'

'Who?'

'The monk and the whore of course! The ones who were caught last night!'

She was taken aback. She'd never experienced anything like this. Even when she'd heard her husband making all the arrangements, she had never imagined what was about to happen. Suddenly she could bear it no longer; she was violently sick.

The guard ran out and after a few seconds ran back in again, dripping with sweat. He announced: 'Dr Qi is busy because Old Chen's wife is also about to give birth. He says he's nearly done over there, he'll be over any moment!'

She burst into loud sobs. The child was killing her. She reached out and grabbed the mosquito net, pulling on it so tightly that it fell down on top of her.

'The doctor said Old Chen's wife was giving birth prematurely...they never thought she'd be giving birth this early...' said the guard; he knew he was about to be sent back to hurry the doctor along.

His remark fell on deaf ears; she had long since lost interest in anyone's pain but her own. She knew by this time that she was going to have to do this by herself – a realisation which, strangely enough, seemed to calm her. She threw the mosquito net down onto the floor. She had to figure out how she was going get through this; how she was going to save her own life, as well as the life inside her.

At that moment she heard a tumultuous roar from the meeting area. Her chest felt heavier and heavier, and she felt as though the unborn child was gnawing at her intestines; her hair and clothes were soaked with sweat. She didn't hear the gunshots that followed – or the uproarious shouting which came after that – she was putting all of her energy into trying to control herself. 'Be strong!' she told herself, 'I must be strong!'

Chapter Fifteen

All the restaurants she was passing had little heating devices fitted into the tables to keep the hot-pots simmering. Business didn't look bad – most of the tables were full. Everyone seemed to be talking about how bad the rat problem was getting. They were saying that there were huge numbers of dead rats rotting in the streets, which was encouraging the emergence of swarms of flies. The flies, they explained, were transmitting a strange disease which gave people a rash on their arms and legs and made them subject to fits of uncontrollable rage.

The discussions became quite heated. Some people were claiming that the poison wasn't strong enough; beforehand a rat would die almost immediately after eating just a small amount, whereas now they just carried on as though nothing had happened. Others were saying that the poison must be strong enough because a few weeks ago a peasant from a village in the mountains had used it to kill off a corrupt village head and when the police had arrived to arrest him he had taken some of the poison himself and had died almost instantly.

The one thing they all seemed to agree on was that hot-pot was the safest thing to eat because it was constantly boiling. That's why all the hotpot restaurants were doing such unexpectedly good business.

Liu didn't think the rats posed much of a threat. There were plenty of other things in Liang which carried infection. That said, she didn't want to take any chances and she made sure she found something hygienic to eat. Fortunately she didn't feel hungry, but even if she had she still wouldn't have dared try Sichuanese hot-pot, a dish notorious for its intolerably hot spices.

Some of the restaurants had chalk-written signs outside: 'Fresh Globefish – Speciality of the Three Gorges'. Her mother had told her that the best time to eat globefish was in May, around the time of the Yellow Brightness Festival. The chefs in Liang were very skilled when it came to preparing globefish; the liver, roe, and eyes were poisonous, so they had to be removed with the utmost care – the slightest mistake meant the whole fish had to be thrown away. Customers usually insisted on watching the whole process to check it was being done properly. Liu joined a group of people crowding round one of the chefs to get a better look. The locals could tell that she was an outsider and tried to persuade her to taste one. She declined with a smile; she thought she was best off eating at the hotel. A few minutes later she came across a small bookshop. It looked smart by Liang's standards and had a huge sign outside exclaiming, '50% off all new books'. She went in. It had all the latest bestsellers – every one of them a pirate-edition. She'd read in the papers that pirating was an even bigger problem in the South than it was in the North, but she had never imagined that it would be quite so obvious. She browsed for a while though the mass-market books did not interest her. Something quite different caught her eye – it was a reprint of a little Ming Dynasty novella.

The man behind the till looked very pleased to have a potential customer. He told her that only a pitifully small number of people read books in Liang – he counted himself lucky if he managed to sell a book a day.

She carried on and came to the shiny glass buildings of the New City. Turning the corner she saw the huge ostentatious sign of the Golden Pleasure Hotel.

Everything was waiting for the flooding. Every hope and aspiration was focussed on its success. On the top of Liu's thirty-storey hotel, fixed onto a model of Shanghai's Oriental Pearl Tower, was a giant neon countdown clock which showed the seconds ticking down. Meanwhile, in the Old City, it was as though people were sleepwalking, waiting to be woken one beautiful morning when the rats would turn into princes.

Liu made her way up to the Western-style restaurant on the first floor and ordered spaghetti and beef and mushroom soup. She looked at her watch; no wonder there were no other customers – it was two o'clock already. But despite the time, two rows of waitresses, all dressed in traditional costumes, were

141

still standing to attention, lining two of the walls of the restaurant and waiting respectfully for a customer's signal. They must have been standing there for at least two hours.

She was not used to this kind of service – a vulgar feudalistic custom reintroduced by the nouveau riche. If she walked into a restaurant in Beijing where there were rows of waitresses waiting to attend to her every whim she'd put her head down and walk straight back out. But here she had no option. She thought it a blessing that the poor girls weren't made to kneel, as had become fashionable for waitresses in certain Southern Coastal regions.

The chrysanthemum tea was served. While she was waiting for her food she took out her map, but before she had even opened it up she felt an impulse to look round. She had the feeling that someone behind her was watching her. She glanced back to where the till was; there was a group of people there, but no one was looking in her direction. They, like most of the people staying in the hotel, looked like businessmen or technical engineer; impressive-looking people dressed in immaculate suits. The women staying at the hotel were similarly well-dressed – elegant and professional. She felt very unremarkable-looking in comparison; the only thing that made her stand out was that she didn't know how to make herself look as good as they did.

She preferred clothes of a uniform colour; she couldn't bare anything with a pattern on it. And regardless of whether she was wearing a skirt or trousers, she always wore a loose-fitting black overcoat. Her mother didn't like the way she dressed;

she thought her daughter should show off her good figure a bit more instead of always hiding it in large, shapeless items of clothing, and that the coat made her 'look just like any other working woman.'

She was not arrogant enough to assume that she didn't need any makeup, but she always tried to make sure that no one could see that she was wearing any. She would always use a tissue to try to get off almost all of the lipstick she put on.

She thought people might be looking at her because she dressed so casually.

After lunch she had a little nap during which she was neither fully asleep nor fully awake. When she felt sufficiently rested she opened her eyes, got up and was just in the middle of putting her shoes on when the phone rang.

'Surely that's not him again!' she thought.

She deliberately let the phone ring for a while before picking up. It was not her husband; it was an unknown male voice with a strong local accent. He apologized profusely for disturbing 'Madam Director' and introduced himself as the manager of the hotel. He said he was ringing to ask if Madam had any 'special requirements', which he would be only too happy to oblige.

'Madam Director' indeed! She glanced out of the window at the green mountain. No one could have climbed the tall glass building and be listening outside, surely. She knew there was no respect for privacy in places like Liang, and she was well aware that Mr Han must have a network of spies beneath him. But what would be the point of spying on her, now that Li knew where she was?

Unable to figure out why the manager should be phoning her and why he should be being quite so humble and polite, she just replied straight-forwardly by thanking him for his concern and saying she couldn't think of anything she required at that moment.

Just as she was about to put down the receiver he asked if he could trouble her to do him the honour of meeting him in the lobby downstairs, if she could spare a few moments.

She felt she was getting closer to the real reason behind the call now. She tried to suppress her irritation and asked casually: 'Did Li ask you to call me?'

The manager was hesitant and eventually mumbled something quite incomprehensible.

She couldn't help being curious about the lengths to which Li was prepared to go to win her over. Ever since he had given her that perfume it had seemed as though his whole team had been laying siege to her resolve. There hadn't been anything like this before they were married.

'Ok, I'll come down now,' she replied. She wanted to see what they were up to. She took her electronic key out of its socket, plunging the room into darkness. She felt she had every reason to be angry now; she didn't like playing the part of a rat in a trap.

She hurried into the lift. 'Special requirements' – what could they be? Despite the fact that the hotel was only four star, it offered every luxury imaginable. The shadowless lamps in the lift lit up the photos of the hotel's gourmet restaurant, sauna, massage parlour, gym and swimming pool. Even some of the five star places she had stayed at could not have outdone this one.

Everything was spotlessly clean, particularly the carpets. And there were a few nice touches here and there, like the fact that there was a red rose in every bathroom. The manager obviously knew what he was doing.

On the brown leather sofas in the lobby sat a variety of people – male and female, young and old. Some were reading the newspaper, some were chatting, and some were just fidgeting restlessly, obviously waiting for someone who was late. One of them had to be the manager. Liu did not stop to try and work out which one he was, she just walked straight past. Just as she was approaching the revolving doors she heard a gentle voice call out:

'Dr Liu, would you mind waiting a moment?'

At least she wasn't being called 'Madam Director'; here was someone who knew her proper title. She turned round and saw two men and a woman. The woman standing just behind the two men looked like a secretary of some kind. The men were quite young, both smartly dressed with colour-coordinated jackets and ties; they looked like successful new generation professionals, the type that was thriving in the ever-changing political and economic climate.

'I am the manager of the hotel,' the thinner of the two announced, walking forward to shake hands with Liu: 'My name is Zheng.' He reached into his jacket pocket and drew out a gilt business card case. He flicked it open and whisked out a card which,

145

observing traditional etiquette by holding it with both hands, he presented to Liu. Then the other man, who wore glasses, took a step forward. The manager hurriedly introduced him as Mr Wang, the head of some local government department.

'Professor Liu, it is an honour to make your acquaintance.' Mr Wang had done his homework even better; he knew about her teaching post at the Academia Sinica which entitled her to be called 'Professor'. 'May I invite you to have a chat with us for a few minutes in the coffee bar?' he asked.

She glanced over to the far end of the lobby where there was a quiet little coffee bar. She was not sure how to handle this polite Mr Wang; she wished she had paid more attention when the manager had said what government department he was head of. But what harm could there be in sitting in a coffee bar for a few minutes? She nodded.

The two men lead the way. The woman walked with Liu, half a step behind them. She smiled sweetly but remained silent.

The tables and chairs in the coffee bar were made entirely of bamboo except for a piece of glass in the middle of the tables underneath which was a piece of local embroidery. It was only when they had sat down that Mr Wang re-affirmed: he was head of Liang's Resettlement Department.

What could the Resettlement Department possibly have to do with Liu?

Seeing her surprise, Mr Wang began to explain: 'It's like this, you see, your being here is a rare opportunity for us; I don't want to waste any of your valuable time...' He continued, his tone straightforward and frank, neither too humble nor too arrogant: 'We have quite a situation on our hands: there are people trying to cause trouble over the distribution of the money set aside for the Resettlement Programme.'

She'd never been very interested in the Resettlement Fund, but did know that the total budget for the Dam Project was 50 billion yuan, half of which was to be used to resettle the thousands of people who were going to have to leave the area. It was going to cost about 30,000 yuan per person.

'There are people encouraging the peasants out of town to demand cash for their resettlement.'

'Why don't you just give them what the State has allocated them?' she replied straightforwardly.

The two men looked at each other. Mr Wang continued: 'It would appear that you don't fully understand the situation. The 30,000 yuan per head you read about in the papers includes transportation costs, building costs, the cost of building new roads, the cost of providing new local facilities and utilities etc. State policy stipulates that any surplus is only to be given to individuals after they have been resettled. We trust that most people understand the reasoning behind this. Many of these people, of course, haven't earned as much as 30,000 yuan in their whole lives and feel extremely grateful to the People's Government.'

The fresh coffee arrived smelling delicious. Three girls in green silk dresses got up on the small stage in the corner and began to dance under the soft lighting. A singer began to sing the theme tune from the hit TV series 'I Love Both the Land and the Lady'. Liu's eyes drifted in their direction; the girls were dancing in traditional Chinese style, but at the same time with a pronounced Western influence.

She put a sugar lump in her coffee – a habit she'd picked up in America – and stirred slowly. 'So what opportunity is there for anyone to cause any trouble?'

Mr Wang frowned and went on: 'Some bad elements have been spreading rumours that Liang's Local Government has been embezzling funds to invest in stocks and shares, and that, in doing so, huge sums of money have been irretrievably lost. People from the small towns in the area are coming here to demonstrate.'

'Embezzling?!' Liu was no fool; she knew exactly what was going on. 'Who in Liang's Local Government is in a position to embezzle funds? You're the director of the Resettlement Programme, you should know better than anyone, shouldn't you?' Her words were sharp, and with good reason. She stood up: 'Whatever is going on here, it has nothing to do with me. I should go; I wouldn't want to take up any more of your time.'

Mr Wang also became agitated: 'Director Li said we should be more flexible, move the money around a bit – if you just put it in the bank you only get 2%. Investment yields profit; leaving the money rotting away in a bank wouldn't help anyone – the public least of all.'

Liu suddenly turned round and said acidly: 'You go look for your "Director Li". I have never discussed anything like this with him, and I don't intend to start now!' She picked up her bag – it was time to go.

Mr Wang also stood up. Liu thought he was about

to physically prevent her from leaving, but instead he said gently, with the same politeness he had shown throughout their meeting: 'Director Li already knows about the situation.'

That was enough to persuade her to stay. She examined him closely: 'What you mean is...' she continued very slowly, speaking syllable by syllable, '...that Li joined you in your stupid little game, gambling away public money. Do you have any proof?' She went a step further: 'And if you do, why don't you show it to people? Why don't you tell them they should have their demonstrations at the Dam Site instead of here?'

Mr Wang's reply was quick and agitated: 'No, no... you've got the wrong idea entirely, Professor Liu, please, allow me to explain. A small number of bad citizens are trying to make trouble, but we can deal with them. Our concern is that Director Li, when he arrives this evening, might, in some way, misunderstand the situation, that's all.'

'What do you mean, "misunderstand the situation"?' she asked, bemused by Mr Wang's flustered response. She sat down: 'Go on then, tell me, what is there for him to "misunderstand"?'

Seeing that Liu really wanted to find out what was going on, Mr Wang seemed to relax. He began to explain patiently: 'Director Li is coming here tomorrow to meet the Taiwan and Hong Kong trade consortia. The arrangements have all been kept secret, but, by chance, this is the very day that the bad elements have decided to stage their demonstration. Now, I'm sure you can imagine as well as I can how damaging that could be...'

'Surely you're not suggesting it was me who told them?'

'Of course not, of course not... We just thought that as you were here, we might take the opportunity to try to show you how sincere we are in trying to resolve the problem; we really are doing everything we possibly can.'

Liu let out a silent sigh of comprehension; all this fuss just to try and get her to put a good word in for them when she saw Li.

She had a good look at them both. The manager was sitting a bit further away than Mr Wang – and why shouldn't he? The whole business had nothing to do with him, he was just trying to help his friend. She glanced over to Mr Wang; he was smiling knowingly. It was enough to make her want to explode.

'If you think I'm going to tell Li how well you're doing your job, think again! We never discuss his work, and even if we did, what would you have me say to him? I don't know the first thing about the situation other than what you've just told me. I could end up telling him something completely misleading!' She stood up. 'It's not him I'm here to see, anyway. I'm here to see a friend.' She was annoyed with herself – how had she ever managed to get embroiled in this nasty little web of confusion? 'I intend to forget that this meeting ever took place and I suggest you do the same!'

Mr Wang nodded vigorously and said he thought she was absolutely right. He stood up to say good bye, but just as he was about to shake her hand, he added casually: 'We are so glad you're here, I do hope you enjoy your stay – you might be interested to know how the trial planting of Nanqing-3 genetically modified rice has been going? Last year we selected the best seeds from the hybrid plant, using the isotopic elements as the indicator and then selected those with the target-genes. In the large scale tests productivity was up twenty percent.'

Liu was taken aback. How had Mr Wang managed to say all that without making a single mistake? She really did have a genuine interest in Nanqing-3. In fact, she had just read an article in a scientific journal which had challenged the idea that the productivity of this particular type of GM rice was any better than that of non-GM rice. It was very rare to find a cadre who had any interest in genetic engineering, and even rarer to find one who could discuss the subject intelligently. There was more to this Mr Wang than met the eye, it seemed.

'If you had time, perhaps we could go and have look. It's not far, just over on the Western slope. We deliberately chose an area where, ordinarily, productivity is below average. If we go by car, we could be there in less than half an hour.'

The girls on the stage started singing an English song. Their pronunciation was terrible. Liu looked at her watch – it was still early. She had plenty of time to kill before dinner. She'd made her position clear – surely Mr Wang wouldn't dare try and trouble her with any more discussion of the Resettlement Fund. It was a rare opportunity. The only thing troubling her was that she couldn't work out why the Director of the Resettlement Department should be interested in GM rice.

'Maximising productivity is vital to the success of

the Resettlement Programme,' volunteered Mr Wang, as if reading Liu's mind. 'Testing out GM crops is one of the most important aspects of our work.'

She was delighted.

Chapter Sixteen

It didn't take long for Liu to realize she had been duped.

Mr Wang immediately started making a number of calls on his mobile phone. Soon afterwards a silver Mercedes pulled up outside the hotel. Where it had come from or how they had got it there so quickly, Liu had no idea. It stood out a mile in a town like Liang, though it didn't look entirely out of place outside the hotel. The woman who had been so quiet all this time got in the car with them. She introduced herself as a cadre from the Resettlement Department. She was wearing a sensible professional suit but had a playful Pierre Cardin silk scarf draped over her shoulders. She had far too much makeup on; the colour of her lipstick was almost as striking as that of her scarf. Her eyes shone brightly and she smiled amiably. Looking at this expensively dressed executive, Liu was reminded of cadres fifty years ago like her mother and Auntie Chen, whose only 'fashion accessory' had been a leather belt tied round their blue boiler suits. She knew it was an inappropriate comparison, but that didn't alter the way she felt. She was in no mood to make polite conversation, so she got into the front seat next to the driver.

Five minutes after they had set off, just as they were approaching the town square, they were flagged down by a policeman.

The car pulled over and the policeman lowered his head to see who was driving. He asked the driver where he worked and told him that no car was allowed to drive along Rinsing Silk Lane past the Square. When he saw Mr Wang sitting in the back seat he saluted, apologized, and waved them on. Liu didn't hear exactly what Mr Wang's reply to the policeman was, she was too distracted by what was going on a few hundred metres ahead of them. There were almost a hundred people crowding outside the grandiose structure that housed Liang's Government Offices, and they didn't look happy.

The car edged forward and Liu saw that some of the people were brandishing what looked like huge envelopes with writing on them. On the steps leading up to the main entrance there were another hundred or so people sitting in silence. In front of the people with the letters was a row of uniformed police, and there was another row in front of the steps. Their main function seemed to be to keep people from spilling onto the road.

The car stopped. Mr Wang said something to the driver, opened the car door and got out.

It didn't take a lot of thought to work out that they hadn't stumbled across this demonstration by chance: this was exactly what Mr Wang had been planning all along. He wanted a credible witness as he 'explained policy to the masses'. Why exactly this was necessary was unclear.

Liu now realized how stupid she'd been; how could she have been so gullible as to agree to let Mr Wang take her to the GM rice field? In hindsight it seemed absurd to have believed that he had any genuine interest in genetic engineering, and even more absurd to have believed that, despite the immensity of his task of placating the 'bad elements', he should have the time to go driving off to a paddy field. Her profession was her biggest weakness: she was passionate about it. The indifference of laymen frustrated her – she couldn't understand why people didn't show more interest. As far as she was concerned genetic engineering was the most exciting, the most world-changing science there had ever been, and yet, if ever she tried to discuss it with anyone but her academic colleagues, all she saw were blank faces.

She asked the driver where they were going.

'Nowhere,' he replied. 'We're staying here.'

The female cadre in the back, sensing that Liu was ill at ease, said: 'Don't worry, we're quite safe here. Mr Wang will be back presently, and we'll be at the Western slope in no time.'

When Mr Wang had told her that 'bad elements' were 'making trouble' she had imagined the kind of thing you see on the news. No matter where it's going on in the world, it's always pretty much the same – you see people smashing cars, turning them over and then setting light to them. Bearing this in mind, Liu thought that leaving a brand new top of the range Mercedes parked not a hundred metres from the 'bad elements' was asking for trouble; she was quite anxious for the driver to move it somewhere a little less conspicuous. She was no longer interested in working out what Mr Wang was up to; she just wanted to go away and forget the whole incident.

But she had realized something: now that it was known that she was 'Madam Director' she wasn't going to get a minute's peace.

Liu desperately felt like getting out of the car. She had lost all interest in going to see the paddy field. She opened the car door as quickly as she could. The woman in the back reached out as though trying to grab her, but it was too late. Liu had already got out and was walking away. The woman got out of the car as well but then just stood in the road, watching Liu; she didn't follow – she hadn't been told to.

Now all Liu wanted was to escape the role that Mr Wang had assigned her. She hurriedly crossed the road to the side where there were fewer people. As she walked she glanced over at the crowd. She caught a glimpse of a familiar face flickering in and out of sight right in the middle. She stopped. The pavement was slightly higher where she was standing. She could also see Mr Wang. He was speaking animatedly in the local dialect, shrieking so loudly she could make out bits of what he was saying despite his being almost a hundred metres away from her. The people who had been sitting on the steps had all stood up. Most people were listening attentively. A small minority were trying to challenge what he was saying. People were becoming increasingly agitated and everyone started pushing and shoving. Whose was that face she kept seeing? Who could it possibly be? She didn't know anyone here. She carried on watching; away from the cadres she felt quite safe and perfectly anonymous. There was no need to run away and hide.

She remembered whose face it was she'd seen in the crowd: that supremely ordinary looking county-town face, the flat-topped crew cut, the modest expression – it was Auntie Chen's son, whatever his name was. Why wasn't he up at the Temple doing his landscapes?

She deliberately kept herself out of sight as the Mercedes drove past. She stood on the steps of a photography shop with a Kodak sign outside, turned her back to the road and pretended to be looking in the shop window.

The familiar face became less and less visible as people jostled about in the crowd. She was certain now: it was Yueming, still wearing that old tunic suit, though it was cleaner this time – not an ink spot to be seen. Maybe it was different to the one she'd seen him in at the Temple.

What was he doing here? She walked down the three steps to the pavement, crossed the road and walked into the crowd. Most of the people there were men, and she could smell the stench of sweat. She could see now that Yueming was one of the people holding a letter, in a huge brown-paper envelope. He remained silent as the noise made by the crowd grew louder and louder. He looked anxious. Liu squeezed in to get a bit closer. The people holding letters were standing in a row. There

157

were only six of them. Some of the envelopes had been written with a calligraphy brush: 'To Liang County Local Government: r.e. such and such a problem in the handling of the Resettlement Fund.' She couldn't read exactly what the problems were because everyone around her was pushing too much, and some of the characters were written too small; one envelope seemed to say something like 'Funds destined for foundation engineering work withheld' and on another 'Funds for house-building withheld'. She moved about to try to see what was on Yueming's envelope. Eventually she found a place where she got a good view in between two people's heads: 'The education of primary school children'. She remembered now that Auntie Chen had told her that he used to be a primary school teacher somewhere in the suburbs.

She couldn't understand why the people with letters weren't holding them up high above their heads instead of holding them modestly in front of their chests.

Yueming called out a question to Mr Wang.

Mr Wang replied, speaking much more loudly than Yueming: 'The children of resettled families will all, without exception, go to schools in the areas in which they have been resettled. This is official policy.'

Yueming replied: 'Yes, but it is also official policy that funds will be made available to provide education for children whose families are being resettled in areas where educational facilities are insufficient.'

'Well, that depends on what both sides decide; I can't give you one answer which will apply to every single case,' answered Mr Wang, pushing up his glasses. Someone else grabbed his attention and asked another question.

'The children can't wait – any delay and they miss a whole year of schooling, and if they miss more than a year they will drop out all together. It's hard enough as it is for poor families in the countryside to send their children to school – it's a problem at the best of times!' Yueming shouted back at Mr Wang. But everyone was making such a racket he probably did not even hear.

Liu was certain Yueming had a point, but when people were being resettled on such a grand scale, children missing school was going to be hard to avoid. Giving schools in the resettlement areas compensation would certainly help, but no one seemed keen to provide the funds – however paltry the amount. Yueming's speech was becoming increasingly animated; he didn't seem to worry that no one was listening to him. He was talking quickly in dialect and she was finding it hard to understand. She found herself edging forward, trying to get closer in the hope that if she could hear better she might understand more. There were hardly any women in the crowd and as soon as the men saw that she was a respectable lady from out of town, they instinctively shuffled out of her way.

Mr Wang gave off the impression that he was being extremely patient and understanding. He no longer even looked like a young member of the political elite that he had been in the hotel lobby. Now he was behaving more like a local cadre – speaking the local dialect and gesticulating just like the ordinary people she had seen sitting in the

159

restaurants by the river.

It wasn't long before she lost sight of Yueming as the swelling crowd swallowed him up. But she could still see some of the other envelope-bearers – they seemed to be trying to get Mr Wang to accept their letters. He refused point blank, putting his hands behind his back and saying he wasn't allowed to accept letters directly from the public. All letters should be submitted to the relevant department.

'But you are the "relevant department"!'

'No, all letters of this nature should be submitted to the Correspondence and Visitation Department,' replied Mr Wang, calmly. 'Many of the issues raised here have nothing to do with the Resettlement Department – primary education, for example.'

People started shouting even more angrily than they had been before. Mr Wang waved his hands frantically, repeating that he definitely was not responsible for receiving letters. At that moment Liu suddenly heard the sound of a police siren – no, four police sirens – four police cars all approaching the square from different directions. They braked almost simultaneously and policemen jumped out even before the cars had stopped. Before she had realized what was happening, dozens of them had run up to the Government Building and surrounded the demonstrators on all sides, standing closely together holding up their batons.

Looking round Liu realized that the crowd was now perhaps almost ten times as big as when she had first seen it, though many of the new arrivals seemed to be just spectators. The two groups, one on either side of the road, had long since merged into one.

Some people had even brought their children and elderly members of the family along with them; they were the ones who looked the poorest – they probably came from the shantytowns down by the river. They were holding up scraps of paper with badly written characters stating their demands and explaining their difficulties.

Some of the more senior-looking policemen had started shouting: 'Disperse! Go home!', then one of them blew a whistle and immediately the police charged into the crowd, waving their batons about and hitting people indiscriminately. There was only one side which was not blocked by police; that was the way everyone was trying to run. There were more police waiting for them a little further on who showed them which way to go by gesticulating with their batons. Once people were a safe distance away they stood still, waiting to see what would happen next.

Liu couldn't decide what she should do – should she run or should she hold her ground? She didn't feel it was necessary to run away, since she was only a spectator. Of course, most of the people running away were only spectators too, but she felt that running away would suggest that she had done something wrong, which she hadn't.

As she stood there hesitating, she realized that she was one of a handful of people who still hadn't run away. Even the men with the giant envelopes had gone, leaving their letters lying on the ground. Still in a bit of a daze, she found herself, together with the others, surrounded by a small group of policemen. She turned her head to see if she could see Mr Wang, but there was no sign. He was probably long gone. She saw two policemen violently kicking someone by the stone steps. Yueming was standing some distance away, with the spectators. But as soon as he saw that Liu had been caught, he ran over to help her. Immediately he too was caught, beaten with a baton and forced to the ground.

Liu was worried and instinctively tried to run in his direction, only to be held back by two policemen. Just as all this was going on a prison van pulled up.

The police of Liang may have been smartly dressed in new uniforms and well trained in crowd control, but their prison van looked about twenty years old – its paint was peeling and its doors looked like they were about to fall off. The young policemen with their nice shiny shoes were unnecessarily rough in the way they threw the prisoners into the van. One of them twisted Liu's arm so much she couldn't help crying out in pain.

'Don't you dare make a noise!' he said, raising his baton to teach her a lesson. But, fortunately for her, he saw that she was a woman from out of town, so he thought better of it.

The police continued shouting and pushing people into the van. The spectators had moved even further away as soon as they saw that people were being arrested and the demonstration was over. Liu was in the prison van. The door was slammed shut and bolted from the outside. They even shut the tiny barred window, plunging them all into darkness.

Chapter Seventeen

This was the first time in Liu's life that she had ever been arrested. She had never imagined that one day she'd be locked in a police van like a criminal.

As the van drove off she could feel that they were going down a steep incline. The road was full of bumps and potholes so they went slowly. Nevertheless, it was an extremely bumpy ride. The siren on the roof made a piercing sound – so unpleasant in fact that she ended up putting her fingers in her ears. The police had made them sit in two rows, one on either side of the van, and had put Liu – the only woman – in the corner. Two policemen stood in the middle to keep an eye on them, holding on to the two iron support bars. Next to her was Yueming who was trying desperately to keep his distance for fear of bumping into her, while at the same time trying to keep his balance.

Driving behind the van was a police car which also had a deafening siren.

Suddenly there was a violent jerk, possibly caused by a very large pothole. The policemen almost swung

full circle as they desperately tried to keep hold of the
iron bars, and the two rows of prisoners were flung
together and then flung back. Yueming almost ended
up on top of Liu who, having had her fingers in her
ears, was even more unbalanced than the rest of
them. He tried to grab hold of her but didn't manage
it in time; she ended up knocking her knee against
one of the iron bars, letting out a loud scream.

The policemen started swearing that the driver
must be blind. The only good that came of the
incident was that the siren stopped, probably
damaged by the jolt.

Yueming, like the rest of the men, stank of sweat.
Being a single man, he probably didn't have anyone
to wash or darn his clothes. His sleeves were filthy,
his shoes wet and his laces undone. He seemed to
realize what Liu was looking at and bent down to do
them up, revealing some nasty welts across his back,
probably made by a baton.

She did not look at his face, nor did he look at
hers. Eye contact would have meant conversation,
and a prison van was hardly the place for
exchanging pleasantries.

When they got to a smoother stretch of road most
of the prisoners started telling the policemen that
they hadn't been the ones holding the letters and that
there had been a mistake. The policemen were very
young but nevertheless remained silent and
expressionless. The prisoners repeatedly proclaimed
their innocence. Only Liu and Yueming said nothing.

In the distance they could hear the siren of a fire
engine coming closer and closer, a sound rarely
heard in rural areas. It made them apprehensive, all

the more so because they couldn't see what was going on.

After twenty minutes jostling about in the back of the van they finally arrived. At least the journey had been a short one – that was one thing to be said for small towns.

The door was opened and the two policemen got out first. There was no ladder – everyone had to jump down one by one, before lining up outside.

Liu had not realized how high off the ground the van was; she had not been paying much attention when the police had bundled her in. She thought that there ought to be a policeman there to help people out and to make sure no one ended up flat on their faces.

She could hear an incomprehensibly crackly message coming through on one of the walkie-talkies. The policemen were probably making arrangements for the prisoners.

None of the policemen had realized that one of the people arrested was a woman, and there were no policewomen on duty. When Liu was the only person left in the van, seeing that she was anxious about jumping out, a policeman stepped forward to help her down. She moved forwards then suddenly recoiled; she may have been under arrest, but she was not going to sacrifice her dignity and let herself be manhandled. The policeman stretched out his hand as though to pull her out, but she simply moved further back.

Her refusal to budge embarrassed the policeman. He looked no older than eighteen or nineteen. He would certainly never have come across a local who would have dared to behave like this. Copying the older policemen, he began swearing at her, though he stopped as soon as he noticed her expensive clothes and out of town appearance. She knew he had been shouting something obscene, but she was not sure exactly what it was: he'd been speaking in his dialect and it had been too fast for her to catch. She sat down point blank refusing to jump.

The compound had an extremely high wall, topped with rusty barbed wire. The old wooden gate was so heavy that it took two men to push it shut. The building itself was small and old-fashioned; it was made almost entirely of concrete and was only two storeys high. It looked as though it had originally been painted red, then white, but now, after years of big black slogans, it wasn't really any colour at all. Layers of ever-changing policy had left the building a dirty grey colour.

Seeing that she wasn't going to budge, Yueming stepped forward and reached out his hand. She accepted his gesture willingly and jumped out gracefully.

She blushed a little but luckily no one seemed to notice. She would never have imagined he would do a thing like that. As his hand touched hers she felt a kind of affectionate warmth – something she hadn't felt in a long time – the kind of feeling you get when you hug a close relative – solid, reliable, trustworthy.

Being arrested when you are innocent is the kind of thing that makes you seethe with indignation, but she wondered if it weren't perhaps a good thing after all: not only a completely new experience, but also the best possible way to get away from that

166

ghastly Mr Wang and his rice field. In any case, there would have been no way of knowing whether or not the field really was GM rice; cadres here could lie about anything.

At least this way she wouldn't have to worry about Yueming and go running off to Auntie Chen to tell her what had happened. Poor Auntie Chen had enough in her chaotic life as it was with a cancer patient to look after, without having to dash about asking for help in getting her son out of jail! No, she didn't regret her involvement in this messy little affair in the slightest. Strange though it might sound, it all felt so right.

She congratulated herself for not having worn high-heels. She wouldn't have wanted to have stood out any more than she did already. The ones she was wearing were not her most casual, but they were comfortable and good for running and jumping.

Just as Liu was beginning to feel better about her predicament, the policeman who had tried to help her out of the van walked up to her with a sneer on his face. He grabbed one of her wrists and before she knew what was happening she found herself handcuffed. Yueming was outraged and protested: 'You can't do that! She's not one of us, she's from Beijing.' No sooner had he finished his sentence than one of his hands was grabbed and handcuffed – what's more, handcuffed to Liu. 'You two scumbags seem to be a bit too chummy – well, I've news for you: you're in custody now and you'd better start behaving yourselves. This one's from Beijing is she? All the more reason to keep an eye on her then!'

When Liu looked down and saw her left hand

tied to Yueming's right she was incensed. But
before she'd had time to react the pair were
marched off and thrown into a cell, the door of
which was slammed shut.

It was the worst cell in the whole compound –
smelly, dirty, damp, lightless and airless. It was a
place reserved for prisoners who needed disciplining.

The sun was beginning to set. Several hours elapsed
before they were hauled out and dragged into the
room where the other prisoners were waiting.

This was the old police station which was only
used in special circumstances. It was completely
deserted. Even the glass in the windows had long
since been smashed. The toilet stank so badly you
could smell it even if you were right at the other end
of the building. They had been moved into the only
functional room in the whole place – there was a
table and two wooden benches, parallel to one
another. They were led to the only two remaining
places – one on each bench. All the prisoners were
ordered to sit down. Still handcuffed together they
had no option but to sit one behind the other. The
other prisoners were all staring at them, maybe
because they considered them dangerous. The people
sitting either side of them inched away, trying to
keep a safe distance.

Most of the other prisoners were still protesting
their innocence, saying they'd just been passing and
stopped to have a look. Realising the futility of
directing their pleas to the younger policemen, they
were all trying to talk to the older sergeant who
looked more authoritative. He was standing guard

by a door which, presumably, led to the interrogation room. He shouted at them to shut up, his manner straightforward and unsympathetic: 'Silence! No one that ends up in here is ever innocent! We know that – the only thing we care about is how people behave once they're here. When you go through that door you tell our bureau chief what's happened – confess – and don't, whatever you do, start mouthing off about being innocent!'

The prisoners were summoned into the inner room one by one – some staying for longer than others – but none of them were told they were free to go when they came out; they were ordered to get back to their seats and wait for the bureau chief to make the final arrangements. Some people were still muttering but no one was shouting like before, they all seemed to have been awed into submission by the interrogation. Yueming and Liu were of course the last to be summoned. She lifted her head and looked at him; he turned and smiled.

This struck her as strange. She couldn't recall having seen him smile before – most of the time he either had an expression of humility and respect on his face, or else he had just looked indifferent – detached and cold. Why had he chosen now, of all times, to start smiling? What's more, it was no ordinary smile – it was a smile exuding calm and inner peace; his eyes seemed like the clean shining mirrors.

Another odd thing was that they were the calmest two there. She knew she'd be let free, but what about Yueming? It was quite possible that he was the only letter-bearer who had been caught, so if they were after a ringleader it was sure to be him. And yet here he was – apparently calm. He seemed to be detached from everything around him. While they had been in that dark cell she had been terrified – the kind of terror that you cannot control, that makes your heart beat so loudly you can hear it. She had asked Yueming what might be in store for them, but before he'd had time to answer the guard with the frightening face had opened the little hatch in the iron door and had barked: 'No talking!'

She didn't know how to go about helping Yueming. Maybe she should insist on having her interview alone, before him; she could surely kick up such a fuss that they would have to let him go. If she didn't do something he could end up being given an extremely long sentence or even being sent to a labour reform camp for life – the crime of organizing a riot would be taken very seriously indeed. After all, his complaint had been fairly minor: the problem of children not going to school in rural areas wasn't exactly new – it had been going on all over China for almost twenty years. The only effect the Resettlement would have on the situation would be that it would make it even easier for families to pull their children out of school.

No one could deny that Yueming had a point. What's more, not talking about education would surely be much more harmful than talking about it, and besides, however much it was talked about, it was hardly a topic which was likely to lead to mass riots or national instability – the vast majority of people couldn't care less.

Liu began to analyse the situation: the worst thing that any of the people who had been arrested had done was to try and give a letter to their local government. Nevertheless, someone must have been organising the event; how else would the six letter-bearers, each with different complaints, have ended up in the same place at the same time, each with a giant envelope? By trying to 'pacify' the protestors, Mr Wang had in fact made the whole event a much bigger affair. His refusal to accept the six letters meant that the protestors had refused to leave, and his shouting and marching about caused passers-by to stop and stare, making it look as though there were many more protestors than there actually were. The huge crowds blocking the roads had given the police an excuse to use force. Could it be possible that Mr Wang and his cronies had engineered the whole thing?

The last person walked out of the interrogation room. Liu stood up before Yueming was ready, pulling him up too. She started shouting that they demanded to be uncuffed. Before standing up she had forgotten all about the handcuffs – keeping her hand so close to his seemed the most natural thing in the world.

At that moment she heard Mr Wang's voice coming from somewhere down the corridor. It was getting nearer. The door was open; there was a fully armed policeman standing guard. They were close enough now for her to hear every word of what was being said:

'How ridiculous! How absolutely ridiculous! What the hell did you think you were doing!?'

Between these outbursts came the timorous

explanations of the police chief, but he was mumbling too quietly for Liu to be able to catch his exact words – the gist of it was along the lines of: 'I was only following orders... I was told to make sure that most of the protestors ran away and that a small group got arrested, like catching fish in a net. That's the standard procedure – you don't catch the ringleaders, you catch the people who can lead you to the ringleaders.'

Then came the sound of a door being slammed shut followed by footsteps getting closer and closer. A group of people appeared in the doorway. Standing at the front was Mr Wang and a senior police official with insignia on his collar. Mr Wang gave him a nudge and he walked into the room.

'I would like to apologize to you on behalf of all the officers on duty. The chaos of the situation has lead to regrettable complications.'

His apology almost seemed to be denying responsibility. He took the key from the guard and immediately uncuffed Liu and Yueming. She rubbed her wrist – it felt much more painful now it had been released.

Mr Wang walked into the room and held out his hand to help her stand up. 'We have been extremely negligent to allow such a serious mistake to have occurred. I'm sure you will understand and find it in your heart to forgive us.'

Everyone – policemen and prisoners – had turned round to watch this strange scene. Only the guard in the doorway remained dutifully where he was, blocking the door with his hands on his hips.

Liu folded her arms, indicating that Mr Wang

shouldn't try to touch her. He had a speck of dirt on his glasses. The people standing behind him shuffled forward and started all talking at once – each of them trying to outdo all the others in sincerity and humility as they apologized over and over again. Liu stood there in total silence. When they all seemed to have finished she looked at them more closely – every one of them was smiling in embarrassment – and asked:

'So, what you're saying is, you arrested me by mistake?'

Mr Wang didn't answer; he knew she was trying to trick him into saying something he didn't want to say.

'Definitely! There's no question about it!' volunteered the police chief.

'What makes you so sure?' she asked slowly.

'Well... the fact that you are not a troublemaker.'

'So who are the troublemakers you meant to catch then?'

'Some of the people here are probably troublemakers, though some may just be harmless bystanders. We're still investigating at the moment – just taking some names and addresses,' explained the policeman who had been sitting in the inner room.

'Good answer. At least this comrade is not trying to blame anyone else for his own mistake.' She turned round and asked the police official: 'So, could you perhaps tell me who the troublemakers are?'

'We are still trying to find out...' the chief answered hesitantly. 'These things take time...'

'What I meant was: what is your definition of a "troublemaker"? What counts as "making trouble"?' Liu replied.

Silence. Liu turned round and pointed to Yueming: 'This comrade, for example, was trying to present local government officials with a letter drawing attention to the fact that resettlement could cause severe disruption to primary education. Is that an arrestable offence?'

Everyone turned to get a better a look at Yueming. He was sitting in a corner – his face expressionless – his right wrist still handcuffed. He lowered his head, apparently embarrassed by all the attention.

'If you still don't know for certain what a "troublemaker" is, how did you know who to beat up? How did you know who to put in the punishment cell? How did you know who not to release?' Her voice rose in anger: 'One person still has handcuffs on even as we speak!'

This was the last straw for Mr Wang: 'Get those handcuffs off that man – now! Release all the prisoners!' His face was red with embarrassment. 'Come on now, go home, everyone, go!'

The only person who seemed not to understand was the officer who'd been interviewing people in the inner room. He walked up to Yueming and said: 'Comrade, would you mind just staying for a couple of minutes so I can take your details? You're the only one left – she doesn't have to because she is known to the chief. If you haven't done anything wrong you've nothing to fear... I'm not putting you on trial.'

Mr Wang, red now from fury rather than embarrassment, stormed over and yanked him to one side: 'What the hell do you think you're doing!?'

Yueming stood up and said: 'Don't worry, I'm here so I should really be registered – our police comrade

174

will need a record of everyone who's been in custody.'

Yueming and the officer walked into the inner room. The other policemen urged everyone else to leave, but now that the 'prisoners' realized they were out of danger they didn't want to leave; they were having a great time watching senior officials and policemen squirming with embarrassment – a rare treat indeed. So the police started to push them out by force, carefully avoiding any physical contact with Liu. When they'd finally managed to get everyone out into the corridor, Yueming emerged from the inner room. They grabbed him immediately and dragged him out with the rest of them. He just had time to turn and smile to Liu; she couldn't tell if it was a smile of encouragement or of gratitude.

The only people left in the room now were Liu, Mr Wang and the police chief. They were waiting for her to leave, but she just carried on sitting there, her eyes lowered. She wanted to see what their reaction would be: they wouldn't dare push her out like they had everyone else.

After a couple of minutes they got up and walked out into the corridor. They started talking in a whisper, discussing what to do next. Liu thought she could hear footsteps and the sound of somebody moving about upstairs. Mr Wang and the chief walked over to the other end of the corridor, still whispering. The female cadre with the overly made-up face poked her head round the door, but quickly withdrew it as soon as she saw Liu's furious eyes glaring back at her. The officer in charge of registration popped back for a few moments, but only to collect his notebook.

Gradually people seemed to disappear, until

eventually the whole place was eerily silent.

Liu was completely alone. She pulled up her trouser legs to have a look at her knees – as she'd expected, both were bruised. Fortunately she hadn't been wearing a skirt.

She felt strangely relaxed now she was on her own. She did not feel like arguing any more, but nor was she prepared to give up.

It was getting dark. Nightfall brought with it an intense kind of stillness – an ever more pervasive silence.

The only light on was the lamp in the corridor but it was very dim. She sat on the bench and stared at the old table and the peeling paint on the wall in front of her.

Why had she decided to stay here? And, stranger still, why did she feel so comfortable here? Was she playing the part of a spoiled child waiting for sympathy, or of 'Madam Director' plotting revenge? Definitely not. It wasn't in her nature. She knew that her seeing the 'troublemaking' must have been part of some more sinister plan – a plan which had been complicated a great deal by her unforeseen arrest. She felt quite justified in wanting a full explanation.

The world seemed to be a crazy place. None of the events of the last few days made much sense. What would happen if she were to act irrationally too?

She felt happy here in this darkening room, as if she were somehow cocooned from the outside world. The occasional sound of a boat siren echoed from the far-off Yangtze. The light from the streetlight made a yellow parallelogram on the floor as it shone through the doorway. There was lightening and heavy thunder but, as yet, no rain.

They obviously wanted her to feel lonely, bored, or perhaps even scared in order to make her leave of her own volition. How could a woman like her, used to a life of privilege and comfort, bear to spend a night in a place like this?

Aside from her pride, there was no need for her to stay there another minute. But it wasn't pride that was keeping her there. She felt an attraction to the place which she couldn't explain; she felt much more comfortable here than in some five star hotel, despite the lingering smell of urine and sweat. She felt more relaxed than she'd ever felt – completely alone and completely detached from the strains and stresses of daily life.

She knew the place had once been a police station, but she didn't know what it had been before that. It felt somehow familiar to her – as though she'd sat in that very room at some indeterminable point in the distant past. The sound of the wind whistling through the window seemed to remind her of something – a distant memory, indistinct yet so very familiar.

She wanted to stand up and wander about, just to check that she really was on her own and that she was as safe as she felt. But her limbs refused to move and her eyelids slowly closed. She felt that something inside her was telling her she didn't need to bother, that all she needed to do was to relax; nothing would happen to her here.

She lay down on the bench and curled up in the foetal position.

Very soon she was fast asleep.

Chapter Eighteen

When Liu's mother was pregnant, everyone had thought she was carrying a boy; no girl ever kicked and moved about as much as Liu had.

'You nearly cost me my life, you know. A new life would have replaced an old one. It's strange really, strange that we're not closer, strange that we're so different.'

Liu replied by leaning over and grabbing her hand affectionately and saying: 'We might be very different, but we are close, aren't we? I braved this sandstorm to come and see you, didn't I?'

'Your Highness has done my house a great honour,' she replied jokingly.

Liu knew what her mother meant by the strange comment about 'one life replacing another'. When she was little she had often touched the huge scar right in the middle of her mother's belly. Her mother had told her it was the door through which she'd climbed out into the world. She could still remember how ugly it was; it looked like a huge centipede covered in warts. One night when she was about six she had woken up crying, and when her mother had asked her what the matter was she had said she had dreamt she was being attacked by a giant centipede.

She was never allowed to see the scar again.

Even at the age of 14, quite a while after she'd started having periods, she thought that when a child was born it ripped open its mother's stomach and climbed out, like a chick breaking out of an egg.

When her mother finally explained the facts of life to her, she was cross with her for having confused her so much as a child. It may well have been one of the reasons she had never wanted children herself. The horror of that scar had just been too much for her. Her mother had said that after childbirth she'd never dared to go into a communal bathroom again; she didn't want anyone to see the scar. It wasn't until years later that Liu realized why her mother's expression always changed whenever she said the word 'anyone'; that 'anyone' had probably included her father.

On that day, more than forty years ago, her mother was in so much pain that she had to bite her reed-catkin pillow. When it broke there were catkins everywhere; they flew through the air and landed on her sweat-drenched face and body. The confusion made her lose consciousness for a few seconds. She came round to the sound of horse-hooves in the courtyard. She hoped it was her husband finally coming home to see her; she imagined him jumping off his horse while it was still galloping along, then dashing in to be by her side. And, sure enough, she heard the familiar sound of his footsteps as he came running into the bedroom, a few people following him. She wanted to open her eyes but the pain was too much. She heard he husband shouting:

'Where is Dr Qi!?'

Somebody told him that Dr Qi was with Auntie Chen who was also in the middle of giving birth.

'Get him over here!! I don't care what he's doing, get him here — now! There are two lives in danger!' He roared.

A group of men hauled her out of bed. She didn't know where she was going — or who was carrying her, but she could tell that her husband was one of them; she could feel his strong arm supporting the bulk of her weight. Someone shouted: 'We've got a stretcher! Make way! Make way!' She was lowered onto a bamboo frame. The churning sensation in her stomach had eased off a bit, but her heart was pounding faster than ever. She could feel herself discharging a liquid, and she could smell that it was fresh blood. That, combined with the stench of sweat, made her feel filthy all over, and worse still, made her feel that she was making everything around her filthy too.

Eventually Dr Qi arrived. He felt her stomach and cried out in alarm: 'The foetus is upside down! What the hell can have happened!? Yesterday when I checked everything was fine — head down, feet up — how could it possibly have turned round!?'

She could feel the icy stethoscope moving around on her chest. She summoned up all her will power and managed to open her eyes: Dr Qi's face was dripping with sweat and her husband was shouting orders.

'Hurry! We must send her to Chongqing

immediately! We've got to get her to the Obstetrical Hospital – that's the only place with the facilities to deal with this kind of thing. The life of mother and child depends on it!' gasped Dr Qi, verging on panic. She could hear every word.

'Can she hold on another 24 hours?' her husband asked, his tone icy. 'The boat captain says he'll do his best, but that it'll take at least 24 hours going up stream.' He controlled his fear and took charge just as though he were leading an army into battle: 'Captain, do whatever it takes to make sure we can get there as quickly as possible! Doctor, prepare for the worst – when the time comes it'll all be up to you!'

'But I'm an army doctor – a surgeon – I'm not an obstetrician. I haven't the faintest idea how to deal with this kind of thing!' protested Dr Qi.

She clutched his hand, pulled him nearer. With tremendous effort, she managed to whisper: 'Give me morphine, I beg you...'

Dr Qi raised his head and said something to Prefect Liu. He said something back. The doctor bent over her and said: 'The child can't take morphine. You're going to have to bear it. We'll give you an injection the second the child is born.'

She didn't reply. Her hair was drenched with sweat and her eyes were so filled with tears she could hardly see. She could feel herself being carried out into the street. The sky was a striking bright blue dotted with white clouds. The people carrying her were marching with rapid military strides, making a rhythmical sound as their feet hit the ground. Her head fell to one side and she could see the many mountains which surrounded the town. They flashed past her, one after another, varying shades of emerald green. 'Yes, this is Liang, the place I came to work for the revolution. And now I am dying,' she thought to herself mournfully as tears trickled down her cheeks.

'Come on! Come on!' Someone behind her was shouting.

The people carrying her speeded up. She began to drift into unconsciousness once again, her senses gradually fading into numbness. All she could feel was the blue sky above her, the clouds pressing down on her chest, heavier and heavier; so heavy she could hardly breathe.

'Be careful! Lie down flat!'

She was vaguely aware of being carried into some kind of tent-like structure. The engine started roaring and the iron floor began to shake; she was in fact on a boat. The child in her belly suddenly stopped moving; it just stayed where it was, good as gold; it was as though it knew where they were going, and knew they were going to the right place. But what if it didn't know? What if it had stopped moving about because it could move no more? What other reason could there be? A spurt of water gushed out of her. She fainted in panic.

Dr Qi's voice was remote.

'Her heartbeat is slowing down. She may be suffering from heart failure. Her water's already broken. The umbilical cord might pop out at any moment. It's too risky...there's not a second to loose. We'll never make it to Chongqing in time. I've never done a Caesarean.'

She could see the naked rock of the cliffs and the

luscious green foliage on the mountains. The engine of the boat was humming noisily, but she could still hear the pleasant gurgling sound of the river; it almost sounded as though it wanted to take her away.

'I've only observed one once,' persisted Dr Qi.

'Go on, be brave! The party has great faith in you!' someone said.

Dr Qi's voice was quivering with fear: 'I might be able to save the child but I don't think the mother will make it.'

'If you don't do something soon neither of them will make it. What is there to lose?'

'Two lives are at stake,' said Dr Qi, turning to Prefect Liu, 'Sir, I'll do whatever you order me to.'

Those were the last words she heard; there followed the sound of Dr Qi looking in his medicine bag trying to find the right surgical instruments. The boat slowed down. All she could see was whiteness; the canvas sheet must have somehow been pulled around her to form a temporary operating theatre. She could feel the cold metal on her belly. 'Oh God,' she thought, 'it's really going to happen. They're going to cut me open.'

She opened her eyes in alarm, to be met by the anxious gaze of her husband. He looked thinner than he had the day before. She grabbed his hand and held it tightly. Her eyes were filled with tears. She no longer had the energy to speak; all she could do was shut her eyes and await her fate. Her husband looked away.

Suddenly she felt a sharp pain just above her navel – so excruciating that she started howling like an animal. She struggled, but her wrists and ankles were held down tightly by the people around her. She felt like a bird being nailed to a specimen board – completely unable to move. The whiteness had turned blood-red – redder and redder – there was red lightening and a downpour of blood.

Then, all of sudden, her whole body relaxed as though it had been stretched so much that it had literally snapped apart. She could hear something in the distance – a strange cry – so far away it sounded as though it was coming from deep within the dark mountain forest.

She lost consciousness.

Liu knew a lot of women who had had caesareans. Their scars were neat and scarcely visible, sometimes as short as two inches; after cosmetic surgery you couldn't really see any scar at all. In summer some of them even wore tops which showed their belly buttons. It made her realize quite how much pain her mother must have gone through. That hideous scar was an inerasable record of the horror she must have felt as she was being cut open, cut open like a fully-conscious living sacrifice.

Chapter Nineteen

'Little Liu!' The familiar voice startled her. She moved her head and tried to sit upright but couldn't find anything to hold on to.

'Wakey wakey Little Liu!'

She opened her eyes and saw Li looking down at her. She was still lying on the bench in the old police station, but her head was in his lap and he was tenderly caressing her long black hair. It was still dark. Only the dim light of the lamp in the corridor glimmered through the open door.

She sat up abruptly and put her arms around him, her head pressed tightly against his chest: 'It was terrifying! Absolutely terrifying!' she exclaimed, without really knowing why.

'It's alright, it's alright,' said Li reassuringly, 'I'm here now. Everything's ok.' He was behaving like a big brother, just like he used to when they were first together.

It had started when she was still only a teenager. She would deliberately act like a spoilt child in order to get his attention − it didn't matter where they were – both at home and at school it was always the same: she would exaggerate how upset or frightened she was, and he would come running to the rescue. He was an only child so he was used to having to rely on himself. He had been born by the roadside while his mother was on a Red Army expedition, hence the name he had been given, 'Lusheng', which means 'road-born'. After his birth her health had deteriorated and she had not been able to have any more children.

When Liu left school she joined the army and was posted to a hospital in Inner Mongolia. The time away from home made her much quieter and more introspective. When she came back to Beijing to start university, Li was the only person who could make her come to life; he was the only person she could have a proper chat with, the only person who could make her laugh out loud. Their most intimate moments were walking down the street hand in hand.

Neither of them could have fallen in love with anyone else. He thought her better than any other woman in the world, and she thought him better than any other man. They didn't think of each other as ordinary people, and neither expected the other to behave like an ordinary person. Whenever one of them went to the toilet they would always shut the door tightly, afraid the other might catch them. And whenever one of them did catch the other doing something ordinary or mundane, they would look away in order to save the other from embarrassment. Liu could hardly believe that she could have acted, out of instinct, like a little sister once more.

He was hugging her with one hand and stroking

her shoulder with the other. 'Are you warm enough?' he asked.

She nodded and refused when he offered her his jacket.

How had he found her here? The answer was obvious, and made her suspicious. Mr Wang and his cronies were probably waiting outside. Or even in the next room. Or even just outside in that dimly lit corridor.

She blushed. She didn't even bother to ask Li if she was right or not. She knew they'd been listening the whole time. Liu felt an immense dislike for them. What were they after? She realized she could not yield an inch to them.

She sat up straight, looked her husband in the eye and asked, 'Why isn't the money from the Resettlement Fund being given directly to the people being resettled?'

He was taken aback by her sudden change in manner but it didn't take him long to readjust.

'The Resettlement Programme, including the distribution of the fund, is handled by local government officials in the regions concerned; we consider them competent enough to make all the necessary arrangements and decisions.' He replied.

'Are the people who are to be resettled allowed to complain to their local government if they suspect that the fund is being mishandled?'

'Of course,' said Li, smiling to himself, 'Government officials are the servants of the people.'

'Can presenting letters of complaint be regarded as "troublemaking"?'

'No, so long as there is no breach of the peace.'

'If a small demonstration gets out of control because local cadres handle the situation badly,' began Liu, her anger finally finding a suitable target, 'then who is to be held responsible?'

He knew she wanted him to blame someone, and he knew that dodging the issue would only make her angrier. But he also knew that she was not the only person who would want to hear his verdict. He said clearly: 'Government officials should certainly never make a conflict worse.'

'Well, I am a witness. I saw what was going on with my own eyes, and they were making it worse.' She stood up, as if about to give evidence in court.

Li stood up as well. He was going to have to win her over, and he still had the local officials to deal with as well.

'Come on now, listen, this needn't be a big deal. Let's keep a sense of perspective. Project Headquarters believe that local governments should be able to sort out all civil disputes relating to resettlement.' He repeated, 'All civil disputes relating to resettlement.'

Liu walked quickly out of the room. There was nobody in the corridor. She opened the door of the room next door. Nobody there either. They were cleverer than she'd thought. After all, they didn't need to be there if all they wanted was to hear what was being said; all they had to do was leave a tape-recorder somewhere, or even just a mobile phone.

She'd said everything she wanted to say; she was quite happy with Li's use of the phrase 'civil disputes' – far more accurate than 'riot' or 'troublemaking'. She felt ready to leave the old police

190

station now, but she didn't want to leave Liang quite yet; she still wanted to make sure that Yueming was completely out of danger.

She turned round and walked back into the room where her husband was waiting for her. She walked right up close and whispered in his ear, 'Lusheng, thank you so much.'

There was no one waiting outside, but she did see a black Toyota. The rain had stopped and parts of the courtyard were flooded with puddles. The water glistened under the street-lighting.

Liu decided it was time to ask how he'd got there.

'I borrowed a car from the Golden Pleasure Hotel.' He walked over to the car, got out the electronic key, and pressed the 'unlock' button. He bent down and opened the door for Liu, saying, 'I asked the driver to stay behind.'

She was glad that he had come by himself. She glanced back at the gloomy courtyard; it looked as though that little light in the corridor was the only light in the whole building. She couldn't for the life of her understand why she hadn't been more scared.

After she had climbed into the car and closed the door she asked, 'So where are we going?'

'I'm staying in your hotel room,' he fastened his seatbelt, 'so long as you don't have any objections, that is.'

'As long as you pay your share of the bill,' replied Liu, laughing.

Suddenly she remembered the 5,000 yuan she'd asked for. 'The money you said you'd bring me...did you remember it?' she asked anxiously.

'It's in the hotel. It's not like you to want to buy a painting. You must show it to me when you have bought it.'

'So you can ask for the money back if you don't like it?' She didn't tell him anything about the painting; she didn't want to end up having to tell him the whole story.

Li started the car, turned the car round and drove out of the large wooden gates. He turned to the left, put his foot on the accelerator and sped out. A policeman closed the gates behind them. It was the first time she'd seen anyone in the courtyard; it put her on her guard.

She thought to herself that if the car really had been borrowed from the hotel, then surely there could not have been enough time to bug it, but she put the radio on just in case. The news was on; they were talking about a special event that was being put on in Chongqing in order to 'sing the praises of the Three Gorges Project and raise morale'.

Liu cut to the chase: 'That Director Wang is bit of a sleaze-bag if you ask me. He's up to something.'

No reaction. There was not the slightest indication of surprise on his face. He didn't ask Liu what she meant, nor did he volunteer any information himself. All he said was:

'Resettlement is the biggest headache of the whole project. Project Headquarters gave all the money to local governments right at the very beginning – no one at the top wanted anything to do with it. Think about it, this county only makes 6 or 7 million yuan a year and now, suddenly, local officials have got three hundred million to play with. It's hardly surprising if it's gone to their heads a bit...'

They turned into the busy high street of the Old City. People were walking in the street completely oblivious to the thunderous traffic around them. Li had no choice but to slow down. 'Let's just hope nothing really serious happens...'

'You mean you knew that local cadres were embezzling money from the fund?' Liu had never had this kind of conversation with her husband. He'd never talked about work, and she'd never asked. She had never really been very interested.

He laughed, turning the steering wheel slightly to the right as he edged forward. He had learnt to drive in America; he never hooted the horn or leant out of the window to swear at the person in front like most Chinese drivers.

'Project Headquarters could not possibly have distributed the money to each resident in one go. If people got their money before they moved then there would not have been any incentive for them to go. The local governments will have no option but to build houses and streets in the resettlement areas and the money that's left over, which won't be much, will be waiting for the settlers when they arrive. If you gave the money directly to the peasants they would build mud huts and keep the rest.'

'Why do cadres have such a low opinion of peasants? Treating people like this is only going to cause trouble.' said Liu, getting annoyed.

'My dear wife,' began Li, clenching his teeth as he swerved to avoid a pedestrian who seemed to have a death-wish. He put the headlights on, illuminating the whole street. It seemed to have the desired effect;

no one dared mess with a big car with headlights on. 'This is China! Those peasants have never seen so much money in their whole lives. A family of five would get more than 100,000 yuan. It would be like winning the lottery! After a few days of gambling, whoring, drug-taking and squabbling among relatives all the money would be gone!'

'Well, I fail to see how the money is any safer in the hands of a load of greedy local officials!' She didn't like Li's attitude; it sounded as though he was just trying to make excuses. Cadres always try to protect one another.

There was a crowd of people in front of them. They all seemed to be desperately trying to get into one particular shop. Others were filing out with large bags on their shoulders. Li stopped the car. There was rather nondescript Sichuanese opera on the radio, the modern stuff that's supposed to be amusing. He turned the volume down a bit and said:

'The People's Congress gave us five billion, which is only a quarter of the cost of the construction work alone! But we accepted because we knew that money makes money. My company has had to turn that five billion into what it is today, and has depended on the cooperation of all the local governments in the Three Gorges region. Now if I deny these same local governments the opportunity to make money, then how can I possibly expect them to listen to me?'

'So the whole project is just a big feast as far as you're concerned!' Liu had finally realized what was going on. 'Everyone gets a nice fat slice! You've had your slice, so you've got to let them have theirs!' She added icily.

Li seemed unmoved by his wife's cynicism. He started trying to push his way through the crowd, but now not even the headlights were enough to get people to move out of the way. They could both now see what all the fuss was about: eiderdown quilts were being sold at a huge discount. Eventually he lost patience and started tooting the horn. People slowly moved out of the way and let the car pass through.

'Don't you worry,' he said curtly, 'If anyone's taken a bite, I'll make sure they spit it right back out!'

Driving in the Old City was virtually impossible. He revved up and turned into one of the steep roads leading up to the New City. The main road in the city centre had six lanes; there were cars parked on both sides, in front of the brightly-lit restaurants, but there was still plenty of room to get some speed up.

Li breathed a sigh of relief, either because he had escaped the hazardous driving conditions of the Old City, or perhaps because he had put a stop to his wife's relentless interrogation.

After a couple of minutes they arrived at the Golden Pleasure. There were quite few people standing in the car park. They looked anxious – some were looking at their watches, some were talking into their mobile phones and some were just pacing back and forth.

Li looked at the clock on the dashboard. 'Sorry, I'm late!' He stopped the car and jumped out. Mr Han came rushing over to greet him, a calm obsequious smile on his chubby little face; he didn't look worried like the rest of them.

Li turned to tell his wife, 'I've got some important

business here. You go on and have dinner without me – don't wait up.'

'Do whatever it is you've got to do, but give me the money!' replied Liu in a whisper.

Li laughed apologetically. He beckoned Mr Han over; they exchanged a few words and disappeared.

She'd didn't have to wait long before he came back with a black leather suitcase which he handed over. She was left standing in the luxurious marble-floored lobby all by herself, facing a huge vase filled with a selection of incredible fresh red and yellow paradise-bird flowers. She felt lonely and wondered whether she wouldn't have been better off spending the night in the old police station. Anything would surely have been better than feeling as confused as she now felt.

Every time she came back to the Golden Pleasure she felt as though she'd come to the wrong place. She felt it inappropriate that, despite all the poverty of the region, Liang should still boast this kind of luxury hotel.

Chapter Twenty

It wasn't that she felt left out; she had no desire to spend any more time than was absolutely necessary with her husband's cronies. Li leaving her on her own so he could get on with his work was hardly anything out of the ordinary – she often treated him in the same way when she was in the middle of an important research project. What was making her so uneasy was the fact that seeing him again had reminded her that she still loved him. And, at this crucial moment in their relationship, all he could say was 'You go on and have dinner without me' and disappear! She felt she'd made too many compromises, given in too quickly.

Liu pressed the lift button and the steel doors opened immediately, silently gliding apart, as if they'd been waiting for her.

She thought back to the time when she was on her own in America after Li had already left. She'd had a roommate to save money on the rent, a very likeable American-born Chinese girl who had been studying computer science. She'd once asked Liu: 'Haven't you ever thought of getting yourself a boyfriend now your husband's not here to keep an eye on you?'

'I could never do a thing like that,' she had replied.

'You Chinese girls are all so brainwashed! I really feel sorry for you.'

Liu had explained by saying that she loved her husband very much, they'd been childhood sweethearts; no one in the world could have a better husband.

That evening she wanted to call Li and tell him how much she missed him, but she decided against it. She thought she'd wait until she actually had something to tell him.

Liu's roommate used to tell her everything, including the details of her numerous relationships. The latest one was a work colleague; she said he was nothing serious, just a fling. The man's wife found out and came round and threw a flowerpot through their window. The next day the man came round to apologize. The roommate told him that the affair was over and sent him on his way. Liu felt quite sorry for him.

The roommate said it was time the relationship ended in any case. Time for a change, time for a new boyfriend.

Liu didn't voice any disapproval, but she didn't think much of people being quite so casual about their relationships. She never thought that sex could ever be important enough to justify losing one's dignity. That was the reason why she had always thought Li would never have an affair. She had certainly never imagined she was going to end up as a betrayed wife.

'No,' she thought to herself, 'I shouldn't think like that. I don't need any one's pity – least of all my own.'

The first thing she saw when she opened the door to her hotel room was a big bunch of yellow roses in a vase. There was a card which she picked up curiously. To her surprise they were from Mr Zheng, the manager of the hotel.

He wrote that he hoped she might be willing to give him a ring when she was fully rested. He was hoping she might do him the honour of dining with him.

The roses had a beautiful fragrance. The flowers were unusually large with petals like silk. They almost looked too good to be true. She recognised them instantly as Italian campaniles. How on earth had Mr Zheng managed to find campaniles in Liang?

She was feeling rather dirty and smelly. The stench of urine which had pervaded the old police station seemed to have stayed with her. She went into the bathroom and had a quick shower. When she'd finished she sat on the sofa and tried to open the leather suitcase but found it locked. Of course, it was supposed to be locked. Now she remembered that Mr Han had slipped a key into her hand. She felt in her pockets. Sure enough, there it was. All the rushing about and general chaos of the day were beginning to affect her mind.

The only thing in the suitcase was a small brown paper bag. She opened it to find a neat wad of a hundred 50 yuan notes. She could tell from the way it had been tied that it had come straight from the bank. Next to it was a wad of ten 100 yuan notes. He even knew to bring some extra.

Maybe he had asked Mr Han to get the money.

She started to worry: where had the money come from? Had it been embezzled from public funds?

She shuddered. On the way over they had been talking about millions and billions of yuan – surely not, surely Li was not that kind of person. His salary was more than enough, and he was not a big spender. No, of course he'd be able to spare a measly 6,000 yuan out of what he earned.

Nevertheless her immediate reaction was to put the money straight back in the suitcase. Money was the only thing anyone in Liang seemed interested in.

She looked at her watch. It had just gone eight o'clock. She opened the window. She could see the night tourist boats sailing up and down the river, a row of lit-up cabin windows shining in the darkness, brightly coloured lights decorating the decks, the boat dragging a long snake of glittering scales behind it. The mountains in the background had not been completely erased by the night; they stood there dark and motionless, as ancient as the heavens; a pure wilderness, seemingly untouched by the hand of man. All of a sudden one of the boats turned on four search lights, scanning the turbulent waves. The beams were so intensely bright, it almost seemed as though they made a kind of swishing sound as they passed over the water.

She returned to her bed. So much had happened so quickly. She had probably experienced more surprise and bewilderment in the past couple of days than in the whole of the rest of her life put together. She wanted to rest.

She was just about to close her eyes when she suddenly remembered that she had arranged to meet

Auntie Chen after dinner. Tired or not she had to go, not least because she had to give her the money – there wasn't a moment to lose.

She walked out through the revolving doors of the hotel. There was a hotel security guard standing respectfully just to her left as she walked out. He was dressed in a strange outfit and looked like a warlord from the early 20th century. She asked him to get her a taxi, but he didn't seem to know what to do, he just stood there scratching his head with an embarrassed smile on his face; he almost ended up knocking his cap off.

It wasn't hard to tell that he'd probably only been in Liang a couple of weeks. Fortunately a taxi happened to drive up and stop right outside the main entrance. The young man walked up and opened the door for her. He had turned bright red in embarrassment.

She told the driver to take her to Herring Lane. He repeated her instruction in Sichuanese, just to make sure he'd understood her correctly, and she then confirmed that he had understood correctly by replying in Sichuanese herself. He would have found it strange that anyone staying in a place like the Golden Pleasure could possibly have had any business in the Old City.

The air was unusually clear after the spell of rain. The driver was not very talkative but Liu decided to initiate conversation by asking:

'What are cadres like here?'

The driver was a bit taken aback by the question. He looked around and whispered: 'There are evil spirits in the air here!'

Now it was Liu's turn to be taken aback. Of all the things she'd thought he might say, she had never imagined that. He looked like a perfectly normal young man, not some superstitious geriatric. However, now she'd got him started, there was no stopping him:

'This place is full of bad energy! People round here can be going about their ordinary business and suddenly... wham! They're on the brink of death and their best friend breaks a leg, completely out of the blue. You know what old people say? They say that the housing blocks on the mountainside look like painted coffins! There are evil spirits that will attack anyone, doesn't matter if you're an ordinary worker or a senior cadre. An outsider like you should be careful, make sure you don't let anyone cause you any harm.'

Liu was unimpressed. She tried to change the subject: 'Don't you think this is the most beautiful scenery in the whole of China?'

'Visitors may think it's beautiful, it's different for those of us that live here.'

Liu suddenly realized that his words made a lot of sense. Her parents had 'lived' in Liang. How could Liu, a mere visitor, ever hope to understand why Liang had made such a strange impression on her mother, why she'd never been able to put her memories of the place behind her?

The driver interrupted her train of thought: 'Which house number in Herring Lane?'

It was an unnecessary question as taxis couldn't drive into Herring Lane because it was down a short flight of steps. Maybe he just wanted to try and find out what she was up to.

'Here's fine.' She replied. She paid and got out. When she handed the money over he smiled at her rather mysteriously. It made her feel nervous. His expression was strangely in tune with his preferred topic of conversation – eerie and unsettling.

Liu walked carefully down the steps into the dark little lane. Auntie Chen was standing in her doorway, with her back to the dim light which was shining out of her tiny house. When she saw Liu she shouted out, 'I didn't think you were coming, it's so late already! Have you had your dinner?'

Liu realized that she had in fact completely forgotten about dinner. Li had told her to go and get something to eat, but as it had turned out, her mind had been so preoccupied that she'd ended up leaving the hotel on an empty stomach. Now she came to think of it, she felt ravenous.

She shook her head. Auntie Chen grabbed hold of her and pulled her into the inner room. The wooden table which had been in the main room had been moved into the bedroom and the whole place looked a bit tidier and cleaner. On the small table there was a plate, a cup and a pair of chopsticks.

She sat down on the tiny stool. The house still smelled of Chinese medicine but Liu didn't mind so much this time. The wind from the river was whistling through the open window. Auntie Chen chuckled and said, 'I knew it! How did I guess you wouldn't have had anything to eat?!'

She walked into the kitchen. Liu could smell the

home-cooked food sizzling on the primitive-looking stove. A couple of minutes later she came back into the inner room with a steaming bowl of egg fried rice, a plate of home-made pickles and another plate of dried tofu. 'Diegu went to the hospital; I thought you'd show up, so I asked her to go so I could stay here.'

Liu smiled, picked up her bowl and started eating. The simple food was delicious. She asked Auntie Chen: 'Whatever made you think I might not be able to come?'

Auntie Chen put a cup of tea down on the table in front of her guest and said: 'Yueming came here as soon as they released him. He told me everything and asked me what I thought he could do to help you. He was very impressed by you.'

Liu blushed. She took a mouthful of rice as a distraction.

'I knew they wouldn't dare do anything to you. On the contrary I thought you would be the one giving them a hard time; I don't suppose they were very happy when you refused to leave!'

'Didn't you complain to me earlier that he never told you anything? Sounds like he told you everything this time!'

'He's no fool. He's only stupid when it comes to sorting out his own problems. He's not stupid when it comes to helping other people with their problems. He probably thought of you as our guest and felt responsible for you, that's why he came and told me first.'

'I remembered you mentioning that your husband was coming this evening, so I told Yueming to go to the dock. He knows how to spot the fast boats from the Headquarters.'

Liu was surprised, 'So Yueming met Li and told him what had happened?'

'Well, not exactly,' said Auntie Chen with a chuckle and clap of her hands, 'There were too many people wanting to see your husband, the whole quay was filled with local cadres. They tried to force Yueming to leave but he caught sight of Director Wang and tried to approach him. Mr Wang lost his temper and ordered the police to arrest him again. Then, for some reason or other, shortly afterwards, he ordered his release again – probably didn't want any trouble.'

'What did Yueming say to make Mr Wang lose his temper?'

'He just said: 'Why isn't Madame Director Li here?' Of course, Director Wang knew what he was getting at, but just to make sure you were safe Yueming went back to the old police station and waited in the courtyard. When your husband arrived he came straight back here to put my mind at rest.'

Liu felt very touched. 'It was because of me that he got arrested in the first place...it was awful...they even hit him...' As soon as she'd said it she wished she hadn't.

'And quite right too! Serves him right. That will teach him!' replied Auntie Chen. Her words were harsh, but she was clearly upset; she wiped away her tears with her hand. She glanced over and caught sight of Liu's injured wrist. She pulled it closer and had another look, fresh tears welling in her eyes. 'Does it hurt? Is it serious? It's because of him that you were arrested. Delivering a letter indeed!'

'Where is he at the moment?' she asked.

'He's missed a day's work. He went off to the school to meet up with his colleagues – the other teachers all want to know what happened. When he's done that he says he's got to go back up the mountain to catch up on his work at the Temple. He's got to have a certain number of pictures finished by tomorrow.'

There was so much she wanted to ask. 'He must have had a good reason for wanting to deliver that letter.'

'Good reason my foot!' replied Auntie Chen, annoyed. 'People whose houses are below the 175m mark are going to be resettled, but it so happens that our house is just above the 175m mark, so we'll be staying put. I know it's small, and there's no bathroom or toilet, there isn't even a shower, but I like living here – it's my home. I'm pleased we're not moving. The row about the fund really has nothing to do with us.'

Liu thought of the New City – it was so much better than the run-down area Auntie Chen lived in. Everyone moving there would surely be over the moon. What a pity she and Yueming would have to stay where they were. And yet Auntie Chen didn't seem to care.

'What's more, neither my husband nor I have a pension. We have to rely on Yueming and Diegu to pay the hospital bills. What's the point in us moving to a pretty flat? We'd never have enough money to paint the cement shell. I expect we'd have to fork out almost as much as the value of the house to furnish it. There are plenty of people out there working themselves into early graves just so they can earn enough money to be able to afford to move in. I'm glad we've been spared it.'

'So why did Yueming go on the demonstration then?'

'He went on behalf of his colleagues. I know what was going on. The simple truth is that those primary school teachers were too lily-livered to go themselves; they said it would be better if he went because he had no vested interest.'

'What's wrong with people who have a vested interest going and demonstrating?' said Liu, beginning to realize that she really had no idea what it was like to be an ordinary citizen.

Auntie Chen took off her apron and sighed. 'It used to be power that was the problem, now it's money. Ordinary people will do almost anything for a few hundred yuan, and cadres will do anything for a few million yuan. Yueming stuck his neck out, and for what?'

'So you're saying the cadres here are corrupt?'

'I wouldn't quite say that. There have always been a few good cadres who aren't interested in rising through the ranks. For example, Old Chen was as honest as they come, but look what happened to him! I shouldn't talk like this. You're a visitor here and you will go back where you belong. We've spent our whole lives here and we'll die here. Even with this new reservoir, which will cause change the like of which hasn't been seen for tens of thousands of years, things won't be all that different for ordinary people. You see, you're not like us, and you never will be.'

In a strange way her bluntness made Liu feel much

more relaxed. People are only polite when they don't know you very well, when they don't feel entirely comfortable with you; now that Auntie Chen had said what she really thought, Liu knew she must think of her as a real friend. It was the perfect opportunity to ask a few more questions:

'Does Yueming know about my parents?'

Auntie Chen was silent. She walked into the kitchen to check the front door was closed, and didn't start to answer the question until she had sat back down.

'I've never mentioned your parents to Yueming, or even to my second husband. In fact I haven't said anything about them to anyone for decades. Even when Old Chen was still alive we always avoided the subject.'

'Why was that?' asked Liu.

Auntie Chen let out a long sigh and said, 'There's no rush; all in good time. Eat your dinner first. You're not in any hurry to get back to the hotel are you? We will talk when you have finished your food. I didn't know whether I would ever see someone from your family again. Meeting you makes me feel almost as though your mother has come back. This is your third visit to see me – the neighbours have been asking who you are. I told them you were a distant relative, so distant that this is the first time you have been to Liang.'

She sat down on a stool, facing Liu. She seemed hesitant, wiping her hands on her apron for longer than necessary.

Liu moved the stool next to her and sat down.

'Auntie Chen, surely you can trust me?'

'I'm afraid of upsetting you...'

Liu realized she had to think of something that would convince Auntie Chen to carry on.

'Auntie Chen, I am so tired. I really need to lie down. Do you think I could lie on your bed?' She got up and started walking towards it.

Auntie Chen immediately put her hand out to block the way. 'No! It's too dirty. I can't let you lie on that!'

Liu took no notice and pushed Auntie Chen's hand out of the way. She sat on the bed and took off her shoes. The bed really did smell, the pillow in particular – mainly of sweat. She let down the grey mosquito net. The room was lit by a solitary yellow light bulb in the far corner; with the mosquito net down it was so dark Liu couldn't even see what colour the duvet was. However, lying on this old bed she began to feel much better.

'Auntie, I know you've never told anyone, but it was forty years ago... come on, you know you can tell me.'

'What makes you think there's anything to tell?' said Auntie Chen, trying to avoid the subject.

'I know it's got something to do with me, and if you don't tell me, then I'll never know, and if I don't know, then the story will be lost forever.' She paused. 'Or maybe you'd like to go to Beijing and tell my mother? You could stay a whole month – I'm sure you'd have a lovely time!'

'You're a crafty one, to be sure,' chuckled Auntie Chen. 'Alright, I'll tell you, but on one condition: you mustn't interrupt me, no matter how much you don't like what you're hearing. Questions must wait until after I've finished.'

Liu squeezed Auntie Chen's hand in agreement.

Chapter Twenty-one

As the familiar aroma of medicinal herbs brewing on the stove wafted over from the kitchen, Auntie Chen told Liu about her pregnancy all those years ago. She had suffered from terrible morning sickness. The herbal medicine she'd had to drink wasn't all that different from what Diegu was drinking now. Her stomach always used to be empty – she hadn't been able to keep anything down. She might have a craving for meat, but even if she was lucky enough to get hold of some, she'd only end up vomiting it up. She was sick almost every day and at the same time became fussier and fussier about what she would and wouldn't eat. She felt as restless as a cat's paw.

An army doctor called Dr Qi came and had a look at her. He told her she had an excess of amniotic fluid and that the position of the foetus put the pregnancy at some risk. He prescribed bed rest, but she was far too busy for that.

They had their meals at the Prefectural Administration canteen. She usually asked the cooks for rice soup, to which she added a bit of brown sugar. That was her way of taking extra care of herself and the baby. Fortunately she'd been working in the fields since childhood so she had grown up to be very strong. At night she would fall asleep as soon as her head hit the pillow. She was still young and never slowed down, despite the fact that she was getting bigger by the day.

Her husband, Old Chen, was even busier than she was. He was working hard trying to set up county and township offices for the Department of Military Affairs. He had recently been wounded in the arm during a battle with some of the last remaining rebels. But this was a man blessed with good fortune; altogether ten different parts of his body had been wounded, but had never had the wound been very serious; he had always recovered quickly. Ridding the densely wooded mountain district of bandits was no easy task. Many were killed. Once the large organised groups of rebels had been wiped out, they started the 'Campaign of suppressing counter-revolutionaries' – tracking down dispersed bandits in every village and shooting those who had committed crimes. The smell of gunpowder was all too familiar in the years immediately following the Liberation of '49.

Liu's mother still hadn't arrived when Auntie Chen began to get involved in the 'Campaign to Reform Prostitutes', so she never saw the mass arrest.

The Campaign was launched at night. All the soldiers and militiamen took part – armed with guns and bayonets. First they cordoned off every dock and every street that ran along the waterfront. Then they began a house-to-house sweep.

There were very few female cadres at that time so

Auntie Chen usually took part – fulfilling her duty despite her pregnancy. It was chaos – prostitutes and customers scurrying about like headless chickens. The female cadres arrested the women and the soldiers arrested the men who were only released after they had been 'registered'.

There were problems with the 'Prostitutes' Reform Class' right from the start. Prefect Liu required the female cadres to identify the 'madams' so the class would have targets for their denunciations. But Liang was too small – most of the prostitutes were just ordinary women working illegally. There weren't any 'registered' brothels, so no 'madams' could be found.

One of the prostitutes caught Auntie Chen's notice. Her name was Red Lotus. She was a bit older than the rest, 25 or 26. A few younger girls had asked her to be the head of their little 'partnership'. She was very beautiful – she had an oval face, long eyelashes and a good figure. She stood out in such an unruly crowd. She was also neat and clean and unusually good at needlework.

Both her parents had died when she was young and she had run away from her village because she couldn't accept the marriage arranged for her by her older brother. While making her escape she had been abducted and sold to a boatman, who had in turn sold her to a brothel.

Auntie Chen had also run away from home, but instead of being abducted and sold to a brothel she had come across a band of Communist guerrillas who were hiding in the mountains. She and Red

Lotus had both set out on the same path, but arrived at different destinations for the simple reason that they had come across different groups of people.

Red Lotus had told Auntie Chen time and time again that she was terrified about what would happen to the Reform Class when their re-education had finished – she didn't want to be taken away by some man she didn't know. It would be just like what had happened in the village and she was just as scared. Only this time it would be even worse; before at least it had been a member of the family who had chosen the man.

Auntie Chen tried to convince Red Lotus that being married to a working man was better than being a prostitute. She had to trust the People's Government. They were giving her another chance.

Red Lotus said that at least as a prostitute you knew why you were sleeping with a man. But if you were forced to marry someone, then you'd have to sleep with him forever – and get nothing in return.

Auntie Chen was astonished by her words. She had never thought of it like that. She couldn't deny that Red Lotus had a point, but all she could say was that prostitution was 'immoral'. That evening she told Old Chen about the incident. He said she was an idiot, and when she started to argue with him he flew into a rage, shouting at her to shut-up. He smashed a bowl and tried to slap her but, as a guerilla fighter, she managed to dodge his hand. As it turned it out it was lucky Old Chen had smashed that bowl. If he hadn't she might have been naïve enough to mention what Red Lotus had said at the cadres' meeting, and that would have been a very grave political error.

People might even have suspected her of being party to Red Lotus' subsequent escape.

The evening they caught Red Lotus Auntie Chen was in a great deal of pain. She wanted to go out and perform her duty, but she couldn't even get out of bed. The baby was moving about so much she was utterly exhausted. Old Chen was very worried about her, but he was a soldier. He had no choice but to obey orders. He picked up his gun and left.

She couldn't sleep and her stomach was hurting a great deal. In the end she called Dr Qi. He said it was nothing out of the ordinary. She just needed peace and quiet. If she suffered any more discomfort she was to send for him.

She didn't fall asleep until just before dawn.

Early the next day, sometime between 6:30 and 7.00am, she was awoken by a terrible din being made by the crowds outside. It was far too early for the market but the streets were already packed. Suddenly she heard footsteps in the courtyard. Someone had run in shouting: 'We've caught them! We've caught them!'

A moment later, a comrade from the Women's Federation ran into her room. She told her that the prostitute Red Lotus had escaped but had subsequently been caught. They hadn't found her alone either. She had been at it with Yutong, the Buddhist abbot of the monastery.

'Can you believe it!? Red Lotus was selling herself to a monk! She was caught in his bed! Two fornicators for the price of one! Our intelligence network is amazing!' She continued excitedly:

215

'They're parading them through the streets right now! Come on! Get up and have a look!'

Auntie Chen was stunned. She had heard that Yutong was a very spiritual man, far above such worldly debauchery. What on earth was he doing with someone like Red Lotus, and how had he come to be caught in bed with her?

Something wasn't right.

Suddenly she felt as though there were a balloon of air in her belly. She stood motionless. She could feel the air somehow turning inside her and hardening into a knot. She clutched at her stomach. The pain was overwhelming.

But she got up and slowly followed her colleagues outside, using the wall for support.

There were people everywhere; more and more were squeezing their way through the side streets to get a glimpse of the action. The procession had moved no more than about twenty metres away from her.

As she leaned against the doorframe at the top of the steps, the procession pushed through the crowd and came into view. Four strong men were carrying a long, thick bamboo pole on their shoulders. From the pole hung a man and a woman; both were completely naked. They made a grotesque picture: they'd been tied to the pole in contorted positions in the manner that peasants in the mountainous area of Sichuan had long displayed adulterous couples. This ultimate humiliation was only inflicted upon offending couples if their families and clan leaders all agreed to it.

Their arms and legs were spread out and tied back to back: Red Lotus' left arm was bound to Yutong's right arm, and Yutong's left arm was bound to Red

Lotus' right arm. The thick bamboo pole went in between their backs, forcing their bodies into an uncomfortable arch that exposed their genitals for all to see. As their bound legs dangled in mid-air, their tortured expressions revealed their suffering with horrific intensity.

Moreover, they looked frozen – their lips were pitifully white, their faces a kind of bluish-grey colour. The militiamen at the back were carrying guns pointed straight ahead whilst those at the front had the difficult job of pushing their way through the crowds, and those on either side were trying to stop people getting too close. Everyone could see the two bare-bodied captives. Hoisted a full shoulder's height above the crowd, the naked man and woman remained in full view.

The grey stubble on the monk's bald head betrayed the fact that he was already advanced in years. His eyes were tight shut, and his head lolled to one side. Perhaps he had fainted.

But Red Lotus held her head high with her eyes wide-open, staring. Her hair hung down loosely, a few strands touching the monk's face.

Auntie Chen made her way down a few steps, wanting to follow Red Lotus, when, suddenly, she sensed that Red Lotus had seen her. Yes, she was staring directly at her. Auntie Chen was terrified. Clutching her huge belly with both hands, she went back up a few steps. But Red Lotus was still staring at her, her eyes filled with accusation.

The street was seething like a cauldron filled with boiling soup. People were shouting and cursing and the militiamen were making little headway. Those who had had a good look at the filthy fornicating little slut wanted to cross to the other side to get a better view of the randy old monk, and those who had had a good look at the randy old monk wanted to get a better view of the filthy fornicating little slut. There was a good deal of pushing and shoving as city folk and country folk, who had come to town because it was market day, tried to elbow each other out of the way. Those closest to the couple spat at them or pelted them with rotten vegetables and old shoes. Some even threw sharp stones.

The crowd became so wild that the procession almost came to a standstill. Auntie Chen could see the blood and saliva dripping from the captives' faces. It was such an awful sight she could hardly bear to look. More and more people crowded into the street, and some of the people standing near the front ran forward and started pulling on Red Lotus' breasts and tugging on the old monk's shrivelled penis. By now the guards could see that the crowd was completely out of control and they gave up trying to maintain even a semblance of order. When the crowd realized this things got even worse – more noise, more violence and more attacks on the helpless prisoners. A woman who lived on the street produced a rolling pin and rammed it up Red Lotus' vagina. When fresh blood started pouring out the crowd burst into to cheers: 'Serves her right! How's that for a good fuck then!'

She had bitten her lips so much that they too had started bleeding, but her eyes were still fully intact, scanning the sea of faces in search of Auntie Chen. When she finally managed to locate her, she once again started to stare in the way which had made Auntie Chen so uneasy before – those once sparkling eyes now filled with a strange kind of crazed desperation. But there was no sign that she wanted to be pitied. Red Lotus had always been too proud for pity.

Auntie Chen could not understand why she had been singled out like this. She turned away but could still feel Red Lotus' eyes fixed on the back of her head. Why hadn't she picked someone else to stare at? There were plenty of people she knew there, not least other cadres from the Reform Class. Maybe it was because she had been a bit more friendly to her than the other cadres had; but then again, she couldn't have been that much more friendly – it would never have been allowed. The stare was becoming more and more intense, so intense that she felt as if her eyes were boring right into Auntie Chen's stomach.

Terrified of meeting her gaze, Auntie Chen put her head down and turned to make her way back into the compound. But still she could feel Red Lotus's eyes staring at her. She became panic-stricken. At that moment she felt a stabbing pain in her stomach and her water broke, soaking her trousers as it poured out. The child inside her was kicking violently. She tried to mop some of the water off with her hand but it was red with blood. Suddenly everything went black and she collapsed in a heap on the steps.

Auntie Chen's colleagues dashed over, picked her up and carried her home. Dr Qi arrived almost immediately. She was still unconscious and entirely oblivious to the doctor's frantic preparations. A colleague was asked to run off and tell Old Chen that the life of mother and child were both at risk. By this stage Auntie Chen had come round just enough to get the gist of what they were saying: 'Don't go making a fuss – just tell him it's time,' she murmured.

The commotion outside was as deafening as ever; people had started shouting out slogans. Someone told her the public trial had started. If that was true, she knew Old Chen would not be able to get away. Giving birth is a hardship women have to bear alone. If they are lucky they survive, if they are unlucky there is absolutely nothing a husband can do to help.

But Old Chen did manage to get away in time. He was beside himself with worry. He squatted down by the bed and stroked her head gently, so different from the course gruff old veteran she was used to. The noise outside was rising to a crescendo, but she couldn't tell what was happening. Petrified by the contorted expression of pain on his wife's face, Old Chen got up and started pacing the room like a man possessed. Then suddenly he reached down, grasped her hands, held them to his chest and said that if anything happened to her and the baby he would not be able to go on living.

Hearing this, tears started trickling down her cheeks. A few seconds later Old Chen was called away. She carried on clenching her teeth, desperately trying to endure the pain. Then suddenly she saw Red Lotus standing before her, staring at her just like before. She trembled with fear.

'Look!' she shouted to the woman supporting her legs.

The woman looked round. 'Look at what?' she asked.

Auntie Chen looked again: she was gone. But a minute or so later she was back, staring right at her. She almost fainted in terror.

Suddenly there was the sound of a volley of gunshots, followed by an earth-shaking uproar.

She couldn't make out exactly what it was that people were shouting, but she knew from experience that for some reason or other people always felt the need to make a strange yelling sound at the moment of execution.

Not long afterwards she heard the report of the guns again, but this time she felt as though the gunshots were aimed straight at her; the bullets were coming towards her, closer and closer until they rang in her ears. Between her legs something was trying to force its way out. She shrieked in pain yet still it carried on, but no matter how hard it pushed, it simply could not get out.

This continued for so long that she became convinced she wasn't going to make it. During all this someone else summoned Dr Qi. He gave Auntie Chen's colleagues brief instructions as to how to continue and ran out, not to return. By this stage all she could see was blackness – it was as though she were descending into the depths of hell. She shook her head violently in terror, desperate to escape. Then suddenly her screams ceased; she lost consciousness as suddenly as if she had been shot in the head.

By the time she woke up Yueming had already been born. One of the women held him up for her to see – his plump little body was still covered in blood. Her colleagues told her that Dr Qi had said that the unborn child was badly positioned and that he wouldn't leave until he'd managed to turn it round. But he had been called away before he had managed it. When he left they had virtually given up hope and were standing there waiting for mother and child to breathe their last. But, to everyone's surprise, the baby had managed to turn itself round all by itself before slipping out. No one could understand how the two of them could possibly have managed to escape what seemed a certain fate.

She raised herself up on one elbow and looked round to see where Old Chen was but he was not there. After a few minutes he came running back in, covered in sweat. When he saw the two of them, his expression was a lot less enthusiastic than she had imagined.

'What's wrong?' she asked.

'I let you both down! How can you ever forgive me!' he broke down and cried, hugging her closely to his chest. 'I didn't think you were going to make it!'

No sooner had he arrived than he had to hurry out again. He asked his wife's colleagues if they would mind cleaning everything up so she could have a good long rest.

She'd just managed to doze off when her colleagues offered her a bowl of fermented rice with some poached eggs. She caught a few snippets of their conversation as she ate her food, still feeling dazed and exhausted. They were saying that Dr Qi had been called away to see to Prefect Liu's wife who had also been giving birth and was in similar danger of

losing her life; she had been put on a boat to
Chongqing and Dr Qi had been asked to go with her.

'And the rest you know already. You and your
mother, me and my son, we all turned out fine. It
was all a lot of fuss about nothing really. Your
mother probably suffered the most pain, but Old
Chen and I suffered a different kind of pain over a
longer period of time; he was given a severe
reprimand for 'failing to take a firm stand at the
crucial moment of class struggle.' Old Chen hadn't
told her what had happened that night until weeks
later. On their way up the mountain one of the
soldiers had fallen to his death. Prefect Liu's squad
consisted of veteran soldiers, but none of them, not
even Old Chen, had been told what the nature of the
mission was.

It was a moonless night and as they slogged up the
mountain it had begun to drizzle, making the path
even more treacherous than normal. They had also
only brought one torch. They had to rely on listening
to the howls of monkeys and other nocturnal
animals in order to tell which way was which.
Fortunately Old Chen had ordered their men to
carry nothing more than their pistols, so at least they
could move freely.

Suddenly the soldier leading the way screamed; he
had lost his footing and disappeared over the edge.
The person carrying the torch moved carefully
forward. They could see that the path had become
unexpectedly narrow with a steep drop to the valley
below. The men all started talking at once, saying
that the locals seldom dared venture along this path

after four in the afternoon and that absolutely none of them would ever dream of going along it at night. There were too many evil spirits guarding the way. Old Chen ordered a man to go down the cliff on a rope to try and find their lost comrade and see if there was any way of rescuing him.

Prefect Liu stared at him in disbelief: 'Don't you know how to fight a battle?'

Old Chen muttered back that he hadn't realized that this was a battle. Ignoring the furious expression on Prefect Liu's face he ordered a soldier to stay there, but to wait until it was light before starting to investigate. The rest of them continued on their way up the mountain to Water Moon Temple. When they arrived they found the abbot sitting with a few students in meditation. Prefect Liu gave orders for the monk to be arrested immediately on the charge of harbouring a counter-revolutionary. It was in fact true that a month before there had been some bandits who had spent some time at the Temple. They bound the monk and handcuffed him. As they went back down the mountain path they used a flame-torch to lead the way. They came to an ancestral shrine on the outskirts of the town and, to Old Chen's surprise, waiting there was Red Lotus, handcuffed and surrounded by soldiers.

Prefect Liu began to issue a series of orders: the two criminals were to be taken into the town under armed guard at half-past six in the morning and they were to be paraded through the streets in the manner traditionally prescribed by mountain villagers for the humiliation of adulterers.

'Why are we doing that?' asked Old Chen.

'Idiot!' snarled Prefect Liu. He called the captain over and started directing the orders at him instead. Just as he was about to leave he walked over to Master Yutong, looked him up and down, bent down and said something to him. Yutong went white with rage, replying: 'Eclipsing virtue leads to retribution.' He then closed his eyes, apparently trying to calm himself down.

'Reactionary scum! How dare you!' Prefect Liu screamed back at him. He turned round and stormed off.

Just before the trial Prefect Liu told Old Chen that he wanted him to be in charge of the execution itself, just as he always had been before. But Old Chen had so much on his mind – the lives of his wife and child were hanging in the balance – that he was afraid his aim might be off; he pleaded with Prefect Liu to appoint the task to someone else. This time Prefect Liu was truly beside himself with fury. But, nevertheless, he let Old Chen have his way and put him in charge of security instead.

Having made a few perfunctory arrangements, Old Chen ran back home. While he was away, the crowd erupted into uncontrollable chaos.

After sentence had been passed the captain ordered the firing squad to carry out the execution. As Red Lotus and Yutong knelt down opposite their executioners, Red Lotus shouted out at the top of her voice: 'We're innocent! We've been framed!' Possibly distracted by all the uproar around them, the soldiers' aim was off. They both fell, riddled with bullet holes, their blood-soaked bodies writhing on the ground.

The crowd was horrified. People stopped cheering

and started crying out in alarm.

Prefect Liu picked up his pistol. But before he had time to pull the trigger, the firing squad, realising what they were supposed to do, approached the victims to finish the job off. At close range, they fired round after round straight into their skulls, reducing their heads to a pulp. But the monk's legs were still twitching, so they redirected their fire at his groin. Only then was it all over.

Despite knowing the full story, three months of 're-education sessions' made Old Chen so pitifully docile that it never even occurred to him to speak up in his own defence when he received his official reprimand.

Prefect Liu, on the other hand, earned himself quite a reputation for his remarkable ability to mobilise the masses and fan the flames of revolutionary fervour for class struggle. The provincial government was particularly impressed by his achievements in the suppression of counter-revolutionaries. Encouraged by his success, he went on to lead the enthusiastic masses through a series of campaigns, including that of land reform. His promotion to an important position in the Provincial Party Committee meant that nearly all the cadres he had brought with him got promoted and moved on to jobs in better places.

But Old Chen remained in Liang and was demoted. Unwilling to accept his fate he sent up several petitions to clear his name, with Auntie Chen helping him every step of the way. But in the end both of them were expelled from the party and stripped of their status as cadres on the grounds that they had been found 'guilty of opposition to the party'. They became 'nobodys', eking out a humble existence from labouring. The only blessing was that they hadn't been labelled 'bad elements' and sent to a labour camp.

Old Chen died here in Liang and was buried on the mountain slope. His grave was scheduled for relocation, but when Auntie Chen went to dig up his ashes she found that his urn had cracked – inside there was nothing more than muddy water.

Liu sat in stunned silence, her eyes staring into space. She could hardly breathe; she had never imagined that she had been born amid such tumult and bloodshed. She had seen none of it, been aware of none of it, and yet, as she listened to Auntie Chen's vivid account, she felt as though she had been taken back in time and actually experienced every moment. She was speechless.

It had taken Auntie Chen a full hour and a half to tell her story. After the first few minutes they had both decided it was better to sit up in bed, rather than lie down. The pungent smell of brewing herbal medicine filled the air; Liu was sure that it was one of those potions which was so sharp and bitter-tasting that it would bring tears to the eyes of anyone who dared to drink it. The two women leaned back on the pillows propped against the wall, hugging their knees to their chests, staring straight ahead. In fact, they hadn't looked at each other for the entire duration of the story. Now that the tale was over Liu realized that there were a few things she hadn't quite understood, although while she'd been listening everything had made perfect sense.

There was no denying that Auntie Chen's story fitted in exactly with the facts as her mother had told them. However, hearing a story told from two completely different points of view, Liu couldn't help but come to two very different conclusions. Her mother only knew about what she had seen with her own eyes; she didn't know the details of her husband's actions. Or did she? If she had no idea of what had really happened, wasn't it a bit odd that she and Prefect Liu had never had anything more to do with Auntie Chen and her husband?

Of course, Liu had always known that politics was a heartless business – you put one foot wrong and your career is over. Showing compassion at the wrong time could be fatal, even if you only made the mistake once. But Old Chen's 'mistake' had been entirely her father's fault. Why hadn't he ever tried to make it up to him? Why hadn't he tried to help him get back on his feet again?

Whatever the reason, he hadn't done a thing. He seemed just to want to forget everything about Liang. As far as she could remember, Liu had never heard him so much as mention the place.

And her mother hadn't done anything to help them either. Years later, when Auntie Chen wrote to her, she never even replied. Maybe she thought it was too late to try to right the wrongs of the past. Maybe she felt powerless, or lacking in courage.

Auntie Chen said: 'The year there was that memorial service for your father after his rehabilitation, I thought your mother would write to me and invite me to go and see her, but she didn't. I used to be her best friend; whenever we made a maternity shirt or a dress or something, we'd always make two – one for us both. We could talk about anything at all – we often used to talk about each other's problems and we never kept secrets from each other. But ever since she left Liang in that boat the day she gave birth to you – she's never been back, so I've come to realize that she wants nothing to do with me.'

It wasn't hard to see how upset Auntie Chen was, but she didn't shed any tears.

Liu didn't know what to think. She was still desperately trying to make sense of it all.

'It's not her fault of course. A woman's fate is determined by who she marries, and my fate is a world away from hers – hers belongs to the stars and mine belongs to the depths of the earth.'

It is said that children born by caesarean section lack patience. But Liu could be very patient. It is also said that babies can be affected by what goes on around them while they are still in the womb, but Liu did not think that was true of her; she never felt as though the events of 1951 had made any impression on her whatsoever.

Chapter Twenty-two

If only half of everything Auntie Chen said was true, it still meant that the events surrounding Liu's birth had been sordid and gruesome; not only that – everything had been so wrong, so totally unjust, so horribly confused. Of course no revolution has ever been completely free of bloodshed, and no political campaign has ever been completely free of errors, but there could be no excuse for this kind of evil.

'That old police station you were locked up in today used to be where the militia locked up criminals.'

Liu eyes widened in shock. 'You mean that's where Red Lotus and Master Yutong were locked up before they were executed?' she asked nervously.

'That's right – same building, same dark cell,' replied Auntie Chen. 'Old Chen used to work there at that time. Later they extended it.'

Liu held her face in her palms and said to herself, 'How can that be? How can that be?' Her hands began to tremble, but she managed to keep control of herself. She didn't utter a sound. She didn't want Auntie Chen to see how much it was affecting her, but Auntie Chen could see she was upset – even though she didn't know why – and gave her a hug, softly stroking her hair.

Neither of them spoke for some time. They could hear the sound of fireworks in the distance – perhaps signifying the celebration of some happy event like the birth of a child, or perhaps mourning the death of a relative. It went on for ages; it was as though the whole of the lower City had become silent just to hear it.

Auntie Chen was the first to speak, 'It's getting late, you'd better get back. It's almost eleven o'clock.'

Liu nodded. She had so much to think about, so many questions. She didn't know what to make of it all.

She found her shoes which were lying on the floor and put them back on. If anyone ought to repent it wasn't her or her mother; it was her father. But he had died long ago. If it's true that a soul continues to live after the death of the body and is aware of what's going on in the world, then she was convinced that her father would know she was in Liang. Maybe he was even guiding her, giving her the chance to find out what had happened before she was born.

She felt miserable. As she stared into the night darkness, her heart was crying out: 'Father, if your spirit is here, in this county, do you understand why I am refusing to cry? Have you atoned for your crime, have you cleared your debt?'

The father she remembered bore no resemblance to the unscrupulous power-hungry politician Auntie

Chen had described. She remembered him as the sort of man who liked to keep a low profile and who tried his best to stay out of the power struggles that were raging amongst cadres for all those years. In fact, as far as she could recall, he had avoided political disputes throughout his entire career.

In the fifties he had been promoted quickly – from Liang County to Chongqing City, then to Chengdu, the capital of Sichuan Province. After that he'd stayed where he was, as Deputy Head of the Propaganda Department of the Provincial Party Committee. He was never particularly outstanding in his work; in fact he was rather a grey character. The Propaganda Department had always been one of the most dangerous departments to work in. It was like walking a tightrope; only through a mixture of extreme caution and playing dumb did he manage to survive as long as he did.

At home there used to be a picture of the three of them taken just after they'd left Liang and gone back to Chongqing. Liu was in her mother's arms and her father was standing behind them. They all looked very happy. Her mother was smiling; she looked so neat and pretty, so young and elegant. She didn't look in the least bit wearied by the trauma of having just given birth. Her father looked old-fashioned and rigid. His starchy tunic suit looked like it was still hanging on a hanger. His hair had probably just been cut; his temple hair was extremely short and the rest was so straight it looked as if it had been drawn with a ruler. Today you would never find a high-ranking cadre looking so similar to an awkward country-bumpkin.

Prefect Liu was very good to his wife: when it came to everyday household matters he would do whatever she told him. Liu didn't see much of him when she was little; the school for cadres' children was very strict – they were only allowed to go home on Sundays. Prefect Liu seemed to be in an endless series of meetings; he hardly ever got any time off and even when he was at home he would have to go through his paperwork. It was sad how little time he was able to spend with his daughter.

As a child she had always thought that her mother stole her father's love away from her. At night she would secretly tiptoe along to her father's bedroom and try to push the door open, but she couldn't. It was always tightly shut, so she used to just sit on the floor and try to listen to see if he made any noise. Once she sat there so long she caught a chill. It was only when he asked her how she'd caught it that she told him what she'd been doing. He was so touched he picked her up and hugged her.

One summer holiday he had to go to a meeting near Mount Emei and he decided to take her mother and her along with him. Liu was only in her second year of primary school, so when they climbed the mountain she found it hard work. After the first few flights of steps she started crawling on all fours. Her father let her sit on his shoulders, saying, 'In a few years I'll be too old to do this.'

'Don't worry, when I'm older, you can sit on my shoulders,' she replied. 'I'll do lots of things for you when I've grown up!'

Her mother had added, 'What about doing lots of things for me?'

234

They had a photograph taken on the summit. It was the last photograph ever taken of all three of them together. Her father stood in the middle, with his arms round her and her mother. But it wasn't a very good picture; three quarters of it was taken up by the mountains in the background.

At first the Cultural Revolution threw everything into chaos. Liu had just started at senior secondary school when she became a Red Guard. She never went home because she couldn't face asking her parents what was going on. Maybe subconsciously she knew that she was not very good at handling bad news.

The various Red Guard factions vied for supremacy. Sometimes one was on top, sometimes another; things could change quickly during the Cultural Revolution. She spent every day and every night at her faction's headquarters copying 'big character posters' and slogans. Everything was fine until one day the children of low-ranking cadres decided to stage a coup. They forced their way into the headquarters, declaring that they wanted to get rid of the children of 'capitalist roaders'. After a brawl and a good deal of swearing, each of the former staff was summoned for an interview. Every one of them was told the same thing: 'If this organisation is to survive, we have no option but to change the leadership structure.'

Liu had said she wasn't the 'the child of an anti-Maoist roader'.

A girl who had previously been her subordinate came up to her and said earnestly, 'Do you really not know or are you just pretending? Your father has been arrested. He's been locked up in the detention house. They've been investigating him for months. He was taken into custody the day before yesterday. The courtyard in the Provincial Party Committee head-quarters building is filled with posters denouncing him.' Her voice was filled with genuine concern.

Liu replied that she had known nothing about this; she had not been home.

'You should go and have a look,' she said sympathetically. 'But it's probably not a good idea to go today; the Provincial Party Committee is having a struggle session and your father might be there on the platform.'

That afternoon she tried her best to resist the temptation to go and see her father. Her mind was in turmoil. She walked aimlessly along by the river embankment outside the Old City wall and wept. It was as though she used up all her tears up that day; ever since that day she had hardly ever encountered anything that made her cry. She saw denunciation fliers everywhere, including the one she was holding, the ink of which had smudged all over her hands. She looked a mess but no one seemed to notice; they were all in too much of a hurry to notice a young girl in distress.

She had a clear picture in her mind of what her father would look like up there on the platform: the hair on one half of his head would have been shaved off. There would be a heavy wooden board hanging from his neck on which his name would have been crudely written in big black letters and then crossed out with a thick red line with lots of derogatory adjectives in front of it. His hands would have been tied behind his back by the rebel faction. She felt a sense of utter humiliation.

She had known for a long time that many of the cadres who had fallen from power in previous years hated her father. They said he'd only survived by pretending to be stupid and that in actual fact it had all been just a ruse to increase his own power. His success was ultimately the main reason for his death.

That night she sneaked off back home in the hope of seeing her mother, but the place had been sealed up already. She walked over to the other side of the courtyard to ask the elderly guard what had happened. As soon as he saw who it was he put his index finger to his lips indicating that she shouldn't make a sound.

With great caution he managed to help her open the door. He pealed off the seal carefully so as not to damage it; he would seal it back later when she'd gone.

In the dim light she could see that nothing had been left in one piece. Almost all of their so-called 'politically-incorrect' books had been torn up and thrown all over the floor. The furniture had been smashed and even in her bedroom there was not a single object which had not been broken or damaged in some way.

Liu asked him where her parents were. He said he didn't know; all he knew was that her mother had also been taken away and that her father had somehow managed to leave her a note.

The note urged Liu to leave the city immediately. She should go to Beijing and look up his old superior, Uncle Li, who was still in the army where he would almost certainly be out of danger. The guard gave her 200 yuan that her father had left for her.

She took the money and the letter, turned round and walked off. Her mind was focused on getting out of Sichuan as quickly as possible.

She never went back to her parents' home again. Even when she found out that her father had committed suicide, Uncle Li refused to let her go back to Chengdu; he said it was just too dangerous. Her mother had been sent to a labour reform camp thousands of miles away and was forbidden from going back to see her husband's corpse.

Liu became Uncle Li's 'adopted daughter' and joined an army unit which was working to reclaim wasteland in Inner Mongolia; it was almost like being a proper soldier. All cadres' children wanted to join the army and it had only been thanks to Uncle Li that she had been accepted. She felt a deep gratitude to her father for having made the right choice for her future.

Later the faction that had persecuted her father fell out of favour and he was posthumously rehabilitated which meant she was able to go to university.

The first family reunion was when the Provincial Party Committee held a memorial service for him. Over a thousand people attended, including Uncle Li and his family who made the journey all the way from Beijing specially. But even then Liu didn't dare ask exactly how her father had been persecuted, what it was that had finally pushed him over the edge.

How could he have done all those dreadful things Auntie Chen had said he'd done?

She had no reason to think that Auntie Chen might be lying. What possible motive could she have had? It had all happened so long ago. All the men of that generation were lying in their graves, their widows not far behind them. What would she have stood to gain by fabricating such a horrible tale?

She recalled her mother's eagerness that she should go to Liang and meet Auntie Chen, a person she herself had been unwilling to contact for decades. Perhaps she had been afraid because, deep down, she knew what making contact would have entailed: she couldn't have faced it, so she had sent her daughter to shoulder the burden for her.

At that moment Liu remembered the main reason for her having come that evening. She felt embarrassed. How would it look if she were to hand money over after hearing a story like that? Would it be seen as trying to clear an old debt, or as an act of charity? She didn't want to hear Auntie Chen say, 'You put your money away. I would rather starve than go to your door and beg for so much as a bowl of rice.'

But on the other hand, what reason was there for not giving Auntie Chen the money? This was something Liu herself wanted to do; it had nothing to do with the previous generation.

In the end Liu couldn't bring herself to discuss the subject of money. She went back to her hotel, taking the leather suitcase with her.

Chapter Twenty-three

During the Cultural Revolution, Liu had often witnessed the tragedy of someone hanging himself or jumping from a tall building, but she never associated such memories with her father's death. She never tried to imagine exactly how he might have died. But she always regretted not having gone to see his body.

When she shut her eyes she could visualise a group of youths beating up a middle-aged man. They pushed him up against a wall, punching him and kicking him in the chest. He fell to the ground. They kicked him hard in the face and their shoes got covered in blood. There was the sound of bones cracking. The ground was covered in blood.

Her mother had never been willing to talk much about that period in their lives, and was even less willing to talk about her husband's death. All she would ever say was that after a series of intense public criticism sessions and denunciations, eventually her father could stand it no longer. His mind became disturbed and he committed suicide by jumping from a high building.

The last time she'd ever seen her father was one evening when she was coming home from school. It had suddenly begun to pour with rain and she'd tried to take shelter on a street corner under a shop awning. After a couple of minutes her father appeared with an umbrella. He said he knew she must have been on her way home trying to keep out of the rain. His smile was warm and affectionate but his steps seemed a little heavy. He was wearing a short crumpled jacket. That was her father. She would rather keep that memory in her mind.

She tossed and turned, her head buried in her pillow. The unjust deaths of the monk and the prostitute Auntie Chen had told her about kept flashing before her mind. The firing squad had levelled their rifles. Their victims' eyes were filled with fear. The dark red blood gushed out of their bodies, flowing down the slope. She couldn't understand why there was so much blood. It was as though it were pouring out of a tap. The two corpses were wrapped in straw mats and thrown into a huge pit. A layer of earth was shovelled over them. Most of the people killed during the suppression of the counter-revolutionaries Campaign were buried in the same pit half way up the mountain.

Auntie Chen had said that people always used to avoid that place. They were afraid of incurring bad luck. Later they covered it over with cement and put a fence round it and turned it into the basketball court of a secondary school. The older locals seemed to forget all about the dangers of incurring bad luck after that, and of course, whenever anyone told one of the younger people about the history of the place, it would just go in one ear and out the other. But Auntie Chen still refused to go anywhere near it.

Auntie Chen had accompanied Liu back to her hotel, but she refused to walk through the gate. She said it would be awkward if someone like her, dressed in dirty old clothes, walked into a place like that. When they were saying goodbye at the gate, they heard a boat siren in the distance. Out of curiosity Liu glanced over towards the river. She felt strangely uneasy. Auntie Chen took hold of her hand and said, 'You have a good night's sleep. Sometimes you make me worry, you do, just like Yueming does. He's caring by nature you see, and although he can't look after himself he's always worrying about other people, and he's very good to me. We are so close – closer than anyone could imagine. He's the best thing that's ever happened to me.'

'Could it be...' began Liu uncertainly, almost blurting out the first thing that came into her head.

'Yes.' Auntie Chen was looking at Liu, holding her hand tightly all the while, 'Red Lotus has come back to repay me. It was me who helped her to escape. I never imagined it would lead to her death. For many years I didn't know if she hated me for it or thanked me for it. Now I know she thanked me for it.'

Auntie Chen's words stunned her: it seemed that Auntie Chen believed without question that Yueming could have been Red Lotus. But what did that make Liu?

She was just about to ask for more proof when she saw that Auntie Chen had already walked off into the distance.

The curtains in the hotel were so thick that no light whatsoever could get through, but she sensed that it must finally be light outside. She tried to open her eyes but she couldn't. It was as if her eyelids had been glued shut. Surely there should have been an alarm-call; or someone should have come to clean the room. She just wanted her painful night's sleep to end.

But no one came. Her mind wandered. She found herself completely submerged in stagnant water which smelled of blood, tangled up in long greasy strands of jet-black hair. She couldn't tell if the hair belonged to someone living or someone dead. She was desperately trying to scramble to the surface but she couldn't. The more she struggled, the worse it became. The problems which beset her had come to torment her once again, demanding her full comprehension before they would consent to her release.

She felt that there should be someone who understood her distress, but who? She thought and thought. The only person in her life was Li, her protector, the man who had acted as her older brother for so many years and eventually become her husband. She shouted his name as loud as she could, 'Lusheng!'

She heard him reply.

At last she managed to open her eyes. She felt the pillow; it was sodden from the tears which had poured down her cheeks. There he was sitting at the other end of the room. The light was on. He was reading some documents.

It was the first time she had ever seen him wear glasses. 'Must be reading glasses,' she thought. Had her youthful husband's eyesight really started to fail?

The thought jolted her back to reality.

She sat up, 'You're here?'

He quickly removed his glasses and said, 'I came in last night. You'd fallen asleep already. I didn't want to wake you.' He was wearing his nightclothes with underwear on underneath.

'What's the time?'

He looked at his watch and said, 'It's almost nine. You must have been exhausted after your ordeal yesterday.'

'Yesterday?' thought Liu to herself, 'What about yesterday?' He must have thought that she'd gone straight to bed after she'd got back from the old police station.

He walked over and sat on the side of the bed. 'I really must apologize, I still haven't asked you what exactly happened to you.'

'Oh, don't worry about that. It was nothing really.' She jumped out of the other side of the bed. 'I've forgotten about it already!' She walked into the bathroom and turned the hot water on. She washed her hair again and again. There was a strange smell all over her body. It wasn't the smell of the old police station, she'd washed that off the day before. It was the stench of the blood she had dreamt about. She let the hot water stream down her body, lathering her hair with as many little bottles of shampoo as she could find. After a few minutes her feet were completely hidden under all the foam she had produced.

She wrapped a large, unused towel around her chest, fixing it tightly, and proceeded to blow-dry her hair.

Li felt pleased about his wife's magnanimity. He stood in the bathroom doorway and, smiling, said to her, 'Quite right too. Who wants to waste time arguing with those petty low-ranking bureaucrats!?'

'If an ordinary person like me has already forgotten all about it, how can a high-ranking official like you still be thinking about it?' she said, making fun of him. She turned off the hairdryer and started combing her hair back, leaving no fringe and making her forehead look quite large.

'You're the one who's good at forgiving, not me.' said Li. He walked back to the table and started reading his documents again. Liu looked at him and wondered how many hours sleep he'd got. She hadn't got back till gone midnight. There were no taxis or buses at that time of night, only motorbike-taxis, and she hadn't been brave enough to risk taking one of them. She'd started walking back to the hotel but in the dark she hadn't been able to find the shortcut. There'd been a drunkard singing and swearing as he threw stones at the houses at the bottom of the steps. She was wondering what to do and which way to go when Auntie Chen had reappeared with a torch. She went with her all the way to the hotel before turning back and walking home herself.

Li seemed to be sleeping less and less. Liu knew what cadres were like nowadays. They couldn't do anything in the mornings, at night they would slog their guts out and then they would sleep late the next day. But now Li seemed to be working in the mornings as well – sacrificing sleep to read a pile of documents.

He pulled the curtains open and the room was filled with sunlight. When she saw his face in the daylight, Liu noticed how much he'd aged. He looked so worn out. She feared he probably thought the same about her, the only difference being that age detracts more from a woman's attractiveness than from a man's.

'Would you close the curtains a bit?' she asked.

Li laughed, 'Who do you think is going to see you?' He pointed to the window; there was nothing except the green mountains and the wild waves of the Yangtze lit up by the morning sun. He asked curiously, 'What made you decide to forgive the bad cadres?'

She wanted to say, 'I have more important things to think about,' but she didn't want to let the chaos of the previous generation interfere with her personal life. She thought about it, and decided that there was no need to tell Li or anyone else what Auntie Chen had told her, so she changed the topic of conversation:

'How come all you're doing is reading papers? Why hasn't anyone phoned you with urgent business, or come knocking at the door and dragged you away?'

'I've unplugged the landline and switched my mobile off. And I put the 'Please do not disturb' sign on the door.' He turned and looked at Liu.

'Well, the Emperor no longer attends early meetings with his court!' she said laughingly.

'...for he will only be happy if he sees the imperial concubine coming out of the bath every morning!' He walked up to her.

Liu rubbed his nose with her fingers and said,

'Don't be silly.'

But he walked so close he'd rubbed against her towel and it had fallen down. She hurried over to the bed and hid her naked body under the covers. She didn't like having nothing on. The bed was huge, bigger than the double beds in other rooms. But she'd chosen the room so she couldn't accuse her husband of deliberately planning it that way.

He hugged her, and kissed her. He moved his mouth close to her fragrant clean hair and said softly, 'You left me on my own for too long. It wasn't easy. I've only seen you once in all this time.'

She suddenly remembered the reason why she had hurried over to Liang from the Dam Site. It was that mysterious other woman. Liu still didn't have any proof, and she hadn't been interested enough to go out of her way to try and find out anything more, but she wasn't going to let him get away with feigning innocence. She prompted him:

'Hold on a minute and tell me straight, once and for all: are you really as innocent as you claim to be?'

He hugged her tighter than ever and said: 'Absolutely, one hundred percent innocent. I've just been reading an internal report about cases of large-scale corruption – a few deputy-ministers have been implicated, and I was thinking how a man in my position, with goodness knows how many hundred of millions of yuan passing through my hands, how if my wife were in the least bit greedy, I'd certainly be under investigation, no matter how careful I had been.' He kissed her passionately, 'My wife really is incredible...'

He hadn't answered her question, but she didn't know if he was deliberately avoiding the issue or if he had genuinely misunderstood. He lifted the sheets she was using to cover herself.

'Look at you – completely clean – not a blemish on you...' Then he saw her knees. 'What happened there then?'

She didn't want to say, but he'd guessed already. He sounded genuinely aggrieved that such a thing should have happened to her, 'People round here don't know the first thing about law. You must be even more magnanimous than I thought.'

She was in an awkward position. Should she pursue the issue or shouldn't she? If she did, it wouldn't make her look very good, not after he'd been so nice to her. He'd already taken his clothes off. It was good to know that he was innocent as far as public money was concerned. That was important too.

Of course she still wanted to find out; she wasn't one of those wives who were prepared to tolerate all their husbands' misdemeanours. It was just that, at that moment, she really didn't want to think about what to do.

He had already entered her and her body arched in an instinctive response. She hadn't wanted to go to bed with him, it had just happened. She could ask him when it was all over; there would be plenty of time.

She began to relax. They climaxed at almost exactly the same time. When their bodies separated, they were covered in sweat.

He got a hot towel from the bathroom and gave it to Liu, then he went to have a shower himself. When he came out she said, 'You rest, I'll guard the door for you.'

Li obediently lay down on the bed, watching Liu
pull the curtains shut. He yawned loudly twice in
quick succession. 'No one would dare try to come in,
not after you showed them what you were made of,'
he said, smiling. 'I think we'll be able to leave this
god-forsaken place tomorrow.'

'And go where?' asked Liu as she took a carton of
orange juice out of the fridge. She poured out two
glasses and passed one to Li. She didn't normally like
wasting money on the overpriced items in hotel
minibars, but she thought she'd make an exception
on this occasion.

'Go back to our home at the Dam Site! You must
surely have taken more than three days off.'

'It's still just a hotel room, isn't it?' said Liu
unenthusiastically. She picked up her glass. Deep
down she didn't want to leave Liang, though she had
no idea why.

'They've lent me a furnished apartment.' He
looked at Liu, 'headquarters has been encouraging
employees to settle down there, but I know you
wouldn't want to do that.'

Liu didn't reply. She sipped her orange juice. She
knew he wasn't really expecting an answer. Their
'home' was her flat in the Academia Sinica, but it
didn't have a very homely atmosphere. The sitting-
room and bedroom had so many books in them that
the place looked more like a library than somewhere
to live. One room was filled with nothing but suitcases
and another little room had her old bicycle in it. The
freezer was full of microwaveable ready-made meals
for one. Her career wasn't something she was prepared
to give up just to keep her husband happy.

Li put his glass of juice on the bedside table, lay down and closed his eyes. 'The first thing I've got to think about is the banquet tonight. It's really big. I don't know how, but all the Hong Kong and Taiwanese businessmen seem to have found out that my wife is in town. They're expecting to see you there. They're all bringing their wives. I was wondering if you might be willing to oblige. I've had to work so hard these past few days, this is the last hurdle. I hoped you might help me out.'

Liu sat down on the sofa before responding. 'You know I don't like banquets. I can't stand putting on a fake smile for three hours. It's so exhausting, and I never feel it's worth it. Anyway, what's so important that you need me there? Would it really make any difference?'

He sat up and reached for his clothes on the floor by the side of the bed and started getting dressed. 'I really hate having to talk about work like this. The problem is that the State Planning Commission can't be relied upon to provide all the funding for the project. And, in actual fact, we don't need the State to be our sole investor. I've been selling 'Great Lake Bonds'. It's like borrowing a chicken to get eggs. The Hong Kong and Taiwan trade consortia are both keen to invest. The political significance of their investment would be tremendous. This morning local cadres are showing them round. This afternoon we're hoping they'll sign a contract of intent. And, judging from past experience, the banquet will determine how firm that intent is.'

'So you want me to play a little role? Have I put my research on hold to do this?' she said, deliberately exaggerating her annoyance.

'It won't take long, and it's just this once. You'll be the belle of the ball! I've seen their wives, and I think the taste of those businessmen leaves a lot to be desired.' He put his socks on, staring at Liu's naked feet. 'Well, you did come here of your own free will. Otherwise I would never have agreed to put such a beautiful wife on show!'

'It's the manager of the hotel who gave the game away! He's a spy! He's been listening in to my telephone calls, and he told Director Wang I was here. I never revealed anything!'

Li put his fingers to his lips and said, 'Ssshhh!', then pointed to the door.

They could hear rapid footsteps.

Li and Liu looked at each other and laughed. 'Shall we open it?'

And as if in answer to his question there came a light, tentative knocking.

Li put both arms round Liu, pulled her onto the bed and then pulled the bedding over her. 'I've got to go out now. Why don't you stay in bed a bit longer?' He kissed her on the lips. 'The banquet starts at six this evening in the banqueting hall. I'll come up and meet you at quarter to. Thank you so much for doing this. I'll thank you properly tonight.'

He looked at his watch and frowned. He walked towards the door and, just as he was about to open it, he suddenly turned round and said, 'Everyone always wants a free meal. If they think they can they take a bite out of me, well, they've got another think coming. There's no such thing as a free banquet!' He laughed derisively.

That was the closest she came to an explanation for all the 'spying'. He loved talking mysteriously; he obviously thought it beneath him to make himself clear.

The knocking started again. He opened the door just wide enough to slip out and disappeared.

Chapter Twenty-four

A Director's wife was expected to hang around the whole day waiting to accompany her husband to some banquet. What kind of a life was that?

She couldn't understand women who actually seemed to enjoy such a lifestyle. But it was that kind of woman that seemed to make men happy. Li's mother had always thought Liu good wife material: 'The kind of girl who is willing to go up to the banqueting hall and down to the kitchen.'

But as it turned out she wasn't good either up or down. If she had to choose between a proper meal and instant noodles, she'd always opt for the latter. It was years since she'd cooked Li a proper meal. When she lived with her parents, and later with her foster family, there had always been a housekeeper to do everything. And later she'd always eaten out. She was a bit like a monk with a begging bowl – always relying on other people to provide her with food.

Thinking about food was making her feel hungry. The last time she'd eaten was when she was at Auntie Chen's. She jumped out of bed and had just started hurriedly looking in her suitcase for something to wear when she heard knocking at the door.

'He's gone!' she shouted back impatiently. The knocking stopped.

Then, after about thirty seconds, it started again.

The poor door, all these people knocking on it all the time! She walked over and opened it. There was a man standing in front of it. She looked closely and saw that it was Mr Zheng, the manager of the hotel, the man who had told Mr Wang where she was. But he looked completely different. He was wearing a grey suit, no tie. His self-important manner, so evident the day before, seemed to have completely disappeared.

'He went ages ago,' she said. She was about to shut the door when he began to explain:

'Professor Liu,' he said, almost in a whisper, 'Can I have a few words with you?' Liu immediately wanted to shut the door. 'I don't have anything to do with Li's affairs, just as he has nothing to do with mine.'

He lifted his head up. She saw how tired he looked, his eyes were bloodshot – it looked as though he'd been awake all night.

'Might I be able to have a quick word with you?' he asked pitiably.

'Stop pestering me. Yesterday your plans got me into a lot of trouble but I have let it pass.' Her voice was getting louder. He glanced nervously to either side, afraid other guests might overhear.

'I just wanted to tell you the truth about what yesterday was really all about.' He looked pathetic, like a little puppy with no home to go to.

Liu opened the door wide and walked back into the room. 'You'd better make it quick. I've got things to do.'

The manager sat down cautiously on a chair. He didn't sit on the sofa. The first thing he said gave Liu quite a shock, 'Director Wang has been arrested.'

She raised her eyebrows in astonishment, but she realized what the manager was after. She shrugged her shoulders and said light-heartedly, 'The arrester has been arrested, how funny!'

'The City Discipline Commission had him arrested this afternoon, he has been put under house arrest – they're pressing him to confess.'

Liu thought it served him right for having caused so much trouble the day before. But when it came to things like this she thought it best to just pretend to be stupid. 'What could he have done? Surely they'll release him when he's had a chance to explain himself, won't they? Even if he's embezzled public money, surely he could just give it back and everything would be OK.' Of course, Liu was well aware that it wouldn't be as simple as that; she was just trying to wind him up a bit.

'What I don't understand,' she went on, 'is what any of this should have to do with you. Why did you arrange for me to meet Mr Wang yesterday? And why are you now trying to put in a good word for a corrupt cadre?' It went without saying that Mr Wang and the manager had been working together, they were almost certainly as guilty as each other, and now one was trying to get the other out of trouble. This immaculate hotel could have been the dirtiest place in the whole of Liang. How many dirty deals must have been done in its luxurious suites? Zheng, provider of such a palatial safe haven, must have done quite well for himself.

She'd hit a nerve. His face went bright red, but his tone became bold, as though he genuinely had nothing to hide, as though all he had to do was say a couple of sentences to convince Liu of his total innocence: 'No, no, no, that's not it at all, we are merely the victims of a change in policy!'

'I'm not the Party Committee. What do I know about changes in policy? I think I've heard enough.' Liu stood up. She wanted him to know he'd outstayed his welcome.

But he stayed where he was. He glanced over to the yellow roses on the table. They had been put in her room before she'd got back from the old police station: Zheng must have known things weren't going well even then.

'It was Director Li who changed the policy but he didn't think of the consequences for his subordinates. All he's interested in is promotion. We, who acted in accordance with official policy, are now criminals. Yesterday he told the City Discipline Commission not to arrest Mr Wang until tomorrow, after he's gone, so it looks like it's got nothing to do with him, and so nobody can say it had anything to do with your having been arrested. But the Discipline Commission decided to ignore his order and arrest Mr Wang while Director Li was still here, and so everyone will be able to work out for themselves what's really going on.'

Liu sat down. It was a lot to take in. If she tried

to kick him out now it would look as though she were afraid of hearing the truth.

Liu watched as he took a packet of cigarettes and a lighter out of his pocket. He put them back immediately and apologized. 'I still don't really understand why you ever got me involved,' she said.

He seemed to have relaxed a bit now that Liu's tone had become less accusatory. He told her that things were not as complicated as they seemed: 80,000 Liang residents were going to have to move to a higher gradient in the same area, 40,000 were going to have to resettle in other provinces. The fund really was a huge amount of money, and it would have been imprudent to distribute it to the people concerned all in one go. Liang county government had been given all of the fund in one go, and told it could invest the money in local businesses provided that the fund would be intact when the time came for the money to be used for resettlement costs.

'That sounds fair enough, as long as the fund is intact when the time comes. I can't see that the people or government could have any problem with that,' said Liu.

'The problem is, what does 'when the time comes' actually mean?' He sighed and started biting his lip. 'When you invest it takes time before you get any return. Li, Director Li, sent a memorandum to Project Headquarters saying that 'non-voluntary resettlement' would only lead to problems, that it was a waste of time building houses for peasants hundreds of miles away – all that would happen is that they'd either go back where they had come from or try to move into cities. He suggested that it would be better to give the money directly to the peasants so that they could use it start their own small businesses. That way, he argued, they'd move away of their own free will.'

Liu thought back to the failure of trying to force educated young people from big cities to settle in rural areas during the Cultural Revolution. She agreed with her husband that it was better than paid resettlement.

'Surely that would save everyone a lot of trouble?'

'Right.' He looked at her. 'But where is the money? When you invest in something you can't just get the money back at a moment's notice.'

Liu had never found talking about politics very easy; she didn't feel that much could be gained from continuing their conversation. 'Surely they have given you some time to retrieve the money... haven't they?' she said, a little unsure of herself.

'Even if they had, we still wouldn't be able to get the money back. As soon as the enterprises we have invested in see that we want them to give it back they'll just think up ways of delaying doing so. People will do anything for money. The man on the street would sell his own mother if he thought he could make a few yuan out of it.'

'Well, they would be breaking the law if they refused to give it back, wouldn't they?'

'No, quite the reverse; we'd be breaking our contracts.'

What chaos this was! 'Project Headquarters can't launch an attack on every single cadre in Liang!'

Zheng was gnawing his teeth. 'Of course. That's why there's this proposal to introduce bonds. The investment-recipients could use the money they were unwilling to pay back to buy Great Lake Bonds. That way we'd get back not only what was originally invested, but also some of the profit we'd been hoping for. The businesses concerned would surely be happy to comply. All we need now is a little help from Project Headquarters.'

It was the second time that day that Liu had heard the phrase 'Great Lake Bonds'. What she didn't understand was how these 'bonds' would be worth anything more than an ordinary IOU.

He seemed to guess what she was thinking. 'They'd be company bonds only in name. In reality they would be guaranteed by the State. Project Head-quarters would be taking a mortgage out on the reservoir. They'd be worth a lot. But Li is refusing to sell them to us until we've sorted out the Resettlement Fund.'

'Well, he is right. What's the point in just creating a new debt when the old account is not cleared?' replied Liu, though she was actually getting a bit confused and wasn't quite sure what she thought.

'The bond proposal is the only thing which can enable us to solve the problem of the Resettlement Fund.' He sighed. 'Li wants to sell the bond to Hong Kong and Taiwanese businessmen and foreigners. All he cares about is his own career.'

Liu felt frustrated by her own ignorance. If Li had been there he'd have known exactly what to say to shut Zheng up. She thought it best not to listen to any more. She cut to the chase.

'So you're saying that Li has ruined you?'

'Yes. That's right,' he replied straightforwardly.

Liu thought for a second and then said, 'You

address me as Professor Liu, as a person in my own right, independent from my husband. Since I am a professor, I would advise you to stop underestimating my intelligence.'

She stood up. He followed her example. Neither of them looked very happy. Liu said, 'You are the manager of a hotel. The Resettlement issue has nothing to do with you, and yet you keeping talk about 'us', which proves that the money has somehow gone astray. So far as I can judge, there's a group of people who seem to have used the money for their own ends. You know you're about to be arrested because Mr Wang will tell the authorities that you're involved, so you thought you'd come round here and try to scare me.'

'Yes. You're absolutely right. I wanted to make you both afraid,' replied Zheng, no longer holding back. His expression was one of desperation. 'We're going to write to the relevant authorities that Li has thrown the whole Dam Project into chaos, for changing policy without due notice, for making a profit from issuing bonds and for inciting resettlers to riot.'

As soon as he said the word 'riot', Liu realized what he and Mr Wang had been up to. She was seething. 'You just wanted to try to turn public business into private dealings! You wanted to make an illegal profit out of public money, and tried to force Li to help you cover your tracks!' She turned away. 'I'm not going to say a word about any of this to Li. You'd better start behaving yourselves!'

Zheng roared furiously, 'You helped Li instigate that riot, and if you don't tell him, we shall. We've got proof. One of the rioters was a man named Chen Yueming, who is a relative of yours. You arrived two days beforehand to make all the necessary arrangements. Talk your way out of that one!'

In a fit of rage Liu picked up the vase with the yellow roses in it. What she'd really wanted to do was throw the whole vase at him, but she restrained herself at the last minute, and just threw the water and the flowers onto the man's face. She had never been so angry. She felt as though she was about to burst into flame.

The cold water seemed to calm Zheng down a bit. He stopped shouting and wiped his face with his hands, and shook his head elegantly. 'Professor Liu,' he said, smiling, 'you're an intelligent woman, please don't feel compelled to refrain from telling your husband that he's going to have to start being a bit more considerate to his subordinates. Otherwise, regardless of what else he might have going for him, he's never going to get anywhere.'

Liu pointed to the door and said calmly, 'Please leave.' Having shut the door behind him, she threw herself onto the bed and buried her face in a pillow, trying desperately to stop herself from trembling.

Chapter Twenty-five

After a while she began to calm down. Although her window was tightly shut she could still hear the muffled clamour from the noisy streets below. She stood up and tidied her hair. She had a lot to think about.

At least she didn't have to worry about Li. He was a political animal; he had only to glance at someone to know if they were with him or against him. If these corrupt cadres were really a serious threat, he would have wasted no time in taking the necessary precautions to protect himself.

Nor did Liu have to worry about Auntie Chen. She'd already suffered more than Liu could ever imagine; besides, she had already fallen into poverty and obscurity. There was very little anyone could do to make her life any worse.

The one she was worried about was Yueming. He had nothing whatsoever to do with the whole bond issue and yet, somehow or other, he'd become a pawn in the high-ranking cadres' little game. She still couldn't quite make him out. He looked so ordinary, and yet compassion such as his was a rare quality.

He was vulnerable. She knew that as soon as her back was turned the local cadres would pounce upon him again. The worst they could do would be to accuse him of being the 'ringleader of a riot'; if found guilty he could be given a life sentence in a labour reform camp.

She was wondering what to do when she remembered the money in the leather suitcase. But Yueming wasn't the type of person who needed money, and the money wouldn't be able to save him from arrest in any case.

The previous evening she had put the money in the little safe in her hotel room. She had to take it to where it was needed straight away, before it was too late.

The hospital wasn't far, about 20 minutes away by taxi. She asked if it was the only hospital in the area; she was told that it was. It was on the outskirts of the New City and looked quite attractive – there was a neat row of recently planted saplings at the front and the green mountain slope behind. The midday sun shone brightly on the glass of the windows.

Opposite the hospital were a few newly built two and three-storey buildings: restaurants, hairdressers, massage and beauty parlours. The gift shop was selling high-quality tonics like ginger mixed with red deer antler and liquefied queen bee. There was also an undertaker's with a flamboyant display of wreaths outside which caught Liu's eye; she thought it rather tasteless to have urns and funeral fireworks right opposite a hospital.

She walked in. The receptionist's window was just like all hospitals in China had been since the fifties – you had to talk through a crack in the glass. The receptionist was a very young girl. When she asked who Liu was looking for, Liu suddenly realized that she'd never asked Auntie Chen what her husband's name was.

She stood there desperately trying to think what it might be when five or six people came dashing out of the outpatient department. They were carrying someone on a stretcher who'd been knocked down by a bus. A man in a long white coat was walking briskly towards them. When he reached them he glanced down at the man on the stretcher who was still bleeding profusely. 'Nothing too bad. We'll start work as soon as you've paid,' he said calmly.

This remark infuriated the group of people who had brought him in. They began shouting. Some were protesting in a rational manner and some were just swearing. They explained that they had just stumbled across the man and were merely doing their civic duty. They picked the man up and carried him off in the direction of the hospital offices.

Liu turned her head and knocked lightly on the window and asked where the gastropathy department was.

The girl said arrogantly that she couldn't give non-authorised persons information of that kind, then she lowered her head and continued counting the money in her till. The people queuing behind were beginning to get impatient.

The only option left to Liu was to tell her that she

was from the Academia Sinica. She passed the girl her ID.

'So, you're here on business?' the girl asked.

Liu nodded.

The girl said that she needed to see a formal invitation; her ID wasn't enough.

Liu was not pleased. 'Why isn't ID enough?' she asked.

The girl shouted, 'You're very unreasonable! I'll have to start counting all over again now!', and she slammed the tiny window shut.

Liu was stunned, but she knew she shouldn't have been. In China everyone has to put up with this kind of behaviour. She had grown up surrounded by people like this. In China a small amount of power goes straight to someone's head. Liu had always imagined that people in a small place like Liang would be a little humbler, a little more anxious to please and a little more easily intimidated. It turned out that the opposite was the case. Liu knew perfectly well that if she had brought some piffling local dignitary along with her, even someone like that good-for-nothing manager Zheng, for instance, then everything would have been fine. They would probably even have found someone to escort her to the ward.

She asked a nurse in the corridor. The nurse was friendly and helpful; she told her that the Gastropathy Department was on the fourth floor.

She went up the stairs to the fourth floor and walked around looking through all the open doors. Every ward was full of people; most of them were patients' relatives. The nurses just handed out medication; everything else had to be done by family and friends. It didn't take Liu long to find Diegu; she was sitting with her back to the door in one of the wards. Facing her was a haggard old man who had lost almost all his hair. He was on a drip. From behind Liu could clearly see Diegu's two little plaits and her tiny waist. She was wiping her step-father's face.

Four of the eight beds in the ward were empty, but they were far from clean. Under some of them were un-emptied chamberpots. In the corner there was a large overflowing rubbish bin. How could somewhere that was so impressive on the outside be so squalid within? It appeared that the old hospital, with all its old ways, had done nothing more than move into a new building.

Diegu bent down to rinse the flannel she had been using. She rung it out and began wiping her step-father's face again. She said something to him and he chuckled. She lifted up the bedclothes and was about to mop his body.

Liu made a mental note of the number of the ward and the bed and walked towards the department office at the end of the corridor.

There were four people in the office – all busily working away. No one seemed to notice when Liu walked in. She cleared her throat and said she was looking for the surgeon in charge of stomach cancer operations. One of the doctors in the room raised his head and said that the man she was looking for was busy checking the wards and wouldn't have time to see her. She replied that she was a relative of one of his patients and wanted to see the doctor to deliver his 'operation fee'.

The words 'operation fee' made everyone look up. They stared, first at her, then at the leather briefcase in her hand.

She told them the ward and bed number, and asked if someone might be so kind as to tell her the name of the person who would be doing the operation.

The doctor who'd been answering her questions stood up and pushed open the door to a small adjoining room and indicated that she should go in.

She sat down and explained that she worked at the Institute of Genetic Engineering at the Academia Sinica, that she had many friends in medical circles, and that she had been told that operations were done pretty well in this hospital. She felt awkward showing off in this way but she didn't have any choice: a man's life was in danger. In this kind of situation she should overcome her scruples in order to achieve the greater good.

The doctor nodded in agreement. He said it was all thanks to the Dam Project; the state had decided to make sure that the new hospital had the best possible equipment and facilities. Almost all the doctors had been specially selected from among the graduates of first class medical colleges in big cities.

Liu said she understood that performing an operation was no easy task. She had come especially from Beijing because of her relative's condition. Within reason, she was willing to do whatever it would take to get him cured.

The doctor could see that Liu was well-mannered and intelligent, but he regretted having to tell her in the politest possible way that surgeons weren't allowed to take money directly from the relatives of patients. Removing stomach cancer would need a big operation with a number of surgeons, nurses and anaesthetists. It would take about two hours. There would be no margin for error whatsoever. Once the incision is made, the slightest mistake would entail tremendous complications.

'Of course. I understand,' she replied.

'Most of the fee is to cover costs; the surgeon and his assistants don't get much at all. You needn't worry that I'm going to keep all the money for myself; everyone in the office saw you come in. I told your relative what it would cost – and I quoted her a fair price: five thousand. In bigger cities it would cost more like a hundred thousand. I'm not asking for a bribe or trying to strike a deal.'

Liu nodded. Maybe he was being so cautious because he was made anxious by the fact that Liu was from Beijing. She opened the briefcase and passed him a wad of cash. 'There you go. Please count it.'

'I'm sure there's no need,' he replied. 'Please do believe me when I tell you that people in our profession do everything by the book.'

There was no need to count it. Liu wondered who would dare try to con a doctor.

She stood up, 'One small thing – the money is mine; my aunt would be reluctant to accept it. Would you mind keeping quiet about my involvement when you see her?'

'Of course, I understand,' said the doctor.

'So, when will you do the operation?' asked Liu, just to make sure. She knew she wouldn't be given a receipt so she had to be careful.

The doctor thought for a moment and said, 'Tomorrow morning.'

His answer startled her. What would have happened the following morning if she hadn't brought the money? But after a while she laughed at her own mistake: it was obviously simply a case of first come first served.

She walked back down the stairs to the ground floor. She was impressed by the way they had treated her – yes, the doctors took bribes, but at least they did it with an air of dignity. By contrast, the cadres involved in the dispute over the Resettlement Fund scrambled around after money like starving rats scramble for crumbs to eat.

But then again, she could hardly bear to think what would have happened to the old man if no one had managed to come up with the money. Would the doctors have left him in his hospital bed to die? Just paying the daily hospital fee must have been more than Auntie Chen could afford. Heaven alone knew how many of those facile landscapes Yueming had to churn out to keep the family going. Even Diegu did her bit by going out everyday to do manual labour for a pittance.

At least Auntie Chen had two loving children who did everything they could to make things easier for her.

Liu walked out of the hospital. After a few steps she turned her head and looked back. 'What a relief to be out of there!' she thought. Perhaps, if her mother knew what Liu had done, the burden lying so heavily on her heart would seem a little lighter.

Chapter Twenty-six

Liu found herself at the gate of the Nanhua Mountain Scenic Area. There was one more thing she had to do before she left Liang: she had to tell Yueming that he was in danger and, more importantly, try to work out a way to save him.

She bought an entrance ticket to the park for 50 yuan; it was expensive because it included a ride up to the Temple by cable-car. The wide walkway on the other side of the vermillion gate was lined on either side with dozens of little gift-shops which were all selling exactly the same things, including Yueming's watercolours. Just as before, she found them uninspiring, they were good copies, but nothing more; their only distinguishing feature was the unusually elegant calligraphy in the top left hand corner of each one. None of the shops had any customers; the only other person was a young man behind one of the counters reading a newspaper.

Despite the fact that it was a beautiful afternoon, there were hardly any sightseers around. Maybe most of them came by pleasure-cruiser – there was one which was just about to arrive. Of course it was no surprise not to see any locals buying tickets, the tickets cost as much as ten days wages for a potato slicer.

There was a banner across the gateway with the slogan: 'Make Three Violation Day A Great Success!' Liu had no idea what it meant, or what it was doing hanging in a 'Scenic Area'.

Liu raised her head and saw another bigger banner hanging between two cliffs a few hundred yards away: 'Create an A++ Scenic Area As Your Contribution To The Great Three Gorges Dam Project!' She understood this one, but couldn't fathom what purpose it might be serving. Perhaps the cadres wanted to show that they were working hard.

She was now in the very place her father had come to all those years ago on that fateful night when he had led his men to capture the hapless monk, though of course in those days there would not have been a neat flight of stone steps to follow.

She was the only person in her cable car; all the other little two-person cars were empty. Her cable car was so close to the ground that she could almost reach out and touch the tops of the tall bamboos and luscious pines beneath.

She walked along the path to the Temple, approaching from a different direction from when she had come with Auntie Chen by road. She came across a little hall she hadn't seen before, bearing the name: 'The Shrine of Generals Snorter and Blower' On the pillars either side of the entrance there was a couplet:

Snorter snorts with human heart,
Blower blows with breath in common.

She almost burst out laughing. Was this really something that the cadres in the government office of culture and education had thought up?

Behind it, as was usually the case with Buddhist temples in China, was the Temple of the Jade Emperor. Behind that was the newly-built 'Bridge of Sighs' leading to the Temple of Yama, king of hell. This time the couplet was even funnier:

If you do nothing which might give you a guilty
conscience,
Then a knock on the door in the night will not
scare you.

'Well, it must be tough for them, I suppose...' she reflected. 'After all, they've got to toe the line politically and make money at the same time – a difficult combination of socialism and capitalism...'

She recalled a conversation she had with the hotel manager when he was taking her to see Mr Wang. She had commented, 'Isn't it a shame that the beautiful scenery of the Three Gorges will soon all be hidden underwater?'

'A shame?!' he had said nonchalantly, 'Not at all... we'll just make sure we create some more beautiful scenery.'

This was evidently the local cadres' idea of beautiful scenery.

Just when she thought things couldn't get any worse she came to a slope with a narrow flight of steps, both sides of which were supposed to be lined with eight stone statues of various types of brightly-painted horse-faced and ox-headed demons, according to the traditional Chinese vision of hell. But instead there was a new type of statue, made of cement. There was even a pair of cherubs with broad grins on their faces; their mother was watching contentedly, completely naked except for a scarf covering up the appropriate places.

Liu almost turned and ran. It was not the poor craftsmanship that she hated so much, but rather the attitudes that were expressed. The fact that there was a statue of a naked woman was obviously supposed to prove that the local cadres weren't afraid of westernisation, and the idea of replacing demons with happy families was presumably meant to symbolise the happiness the people should enjoy.

She resolved to avoid looking round after that and walked straight on to the Water Moon Temple which, thankfully, was just as a Temple should be: there were some exquisitely carved Buddha statues inlaid in the pillars outside, and inside there was a huge gold-plated Buddha and incense burner. She walked out through the side door into the back courtyard. Yueming's studio was easy to find.

The door was closed. She knocked but nobody answered. She peered in through the window. No sign of anyone. She decided to ask one of the resident monks where Yueming might be.

But then she realized she'd never actually seen any of the Temple monks. She wondered where they did their sutra-chanting and meditation. She had never heard the sound of the 'wooden fish' here either. The strong smell of incense made her think that perhaps the monks did nothing all day long except flog joss sticks and 'gifts' to tourists. The whole area was a building site – there was scaffolding everywhere; perhaps even Buddhism itself was being modernised and developed by the all-powerful local cadres!

She brushed against the door as she turned to walk away and, to her surprise, it creaked open.

The room was just the same as when she'd visited with Auntie Chen: on the table there were some brushes, jars full of water and unfinished paintings. Perhaps Yueming had popped out to deliver the ones he'd finished to the gift-shops, but if that were the case she would surely have seen him in a cable car going down the other way.

In one corner there were a few crumpled pieces of paper which she eagerly picked up and smoothed out flat on the table. This time, though, they really were nothing more than splodges of ink; there was no chance that these were works of art, even in the most abstract sense of the word. She looked in vain for the two pictures she'd found on her last visit. He'd probably thrown them away.

Crestfallen, Liu sat down on the only wooden chair in the room. She began to wonder if she hadn't perhaps imagined the whole thing; perhaps she had just wanted to believe that Yueming was an undiscovered genius, when in actual fact he was nothing more than an ordinary village primary school teacher who happened to be able to copy a few half-decent landscapes. Surely the local cadres would never so much as deign to look at someone so insignificant.

She accidentally knocked over a cardboard tube full of pencils. She bent down to pick them up and ended up treading on the cardboard tube. As she was putting it back on the table out fell a little slip of paper on which there was a rather strange sketch of an object a bit like a bonsai tree, with tiny lamps hanging from the branches.

Below it was what appeared to be an explanation in Yueming's hand:

The Gilded Peacock Tree: Cultural relic characteristic of the Three Gorges region – a work of exquisite craftsmanship, approximately one foot in height, buried with the dead during the Western Han dynasty (206BC-24AD). The branches are decorated with cicadas, which symbolise rebirth. On the end of each of the ten branches hangs an oil lamp, symbolising the ten suns of ancient times. It resembles a peacock displaying its tail-feathers. This afternoon I had the honour of seeing one with my own eyes; it was like a glimpse of heaven! There is no record of this piece being seen by human eyes. It has only just been discovered – unearthed for the first time in two millennia! What a shame there is no way of keeping a national treasure like this in China where it belongs! The man who found it wants 300,000 yuan for it. Of course I have no way of affording such a thing, and I am reluctant to tell the authorities about it, because my doing so could lead to the man's execution. I wonder where it will end up, and for how many tens of millions of dollars it will eventually be sold. What a tragedy the reservoir project is for such relics!

Peacocks are reluctant to take flight even when approached by predators, for fear of damaging their plumage. This sketch is a record of my sadness.

Liu was stunned by what she had read; she had never considered the Dam Project could have stirred up these issues. And what did he mean about the peacock? Was he referring to his own reluctance to flee even when he knew he was in danger?

As she stared at the peacock-shaped lamp holder, her eyes fixed in an almost trance-like state, she began to have a strange feeling. It was as though it had all happened before. Yes, half a century ago she'd been in this same place, looking at something beautiful, something brought here by fate, something destined to be crushed and destroyed. Nothing could be done. Then, as now, there was an overwhelming feeling of sorrow. Even sutra-recitations had become useless, but at least by reciting sutras you knew the Buddha would be watching you, and after everything had become empty, the emptiness would become full.

She took out a piece of paper and wrote Yueming a quick note to say that she'd come to see him and was sorry to have missed him. Then she crossed out what she had written and just drew a big question mark. But then that seemed wrong too, so she crossed that out as well – a note was hardly necessary; she would almost certainly see him again soon.

Chapter Twenty-seven

Liu didn't get back to her room until quarter to six. Li was there waiting for her. He was wearing a black suit, sitting on the large sofa with his arms folded and staring out of the window watching the Yangtze flowing into the horizon, where the earth merged with the crimson sky.

She knew he had never been one for gazing at beautiful views; he was a rationalist who believed that everything real was provable, and that whatever wasn't provable was neither of value nor of substance. He also believed that ignorance and irrationality were gradually cured by time, making each new generation wiser than the last.

She apologized for coming back so late.

He didn't ask her where she'd been. He told her that the banquet had been postponed until six thirty. The afternoon's negotiations had been successful but had taken longer than expected. He urged her to hurry up and get ready – he'd got her something to wear, it was hanging in the wardrobe. She walked into the bathroom and started making herself look presentable. When she came out she sat down on the bed with a dazed expression on her face. Surprised, Li walked over to her and asked gently:

'Little Liu, you better put some makeup on. I've been waiting for you all this time. Why don't you try on the outfit I got you?'

She opened the wardrobe door and found a bright red silk cheongsam. She turned and looked back at Li in astonishment. He laughed. 'Don't you like it?'

It had been bought specially for the banquet. That afternoon he'd happened to pass the hotel boutique and it had reminded him that Liu would need something special to wear. A business suit would have been fine, of course, but suits are always so dour-looking. The cheongsam had caught his eye. As soon as he'd bought it he had sent Mr Han to get it ironed and make sure it was ready in the wardrobe in their room.

She looked at it for a few seconds, not sure whether she liked it or not. It was fashionable – there were bold slits on both sides and daringly deep-cut shoulders. She had hardly ever worn anything so revealing. She took a pair of brown leather high-heels out of her suitcase and put them on. Only then did she hold the dress up in front of her and look in the mirror.

'I had wanted it to be a surprise,' he said, 'I remember you wearing a cheongsam once in America. You looked incredible in it.'

She had never imagined he would have remembered such a thing. She felt she should say something nice to thank him for the compliment, but all she said was, 'That was before cheongsams were in fashion.'

'I know, I know – and if not before they were in fashion, then certainly after they had gone out of fashion!' he replied laughing, and told her that the boutique had said she could change it if it was the wrong size, but she'd have to be quick as they were about to close for the day.

She'd never worried much about whether something was a perfect fit or not, but she put it on anyway. At first it felt a bit too tight, almost as though she couldn't breathe, but after Li had helped her zip it up, it felt extremely comfortable. It hugged her body beautifully and it was just long enough to cover the bruises on her knees.

Li looked very pleased and said that he must have a perfect memory of his wife's size.

'You've got to help me...' said Liu, raising her arms and looking mournfully at her armpit hair. She asked if she could borrow his razor, the idea of which seemed to unnerve him. 'Let me do it for you, I don't want you to cut yourself.' They walked into the bathroom, and between them managed to do what most women manage by themselves.

She got ready as quickly as she could. 'What a nuisance it is being a woman,' she laughed to herself, 'surely I can't possibly have been one in my previous life.'

But when she saw herself in the mirror she saw a shapely attractive woman in a beautiful outfit. It was the colour that did it – bright but not too garish. She hadn't got dressed up like this in years; she felt proud that in the past decade or so she didn't seemed to have aged much at all, or put on any weight. She was a bit like her mother in that respect; time seemed to have been kind to her.

She could hear her husband pacing up and down outside the door, his mobile ringing incessantly. When he answered his phone, conversations were always short – often consisting of a single word like 'yes' or 'OK'. She felt his patience in waiting for her proof enough that he still loved her, and decided to put him out of his misery: 'I'm ready! Let's go!'

All eyes turned as she entered the huge banqueting hall, arm in arm with her husband. Li almost had to drag her as they walked to their seats. At one point she got so nervous she tried to pull her arm away from his. She found comfort in the fact that Li had told her that all the guests had wanted to meet her. Of course they would stare at someone they had heard about but never seen before! But she knew it was her own fault; she'd allowed herself to be talked into going to this banquet. She resolved to suffer it all with a smile.

When she had sat down she had a good look around her. She'd never imagined that even a hotel like the Golden Pleasure would have quite such an impressive banqueting hall. Two walls were made entirely of mirrors. There was a bunch of fresh flowers on every table and in each champagne glass was a pink napkin folded in the shape of a bird. All the waiters were wearing white dinner jackets and black ties, and they were all young and good-looking. Chopin was playing in the background. She'd never been to such a banquet; even the most formal dinners she'd been to at the Academia Sinica could not compete with this.

There was a local official standing on the stage; he'd probably been waiting for Li to arrive before making any announcements. That was her fault; she hoped no one thought they had deliberately made so many people wait just to show their importance.

The guests consisted of members of the Hong Kong and Taiwan Trade Consortia and a few VIPs from the Project Headquarters. Every one of them had a wife in attendance, which made Liu feel bad that this was the first time she'd shown her face, and she had hardly been enthusiastic. There were about a dozen tables, none with any empty places. A good proportion of the guests must have been local cadres who were in some way involved in the Dam Project. The men from Hong Kong wore English-style black dinner jackets, and the men from Taiwan wore dark suits and carefully-chosen ties, though their ties were perhaps a little more brightly-coloured than the kind of tie that mainland Chinese men would feel comfortable wearing. The women all wore cheongsams, regardless of where they came from. It seemed strange that the women had been even more conformist in their choice of clothes than their husbands, even including Liu.

Everyone on her table was smiling at her, so she smiled back. Some people handed her their business cards and she reached into her bag and gave out some of her own. No one handed Li a business card; they probably knew him well already. Everyone on their table must have been an important person.

She couldn't hear very well what people were saying. One of the Hong Kong businessmen seemed to say: 'The feng shui on North Mountain is superb; does Madam Director have a villa there?'

But before she had time to answer the whole hall went quiet. The chairman began to speak, inviting Mr Li, General Director of the Great Lake Development Company and Deputy Head of the Bureau of Yangtze River Water Resources, to make a speech.

Li walked up to the microphone amidst the sound of applause. Liu had never heard him speak in public before and she was curious to hear what he would be like. She had always thought that Chinese cadres made rather poor orators, doing little more than reading the speeches written by their secretaries. But Li didn't even have any notes.

He began by thanking members of the Liang County Government and certain members of the Consortia, and thanking everyone for putting up with such a long busy day, working so hard to achieve common goals. His tone was gentle at first but changed markedly when he began to talk about the project itself. He began by asking a series of rhetorical questions.

'Is the Three Gorges Project nothing more than the construction of another dam, a little bigger than the Coulee Dam, and a little higher than the Aswan Dam? Or is it, as some people maintain, the greatest engineering project in the whole of human history?

'To be honest, I don't know,' he continued, lifting his hands from the microphone as if about to count on his fingers. 'And I don't much care. What matters is not how great the project is or isn't as a feat of engineering, what matters is its geo-economic significance, and in terms of geo-economic significance, the project is, without question, second to none. The Three Gorges Project is going to become the vanguard of the modernisation of China; it will be the springboard of prosperity for Western China.'

He pronounced every word clearly and correctly, in perfect Beijing pronunciation, with none of the hesitancy that was normally heard in cadres' speeches. The length of his sentences, and the pauses between them, formed a compelling rhythm. After having quietly waited for the applause to die down, he raised his voice and asked: 'Why, you may ask, do I make such a claim? Propaganda? Pride? Advertising strategy?'

His question caused a ripple of nervous laughter to echo round the hall, but his calmly-spoken answer caused even greater surprise. 'Of course not. The Three Gorges Project will mean that China's coast is moved inland by two thousand kilometres; we will have our own inland sea directly linked to the Pacific Ocean!'

The whole hall thundered with applause; even Liu joined in. The actual content of his speech had been somewhat empty, but he had delivered it expertly. She was really surprised; where had Li learned to give speeches like that? Maybe he hadn't learnt; maybe it was just another of his many talents – after all, he was an exceptionally clear thinker.

During the applause a Hong Kong businessman moved his chair closer to Liu's and said: 'What an outstanding individual! A pillar of the nation! It won't be long before he's a Minister, or Deputy Premier and more! The sky's the limit!'

Liu was quite taken aback by the comment. She'd never given much thought to her husband's long-term career prospects. She'd been too selfish. She preferred not to think about it and pretended not to have been listening.

Li continued, 'Some people think that the phrase 'Say Goodbye to The Three Gorges' is inappropriate. I don't really care one way or the other – the only thing that matters is whether or not it's good for the tourist industry.' Liu could guess what was coming next.

'Soon this area will have the most amazing tourist attraction: Lake Tours. The Lake District in England doesn't have cliffs as precipitous; Geneva does not have a lake as wide. The 318 National Highway, and the Chonqing-Yichang and Chongqing-Changsha Motorways, will go right round the Lake Region, linking cities like pearls on a necklace... and Liang county will be one of the brightest of them all!'

He continued by asking everyone if he might be permitted to draw a comparison: 'If the dam waterfall can be compared to the Niagara Falls, then the Yichang-Liang-Chongqing triangle will soon be comparable to the Toronto-Detroit-Chicago triangle!'

His listeners jumped to their feet in a frenzy of applause. Some of the Hong Kong businessmen were even shouting out: 'Excellent! Excellent! Something to make us truly proud to be Chinese!'

He joined in the clapping, indicating that what was to be applauded was the message, not the messenger.

Liu was feeling increasingly ill at ease and wanted to sit back down again. At the end of the day Li's 'inspiring' speech meant nothing at all, but his words were so slippery no one could grasp them firmly enough to realize it. The word 'comparison' meant drawing an analogy – nothing more. Not that there was anything wrong with drawing an analogy, or stirring people into giving rapturous applause; what Liu considered dishonest was the way her husband had used his analogy as his conclusion.

'Liang County becoming China's equivalent of Detroit?!' Liu was unconvinced.

Li signalled for someone to pass him a glass of red wine. He raised it so it was parallel with his chin and said: 'I propose a toast to a wonderful partnership between our company and the Hong Kong and Taiwan Consortia, and to the prosperity of China and the whole of East Asia.'

Just as everyone had raised their glasses and was about to drink, he added gravely, 'Liang County Municiple Government has entrusted me to make the following announcement.' Everyone was standing, glasses half-raised, silent in anticipation. 'The two main streets leading to the two docks will be renamed Hong Kong Street and Taipei Street.'

The hall erupted into loud cheers. As soon as everyone had had a drink, there was more clamorous applause.

Liu was the only person not to join in the toast; she just stared into space not knowing what to make of it all. Had her husband deliberately just misled all these people? Everything he had said sounded so wonderful, so positive. Everyone was so thrilled by it all. The bonds would sell like hot cakes and Liang's two main streets were to be named in honour of it all. What misgivings could she possibly have?

The speech had been especially clever from a political point of view. It had all seemed so spontaneous, although it must have taken months of discussion to get it so perfect, with Li undoubtedly deciding what was to be said and what wasn't. Politics was obviously his vocation. A man like him would never be satisfied working as an engineer his whole life, no matter how big the project. Neither would management ever be enough for him. Winning these people's trust, and inspiring them with such enthusiasm, was more than just a matter of ensuring that they would invest in his company; even success wasn't enough for him. He wanted it to be an outstanding success.

Li was now moving around from table to table with a small group of local cadres, making a little toast at each one. Meanwhile everyone on the top table was talking excitedly to Liu; it was as if they thought that by talking to her they were in fact talking to Li himself. She nodded politely but paid no attention to what they were saying.

Bird's nest, shark's fin soup, stewed abalone with black mountain mushrooms; one delicacy after another was served to each guest individually. Liu glanced over and saw her husband at the other side of the room, the centre of noisy attention. The Hong Kong businessman who had tried to talk to her earlier took this opportunity to try again; he was different to the others – he wanted to try to say something special.

He told her how greatly he admired Dr Liu, and that his unworthy company had been paying keen attention to the progress of research relating to genetic engineering.

Up until this point she had been lost in her own thoughts, but this man's words succeeding in getting her attention. He was elderly, his hair was a greyish white, he wore a pair of rimless glasses and he gave the impression of being highly cultured, a so-called 'Confucian businessman'. She thought back to the business card he had given her; he was the chairman of some company's board of directors. 'I presume Dr Liu has read the news in the papers?'

'What news?' she asked. She hadn't read a newspaper since she'd left Beijing, she hadn't even switched the television on.

'The Rowslin laboratory in Scotland has successfully bred a sheep using clone technology. Instead of sperm, an ordinary cell was used. She's a year old now – completely normal and expected to live to a ripe old age. It was reported yesterday.'

Liu's heart missed a beat. 'Oh, so soon.' Of course she knew a great deal about clone technology, Rowslin, and the competition that existed among the various laboratories around the world. Her own laboratory had been working towards such a goal for some time, though with very limited funding.

The woman beside the man, probably his wife, edged closer to join in the conversation: 'The sheep's name is *Duo Li, 'duo'* as in *'yi duo hua'* – a flower – and *'li'* as in *'meili'* – beautiful.'

'Dolly,' corrected the man somewhat impatiently before continuing with the conversation. Not beating about the bush, he asked: 'Does the Institute of Bio-engineering have clone technology?'

'We're not too far behind our Western colleagues,' Liu replied.

'That's excellent!' He went on to explain that his company had been contemplating investing in clone technology for some time. That morning he had had an urgent telephone call asking him to fly to Beijing and go to the Institute of Bio-engineering at the Academia Sinica. But he'd asked around and been told that he could meet Dr Liu that very night at the banquet, which was a happy coincidence.

Liu explained that she was only a researcher.

The man replied that it was research that they were interested in. Provided that there were people capable of doing the research, everything else would be easy; the company would invest as much money as was needed.

'What is it you want to clone?' she asked, somewhat perplexed. It was extremely unusual to come across someone so keen to invest in her research.

'You're no fool!' He moved a little closer, deliberately turning his back on the woman who had tried to join the conversation. 'Rhinoceroses,' he whispered mysteriously.

Liu was rather surprised by his answer and asked: 'May I ask what your company does?'

'Pharmaceuticals – Chinese medicine to be exact. Our products are sold all over the world. We are the biggest company of our kind.'

Liu nodded. She understood. The rhinoceros only survives in certain African countries, all south of the Sahara. Human encroachments and ecological changes have rapidly decreased the number of herds. What's more, they were unwilling to breed in captivity, and all attempts at artificial insemination had failed. Rhino hunting had long since been banned in Africa; the use of rhino horn in Chinese medicine relied entirely on poaching and smuggling.

The man went on to say that his company had conducted 'double-blind' tests proving that, in sufficient doses, rhino horn was more effective than Viagra, and that Viagra had not yet taken complete control of its potential market. 'Our company is well-reputed for only using genuine ingredients; nothing in our products is fake.'

Liu shrugged her shoulders; there was little point discussing her specialist subject with a businessman who didn't know the first thing about scientific research.

'Our company would like to invest two hundred million dollars in research at your laboratory, if you were willing to take on the responsibility of such a sum.'

'Two hundred million?' she repeated, flabbergasted.

Liu stared at him, speechless. He looked like a gentle old professor but was, in all likelihood, the man behind the infamous large-scale poaching and world-wide smuggling of an endangered species. The illegal sale of rhino horns and tiger bones was what gave Chinatowns around the world such a bad name; and now this man was asking her to clone rhinos in order to use their horns as aphrodisiacs? It didn't bear thinking about.

Continuing in the same vein he added, 'Of course, when you have the technology to enable us to go into mass production, we'll give you more.'

Mass production! What would happen if this man

succeeding in convincing people that rhino horn really was better than Viagra? She thought back to a report she'd read about a farm in Northern China which bred bears; a small hole was cut in chest of each bear, to which a bottle was attached to collect the bile. How were the rhino horns going to be removed from the rhinoceros?

She imagined a huge herd of hornless rhinos lying dead in a breeding farm, swarms of jet-black flies buzzing around the carcasses under the hot midday sun.

The man raised his glass and said, 'Come, let's propose a toast to our cooperation!'

Instead of raising her glass Liu said, quietly but clearly, 'I must apologize, I'm feeling rather unwell, would you excuse me.'

She put her glass down and rose to leave. As she was turning away from the table she caught sight of Li, who was walking towards her, surrounded by his little band of cadres. He looked back at her, evidently confused by her sudden exit. She felt guilty.

Just as she was about to start walking towards the exit, the Hong Kong businessman's wife said to her, 'I know from my own experience that rhino horn works better than Viagra. We Chinese have always said there's a strong connection between mind and body, and that horn has life-force; how could it not work better than all those chemicals foreigners use?!'

Liu quickened her step and rushed out of the hall. It was a relief to get out of the place; she felt as though she was going to be sick from the stench of all that smoke and alcohol. She wanted a cup of tea, just to calm down.

Chapter Twenty-eight

The second she walked into her room the phone started ringing. It was her mother saying that she'd got her message, and that she'd phoned dozens of times and never received any reply. She asked Liu what she thought of Liang.

'It's fine, I've been out a lot, having a good look around.' She didn't want to say what she had actually seen, but her mother knew she wasn't being told the whole truth. Liang had already become more important to Liu than it had ever been to her mother; she didn't know how to begin to tell her what had really been going on.

Liu's mother said that she had been dreaming about Liang, particularly about the compound she had lived in all those years ago.

'You don't happen to know if it's still there do you?' she asked.

'It's been almost totally demolished – soon it'll be completely submerged under water,' replied Liu honestly; she was hiding so much from her mother that she couldn't bring herself to lie about this as well. 'It's been converted into the headquarters for the Rat Extermination Campaign; the whole place stinks of dead rats.'

'What!?' exclaimed her mother, scandalized.

'It's true. There's a real rat problem here.'

'You don't seem quite yourself; I'll leave you in peace. Give me a ring when you have a minute,' she replied without any trace of irritation; she sounded as happy as she always did.

Liu had always admired her mother's positive, easy-going attitude to life, and the way she always made sure everything was as fun and light-hearted as possible. However, at the same time Liu had often suspected that this was all just an act. It wouldn't have surprised her if her mother weren't sitting at home in tears – she could just picture it, curled up on the sofa in that luxurious flat, all alone, crying her heart out. But she didn't know whether her mother would ever truly open up to her. It was almost as though they were strangers and had been so ever since Liu was just a little girl.

The Yangtze looked even more mysterious at night than it did during the day. The New City formed a bright cluster of neon lights whereas the Old City, sprawling and disjointed, stretched along the banks of the river far into the distance. The mountains straight ahead were for the most part pitch-black; the reflections of the few lights there shimmered in the ever-moving waters below.

There was a knock at the door but Liu stayed where she was; she wasn't in the mood to talk.

Then a rather timid voice called out, 'Director Li

is asking how Madam Director is feeling...'

It sounded like that sycophantic little Mr Han. Her reply was brusque and irritable: 'Don't worry, not dead yet!'

This seemed to satisfy him and he said cheerfully, 'Glad to hear that,' and walked off to report to Li.

She still hadn't switched the main lights on. The only light in the room came from a small night-light plugged into the wall which cast a soft luminescence over her body as she walked over to the kettle to make some green tea.

The taste of the tea reminded her of her time as a 'sent-down youth' in Inner Mongolia. She'd just learnt to ride a horse and was serving as the local 'barefoot doctor'. A comrade of hers was running a high fever, so she'd grabbed her uniform cap and scarf, jumped on a horse and gone galloping off to the headquarters to get some medicine, braving the freezing wind and swirling snow.

The grasslands were steeped in darkness. She couldn't see which way was which; in fact, she couldn't even see the road beneath her. There was nothing but an arid blackness in every direction. The cold wind was stinging her eyes; it hurt as much as if someone had been there pricking them with a needle. She held the reins tightly and forged ahead. Eventually she caught sight of a light by the roadside. 'If only it were home!' she thought to herself, 'An oil lamp and four walls to protect me and keep me warm...a place to escape from this desolate wilderness around me...'

She rode on and found herself in a valley. In the distance she could make out a few lights, glimmering like stars in the darkness. Were they homes? Did they contain contented families huddling together for warmth?

Back in the hotel room she suddenly felt overwhelmed with sadness, almost physically weak. All she had ever really wanted was a home, somewhere warm and loving; a home perhaps even as poor as Auntie Chen's – small and poky and reeking of sweat. Deep down she wasn't really a sophisticated upper-class intellectual, she was one of the most ordinary women you could ever imagine; all she needed was someone to understand her. No one had ever understood what she was really like – neither her mother, nor her husband, nor her late father. She had always found them so distant, so cold, like the lights shining in the darkness – visible, yet so very far away.

Just as Liu had finished the fried rice she had ordered from room service, Li came in, opening the door with his key card. She had just seen a report about the cloned sheep on the 24-hour world news, but even that had failed to arouse her interest. She'd long since got out of her cheongsam; it was safely back in its box, and her high heels had been pushed under the bed. The room was dimly lit.

'How's your headache?' He walked over and felt her forehead as he undid his tie.

She turned off the television. The room suddenly felt very quiet. 'I haven't got a headache,' she said calmly. 'I apologize; I failed in my duty as your wife. I let you down.'

'It doesn't matter. I should have guessed what

would happen.'

'What do you mean?' She was curious. Was there no end to the man's arrogance?

'Mr Wu told me. He upset you; he asked me to relay his apologies. He was worried you might try to spoil his plans.'

'I have no intention of spoiling anybody's plans.' She stood up to help her husband out of his jacket and hung it up in the wardrobe. 'I just don't want to clone rhinos so people can make the Chinese version of Viagra, that's all!'

'Rhino horns to stimulate virility?' He grimaced. 'It's one of the great ironies of history that Hong Kong should be the vanguard of China's modernisation. They are so coarse and uncultured. I've even had to learn to greet them with the phrase, "Hope you get rich!"'

Liu smiled; he'd done a very good impression of a Hong Kong businessman as he'd said the fashionable four-character Cantonese phrase. 'It was a brilliant speech you know; by the end of it they were practically hero-worshipping you.'

'Hardly. The only thing they were worshipping was the prospect of big profits.' He poured himself a cup of tea. 'No one ever imagined I would turn the Three Gorges into a goldmine.' He casually kicked off his brightly polished leather shoes. 'For years people thought that building the dam would bankrupt the government. Not many people in China really understand finance, you know.' He undid the top two buttons of his shirt and, looking at Liu, continued, 'You see, now it's not a case of me looking for money, it's a case of money looking for me; investors are actually thanking me for spending their money.'

Formerly, Li would never have used the word 'me' like that in public; he'd always have said 'us', or 'our company', or even passed the credit on to 'the national leadership'. Liu sat back down on the sofa, and watched as he walked over to the bed, lay down and made himself comfortable. 'Rhino horn better than Viagra? Who cares – I don't need either of them.' He reached out for his cup and had a sip of tea. 'We can leave tomorrow morning; we've been here too long already.'

Liu recalled what her mother had told her: 'Power is the only aphrodisiac for the modern man.' Here was direct evidence of that; of course Li didn't need rhino horn, all he needed was to listen to himself speak.

He walked over to the sofa, pulled her into his arms, kissed her and dragged her onto the bed. She did not respond.

'What's wrong now?' asked Li angrily.

Liu realized how little control she had over her own body. Just after Li had confronted the corrupt officials, her body had been quite willing to merge with his, but, now he was back to his normal self, arrogantly wallowing in his own success, her body put up a natural resistance. Now was the time to confront him with the question she had been keeping to herself since the day she arrived:

'That other woman who called, who was she?'

'What are you talking about?' He lay back down on the bed. 'Why don't you hurry up and have a shower and come to bed?'

She tilted her head slightly and said: 'The woman who called when I first arrived at the Dam Site; she said there was something important she wanted to discuss with me.'

Li stood up and said he was going to take a shower. 'Let's just forget that. We should be living in the present and looking forward to the future. We're making history! Remember how public opinion in the West was so much against the project? Now Western banks are begging to lend us money! And what's more, I don't need it. Our economy is better than theirs and our cities are more impressive. I love to see Westerners speechless with admiration; it gives me a special kind of feeling of satisfaction. Don't you feel it too?'

Liu didn't take her eyes off him for a second. 'Are you trying to say that this woman doesn't exist?' Usually when they had a disagreement Liu would just let the matter drop, but tonight was different. The more he talked about how wonderful the future was going to be, the less she wanted to be a part of his future.

'Are you sure you want to know?' Li lowered his face, evidently displeased.

'No... I'm not sure. I just don't like people being dishonest, that's all.'

She seemed to hit a nerve; Li's face clouded. 'Then stop asking me.' There was a certain finality to his tone; it was as though he were giving orders to an inferior.

The two of them fell silent. They listened as a night boat sailed by, sounding a muffled siren as it went. Li walked over to the window and drew the curtains, then he went into the bathroom. After five minutes of gentle splashing sounds, he came back out in his pyjamas, carrying his shirt and trousers which he hung carefully on the back of a chair. He set his alarm clock, climbed into bed and turned his bedside light off. 'You had better get a good night's sleep. We'll be leaving first thing tomorrow.'

Liu sat down on the sofa in the semi-darkness, staring at the floor. 'If you don't think you should tell me then you don't have to, but is it really necessary to speak to me like an employee? It makes me feel ashamed of you!'

Li sat up and banged his fist down on the light switch to turn on his bedside lamp. He'd never been treated like this by Liu before. 'We've been happily married for all these years, and I trust that we will remain so for many years to come.'

'People change,' she replied, 'You for example. You're more and more...capable.'

He knew she was making fun of him. He stood up, his face red with anger. Liu was sure he would never loose his temper like this when he was working; it was only when he was with her that he felt free to let go.

'I know what you're implying,' he said. 'You think I'm relying on China's size; you think that just because we have a large population, getting money is easy. You're not entirely wrong, but the point is, someone still has to do it.'

'Just as someone has to build the Dam.'

'Exactly!' he said, 'The debate before 1992 was a complete waste of time. What the opposition failed to appreciate was that there were already hundreds of thousands of people working on the project. As early as the 1980s various ministries and commissions already had thousands of technical personnel engaged in some aspect or other of the creation of the dam. If the construction itself had been vetoed, what would we all have done? So, you see, the project simply had to go ahead.'

Liu replied, 'I know that. People all over China were looking for something to do – hence the enthusiasm in the project. And all those people needed a leader.'

'But isn't it the same all over the world? How else could it be?' responded Li, ignoring her derisive tone. 'How else could mankind progress? How else could China ever hope to catch up with the West, and finally become the new leader of global culture?'

She felt that Li had hit the nail on the head: he believed that China should become more Western than the West itself, in order to overtake the West and in order to turn Liang into a Detroit. This was the glorious future we were racing towards. She tried to picture the reservoir completed – the Three Gorges submerged in water from the Yangtze River, a new lake, new 'scenic areas'. No doubt even the ancient tombs and rare rock-carvings which were to be flooded would be turned into 'underwater museums'.

The pointlessness of man reminded her of bacteria she'd looked at under the microscope. They keep eating and reproducing until they have eaten all the gelatine in the petri dish, then they all die, leaving nothing but a few spores, neither dead nor alive, held in a state of suspension, waiting for their next life. How can it be that creatures on the highest and lowest evolutionary levels should behave so similarly?

The thought depressed her. 'I'm sorry, I've changed since arriving here – I know I must seem strange. I've not been rational. I know I'm really not suitable for the role of 'Wife of Company President'. You should find someone better.'

Li walked up to the sofa and gave her a comforting hug.

'You are a great professor and a brilliant scientist, I understand that. I just don't want any harm to come to our marriage – whatever happens.'

When he saw that Liu wasn't responding, he stood up and said furiously: 'You shouldn't believe everything your mother says!'

She sat up straight, pale with anger. Li hardly ever mentioned her mother, and Liu had never been entirely sure why he'd always been so keen to keep his distance from her. Her mother had never said much about him either – other than to report the occasional rumour about his political career.

She'd never really examined the reasons for the lack of intimacy between her and her mother. But she'd never expected to see Li display such open hostility towards her. He evidently realized that, if her mother hadn't pointed out the precarious state of their relationship, she wouldn't be acting as she now was. It probably had something to do with the perfume – that woman spy who delivered it must have reported back to him unfavourably.

'I think,' began Liu, slowly and clearly, 'that you owe me an explanation.'

He didn't seem troubled by this request; it seemed

as though he'd been expecting it – perhaps he'd even rehearsed his reply a few times. How could it have taken her so long to realize that his approach to marriage was the same as his approach to politics?!

'I treasure our marriage; I don't want us to end up like your parents.'

Seeing Liu almost jump out of her chair he put his hands on her shoulders, making her sit still. But she violently pushed his hands away. This so-called husband of hers seemed to be about to play his trump card. Excellent: she wanted to know what kind of person she'd been married to for the past twenty years.

'What do you mean?'

Li sat down in a chair opposite her and said, calmly and unhurriedly, 'I only found out myself relatively recently. My father told me from his deathbed. He hadn't wanted to say anything before for fear that it might affect our marriage – though he needn't have worried. I've never had any trouble keeping the affairs of different generations completely separate in my mind.' He seemed reluctant to continue, but forced himself, knowing he had no other option. 'Your father often used to complain to my father that your mother hated him; that they hadn't been husband and wife for years, that it was a marriage in name only.'

Liu was now shocked as well as angered: what her husband was saying simply wasn't possible. Many people had tried to find her mother a new husband after she became a widow, but she had never been interested. She would say to Liu: 'There is only one man for me in this life, and that was your father.'

But maybe, just maybe, Liu had got her parents entirely wrong.

Li said that his father had asked him to go to Sichuan to see an old army friend, who was at that time working in the Sichuan Party Personnel Department, to sort out a few of Liu's father's files. His father had said that there were a few things which needed to be cleared up because otherwise they could be used to cause trouble, as had happened in East Germany after the fall of the Wall. Not being a member of the Personnel Department, Li had no right to look at such files, but he dared not go against his father's dying wishes. It was summer and the South was unbearably hot. Li took a train to the provincial capital, Chengdu. When he had found his father's old friend, he agreed that the files should be dealt with as soon as possible. However, the Personnel Department thought differently: the longer they held on to the files the better.

The two of them agreed to meet again at the office the next day, because it was a Sunday when no one would be around. The Personnel Department officially required two cadres to be present whenever files were looked at, but there are exceptions to every rule.

When Li arrived at the office the following morning, his father's friend was already there waiting for him. They hunted through several dusty old cupboards and eventually found all of Liu's father's files — five huge bundles. 'Well, do you want to have a look, or don't you?' asked the old comrade.

Li pondered a while and said, 'I'll just a have look

at the titles; there's no need to read them from beginning to end.'

Most of the files dated back to the Cultural Revolution. Some of the documents had been written by Liu's father himself: self-criticism essays mainly, some of which were tens of thousands of characters long, and none of which were less than a few thousand. The rest of the documents were mostly reports of his various 'crimes', written by informers. Li wondered why he had had so many enemies. One of the reports caught his attention and he decided to sit down and read it because, to his astonishment, the informer had been Liu's mother.

'I know what you're getting at!' interrupted Liu, standing up, 'You're trying to tell me that the reason my father committed suicide was because my mother informed on him!'

Li did not appreciate the interruption: 'I never said any such thing. How could I possibly come to such a conclusion? I have absolutely no way of knowing if your mother was forced to write the report or if she did it out of spite. All I'm saying is that a fire which starts in one's own bedroom is the worst thing that can happen to a cadre. Didn't that famous writer in Beijing commit suicide because someone in his family informed on him?'

Liu recalled the centipede-like scar on her mother's stomach and the strange expression on her face when she had told her what had caused it. She couldn't help shuddering. Was it possible that her mother really had hated her father because he had chosen to risk her life for the sake of the life of their unborn child?

In her mind's eye she could see the boat on the river, her mother lying in the cabin, looking at her husband in despair. 'No!' she kept saying to herself silently, 'No, don't say it, I can't stand it!' But, looking at Li, she said calmly, 'So you want me to pledge my loyalty, to promise not to 'set your bedroom on fire'? Well, what about your loyalty then?' Her voice was heavy with sadness as she repeated, 'What about your loyalty...?'

He replied: 'I've always said it is only with an unsullied wife like you that I can be an incorrupt official.'

He was pretending to miss the point yet again. But Liu had had enough and she didn't feel in the mood to press for an answer. She was more worried about what he'd said about her parents. 'If you've got anything else to tell me, please tell me now,' she said, 'because you won't get another chance to reveal any more of my family's "secrets"!'

'There's nothing else. Absolutely nothing else.'

'So I suppose you know how my father killed himself as well?' Liu had long ago learnt to read the truth behind Li's reassurances.

'If I tell you, you mustn't get upset.' He paused. 'He was beaten until he was almost dead. His attackers thought he couldn't move so none of them stayed back to keep an eye on him; they just left him on his own where he was, the result being that he crawled over to the window and fell from the eleventh floor. I saw his death certificate in his files – there was even a photograph to prove it was true.'

Tears had begun to trickle down Liu's cheeks. She didn't need to see the photograph; she could see it all with horrific clarity in her mind's eye – his skull cracked open, his eyeballs damaged beyond recognition, white bits of brain lying in a pool of fresh blood. Her fingers and limbs went numb and she couldn't help trembling.

No one had ever wanted to tell her the details of her father's death and she had never pressed the matter. Li hadn't told her for her sake, but for his own. He wanted to keep the marriage going: he didn't want any kind of sex scandal at this pivotal moment in his political career. She knew she was expected to keep in mind the big picture.

A part of her wanted just to forgive and forget as duty demanded. But she just couldn't bring herself to do it. Her whole life seemed such a mess.

She heard it start to rain outside. It was pouring; large raindrops were hammering against the glass of the windows. The weather is very unpredictable in the Three Gorges. Liu's mind began to drift back in time.

The train was whistling loudly. The whole carriage was filled with Red Guards of about the same age as her. They were all excited about going to Beijing on a pilgrimage. But she had been stripped of her status as a Red Guard. The train was so packed she didn't manage to get on until it had already started rolling out of the station. She found a tiny space and curled up on the floor in the gangway. It took two days and three nights to get to Beijing. It was her first time there, and it took a long time to find Uncle Li's house. It was a detached house with a courtyard. The armed guards wouldn't let her in so she got out her father's letter to show them, but they refused to look at it and refused to report that she was there.

She was tired and hungry. She sat down on the stone steps and felt her body slowly lapse into a fever. Her head was aching terribly. She felt so weak that she lay down, feeling as though she may slip away at any moment and die in a strange place where nobody would care, where nobody would even notice. All the guards did was try to get her to move away.

She was seeing herself when she was sixteen years old. She had become a protégé of the Li family and, although until now the thought had never occurred to her, it suddenly became obvious: all these years later Li still thought of her as his protégé, as someone who owed him eternal gratitude. Of all the people she had encountered throughout her life, not one of them had really made the effort to engage with her soul. From the age of sixteen she had kept her inner pain carefully hidden – the loneliness, the terrible, terrible, inescapable loneliness.

She walked into the bathroom. She needed to be by herself. Her hands and feet felt as though they had been plunged into ice-cold water and her chest felt crushed as though it were being pressed down by the weight of a huge stone slab, forcing the breath out of her lungs.

Li was completely silent. He didn't come to the bathroom to try to talk to her as she was half-expecting he would. Surely he couldn't have fallen asleep? She didn't hate him, but she didn't know whether or not she still loved him. Her feelings for him were complex; she feared it would take longer than one night to work out what she really felt. She began to imagine what it must have been like for her mother. She was sure she hadn't hated her father at first – but she would never have had the opportunity to talk to him about her feelings, and consequently would never have sorted things out. And then, in the end, she had let it all out – at the worst possible time, to the worst possible people, in the worst possible way.

How could she hope to escape what had happened to her parents all those years ago, in this very place? Back then her mother had been swamped by helplessness and despair, just as Liu was now.

She still couldn't believe what Auntie Chen had said that night about past lives but, if such a thing were possible, then maybe she was the reincarnation of the old monk, Master Yutong, reborn as Liu so that he could see her father suffer the karmic punishment for his crime.

She suddenly began to feel afraid; the coldness of the world made her whole body feel gripped with terror. She began to shiver uncontrollably.

Was there anyone she could talk to?

She didn't know; all she knew was she had to find someone. She opened the bathroom door. The rain was still battering against the window. Li really had gone to sleep but the bedside light was still on. She walked towards the bed, looking for her shoes. It was time she left.

Suddenly Li's mobile started ringing. He reached over to his bedside table and turned it off without even opening his eyes, but he sensed that Liu was standing there. As she was tying up her shoe laces he asked, 'Where are you going at this time of night?'

'I don't think that's your concern,' Liu replied coolly.

'I am your husband! Of course it's my concern!' He screamed back at her, jumping out of bed.

The phone began to ring. Li picked up the receiver, listened for a couple of seconds and put it down on the table. Liu could hear the person on the other end still yelling.

'Actually, I know where you're going,' he said making every effort to restrain his fury. His tone was that of an experienced police officer.

Liu turned her head in surprise: how could he know something she didn't even know herself?

'It's that Chen Yueming isn't it!' So that was it. He'd fired his last bullet. 'I don't intend to interfere, I just want to say one thing: don't get carried away with the idea that you're too good to be true and I'm just a wicked, bullying, betraying husband. You're not half as perfect as you think you are!'

Liu felt so enraged it was as though someone had just poured flaming petrol on her head. She wanted to scream back at him, 'Have you no shame?!' but she didn't; to express her anger would have been to dignify her husband's outburst. He had never seemed such a stranger to her as he did at that moment. He may have had at his command a sophisticated, almost omniscient spy network, but if his ability to assess a situation were so poor that he should immediately jump to such an absurd conclusion, then he was hardly likely ever to go all the way in politics. She turned round and carried on getting ready to go out.

At that moment another phone started to ring. The

sound was coming from the wardrobe. Li dashed over and took a mobile out of the inside pocket of his suit-jacket. Liu guessed that it was his 'special' phone, the number of which was only known to a small circle of his cronies. He drew the curtains open just enough to be able to look out as he listened to the person on the end. It was still pouring with rain; there was a quick pitter-patter sound continually battering against the glass of the windows.

'Landslide?' he asked.

The person on the other end started shouting something, obviously in a state of panic. Li had no option but to listen carefully. Eventually he said, 'Let the local authority deal with it.'

The person on the other end started saying something but Li interrupted him: 'If the whole mountain is sliding away then not even the gods themselves can do anything about it. If we fix the problem now and it starts sliding away again after the flooding, then everyone will blame it on the project.' He snapped his mobile shut.

'Where are you going?' said Li turning round. He stared at her wide-eyed and began shouting at her. 'I'm telling you, this Chen Yueming's background is, shall we say, "complicated". His family has a history of colluding with a kind of local cult; he himself has played prominent roles in various illegal activities. The local government has been given authorization to investigate.'

Another trump card, and what a convoluted one! But Li had lost the ability to shock his wife; she had finally realized beyond all doubt that they would never speak the same language. All words were superfluous. The stage of petty jealousy had passed; Li had gone too far.

'I'm only telling you for your own good,' he said, blocking her way. 'I don't want you to find yourself mixed up in politics you don't understand.'

His 'secret' mobile had started ringing again. He hesitated for a second and Liu walked briskly out of the room without so much as a backward glance.

Chapter Twenty-nine

She rushed out frantically into a world that seemed to be in the process of being washed away by torrential rain.

She felt as though she could see the scene that Auntie Chen had described to her: the woman is pressed down onto the ground, the person pressing her down wants her to kneel but she doesn't want to, and the man behind her is pushed on top of her. His face gradually becomes clearer, despite the heavy rain. But, for the time being, she does not want to see who it is.

She hadn't taken any luggage with her: she hadn't decided where she would go, or whether or not she would ever go back to the Golden Pleasure. She walked quickly through the streets, forging ahead against the heavy rain. Many years of resentment and repression were welling up inside her; she was aching to scream all the misery away, to scream and scream, to howl like a beast in the wilderness.

She now realized that what had just happened that night had been bound to happen sooner or later. In fact, she'd had a feeling it would happen ever since she had smelt that disgusting perfume.

There wasn't a soul to be seen on the streets of Liang. She walked from the New City to the Old. Strips of light from the streetlamps fell slanting on the roads beneath, doing their utmost to illuminate the decrepit buildings on either side of the road. Even the mah-jong players had given up and gone home.

Liu walked wherever the streets took her; the rain was far too heavy for her to be able to work out where she was or where she was going. When the rain eased a little she could just about make out that she was at the foot of Nanhua Mountain. She'd gone the right way after all. The searchlights from the riverboats glided over the dark mountains on either side. Suddenly a beam of light brushed across her face: it made the rain look like a dense curtain of silver needles, glistening as they hurtled towards her.

She reached the entrance to the 'Nanhua Mountain Scenic Area'. The huge gate posts were engraved with dragons and phoenixes and there was a jade arch. In the wild wind and violent rain the self-important slogans and the map of the scenic area were entirely invisible.

The cable car had stopped running hours earlier and the road up the mountain was only blocked by a single horizontal bar which she stepped over without any difficulty.

She didn't speed up; she knew that when going up the mountain she should make her steps slow and steady, especially in heavy rain.

The temples on the way up made the place look

strange and otherworldly. It was very dark except for occasional bolts of lightening which created brief flashes of light. This was how the place was meant to be seen. The halls, which were brightly painted with gaudy gold leaf, looked ridiculous by day but now seemed to come into their own. They were brooding and malevolent, home to creatures of darkness. The red-faced King Yama, flanked on either side by Generals Blower and Snorter, was staring right at her with fierce white eyes and seemed to be laughing hideously. Her shoes were wet through and her feet numb with cold.

She could feel the eyes of the statues on the back of her neck as she pushed onwards. She was the sole night-traveller on the mountain road; she felt like a criminal on the run.

She wiped the rain-water from her face and strained to look into the distance. There seemed to be a light on the final set of steps. Yes, beyond the Hall of Shakyamuni, which was shrouded in darkness, there was a light. Considerably cheered up by this, Liu quickened her step. She could just about make out the shadow of the stone lions, poised to leap up as though itching to greet an old friend.

She relaxed a little; everything was familiar. She had been here before. Perhaps here the stains of worldly sins could be wiped clean. The black clouds sunk behind the trees and the rain gradually began to abate, its clatter giving way to the whistling of wind in the leaves above, like the sound of sutra-streamers fluttering in the breeze.

Her eyes fixed on the light behind the hall. She

walked round the Buddha's Lotus Throne and out through the back door. The light was coming from a house at the back of the complex. She could hardly believe what she was seeing; she had scarcely dared hope that he would be up the mountain in the dead of night.

But then again, why should she be surprised? The very reason she had climbed the mountain was because there was nowhere else in Liang she could have gone. And Yueming would of course have known that, so where else would he be waiting for her? She was almost certain the light was coming from his studio. And why use such a bright light? Perhaps to guide her...

She tiptoed towards the door not wanting to disturb the person working inside. She looked through the window and saw Yueming at work, paintbrush in hand. He must have been there some time: there were several dozen pictures spread out on the table and the floor. She wondered why he had been so keen to get so many done that night in particular.

The door hadn't been shut properly; a crack of light was streaming out.

She looked down at her shoes: sodden and covered in grass, but not as muddy as she had been expecting. Nevertheless, she thought it best to take them off before going in.

The door creaked as she slowly pushed it open. Yueming raised his head and looked at her, smiling without the faintest trace of surprise. Then, as though seeing her in his studio in the middle of the night was the most normal thing in the world, he said: 'So, you're here then.' She nodded.

'You're drenched,' he said, with a tone of genuine concern. 'You got caught in the rain. Hold on a minute.' He walked into the small adjoining room and came out with a dry towel, a pair of straw sandals and a monk's Kasaya robe. 'I don't know whose it is, but it's clean. I'm sorry, you'll just have to make do for the time being.' Liu took the clothes and Yueming went out to give her time to dry and change in private.

The sight of Liu in the monk's robe made Yueming chuckle happily. He hadn't seen her since their confinement, and although that had only been the afternoon of the previous day, it seemed as though an age had passed: so much had happened.

Liu laughed along with him. 'Funny, is it?' she said as she dried her hair with the towel.

'Suits you,' he replied, sitting back down at his work table.

The paintings strewn across the floor and table attracted Liu's attention. They were still rocks and waterfalls, the unchanging mountains and water, water and mountains, but they looked strange on the rice paper: misshapen, distorted beyond recognition, covered in bold splashes of highly concentrated black ink, not the same as the two destined for the bin which had caught her eye before. This time Yueming couldn't possibly claim that they were all just 'mistakes'; there were too many of them. The calligraphy was free and unrestrained, disregarding the fetters of orthodoxy. The texture of the cliffs seemed to flow directly onto the paper as though bursting forth from the primeval chaos of the cosmos. The coloured dots, intended to portray

319

green leaves and red fruit, looked more like magma streaming out of a fracture in the cliff-face, radiating brilliant light in all directions and gradually revealing dizzying depths of remoteness. The paintings showed a symphony of wind and cloud the like of which only the most beautiful peaks could boast.

Liu couldn't take her eyes off the paintings; it was all she could do not to shout out in joyful surprise, not to explode with feelings of deep admiration. 'When the Three Gorges have disappeared,' she pondered, 'the only comfort will be to know that there are paintings like this; a true record of their magnificence.'

But Yueming, his head dripping with sweat, continued to wield his brush, an expression of great anxiety on his face. Watching the vivacious watery strokes of the artist's dancing hand made Liu feel thirsty, so she took the hot water flask on the table and poured herself a glass of water. She wanted to pour out another glass for Yueming but all the other glasses contained inky water, so she decided to give him the glass she had poured out for herself, saying:

'Why don't you have a rest?'

Yueming turned his head and said apologetically, 'I am sorry, what am I thinking? I am not a good host. Please, do sit down.' He grabbed the only other chair in the room and dragged it over.

'What's on your mind?' asked Liu curiously.

He explained that his mother had come to see him earlier that evening. She had been quite upset: she had chastised him for wasting time fighting battles for school children who were nothing to do with him. The hospital had just told her they were going to operate on his stepfather the following day, which had taken her completely off-guard: obviously they were expecting the money straight away. Where on earth could they find so much so fast? He had to find 3,000 yuan before nine in the morning. Auntie Chen would run around and see if she couldn't borrow the rest.

Liu breathed a sigh of relief. Just as she had requested, the doctor had made no mention of money, though she had never imagined that the secrecy would end up sending the whole family into a panic. While she had been at that banquet at the hotel, the Chens had been running around frantically trying to borrow a few jiao here and earn a few yuan there in the vain hope that they might somehow manage to lay their hands on 4,000 yuan. The swallow's nest, the shark's fin soup and that absurdly expensive foreign alcohol, the Louis XIII Cognac…the money spent on the food and drink on one table alone would have been several times the sum that Auntie Chen had been struggling so hard to muster.

But she couldn't tell them the truth, particularly not Yueming, so all she said was: 'So have you worked out what you're going to do?'

'I had a word with the boss of the gift shop. He said that since all the old ones had been sold he could give me one thousand, and if I give him the fifty paintings I promised him, he'll give me a pre-payment of another thousand. He also said that if he's satisfied with the quality he might be willing to lend me a bit, in which case I'll have enough. The problem is I just do not think I can finish in time.' He pointed to the pictures strewn across the floor, an expression of embarrassment on his face: 'I've never been so careless in my work; it's a race against time.'

Liu stood up and walked around barefoot looking at the paintings, careful not to tread on any. She really did love them – she loved their vivacity, their individuality – but it seemed that Yueming genuinely had no idea how brilliant they really were; his genius had only emerged because of the extreme pressure he had been put under by his family's plight. On reflection it made sense: his conscious mind showed no signs of recklessness. On the contrary, he was by nature very meticulous. Perhaps he really was the reincarnation of the brave prostitute Red Lotus that Auntie Chen had talked about. Perhaps a part of her was still active in some shadowy region of his brain, guiding his hand in his hour of need.

'I don't know why you are worrying so much – whatever they say, if they have decided to operate, then operate they will, come what may. It's unlikely they'll be expecting to be paid straight away.' she said, as casually as she could.

Yueming said that that was exactly what he had said to his mother: doctors must have some kind of professional ethics – they are not going to cut someone open and then sew them up again without doing anything first – but his mother had told him he was an idiot who had no idea of the harsh realities of today's society.

How could Liu hint to Yueming that he really need not worry? She could not bear to see him in such a mad rush unnecessarily, even if it did mean that he was painting better than ever. After a good deal of thought she said: 'You know... I'm afraid that you might be hurrying in vain – the pictures will still have to be left to dry and to be mounted, which is going to take a few days...'

Yueming explained that that didn't matter; the manager of the gift shop was only concerned about whether or not the paintings themselves were finished. He had agreed to give Yueming the money as soon as he saw that he had done them all – mounted or not. Yueming looked down at the pictures and wrinkled his brow. He said he was worried about the quality – each painting was more disfigured than the last. If this tendency continued until morning, he was afraid that the manager would be unlikely to accept them, let alone lend him any money. The shop's business was not very good and the customers knew the difference between a good painting and a bad one.

'Then what is the point in going on like this?' She looked at her wristwatch. 'It's morning already and you must have more than fifty here.'

'They're not all up to standard.' He wiped his hands with a small towel, had a drink of water and looked around at the chaos of his room. He lowered his head in embarrassment and reverted to how he had been the first time they had a met: a humble village school teacher.

Chapter Thirty

This time Liu was determined not to leave it at that. She wanted to know once and for all what kind of person this man really was. There was no doubt that he was kind-hearted. What she now wanted to know was whether, deep down, he was just another ordinary person or whether, as a part of her secretly hoped, he was someone of courage, vision and perhaps even wisdom.

She was debating whether or not to ask him whether he had any idea what had happened on the day he was born. Auntie Chen had told her that he had never been told about it for fear that it might all be too much for him. But Yueming didn't strike Liu as being the sort of man who would be unable to face realities.

But she also had a feeling that Yueming was not the sort of person who needed to be told things; perhaps she was best off not telling him things he probably knew already.

'Do you regret joining in the protest?' she asked bluntly.

Yueming scratched his head and replied: 'I felt that the attempt to hand in a petition was turned into a weapon to be used by the cadres in their internal squabbles. Nevertheless, I still believe that I did my duty that day. I shall never regret what I did.'

Liu continued to question him. This time she was even more direct: 'I mean, do you think the Three Gorges Dam should be built?'

'The pros and cons of something before it's been started are likely to be very different from the pros and cons of the same thing after it's been finished. And after a hundred years, or even a thousand years, the pros and cons are going to be more different still.'

Liu's eyes lit up. Here was the answer to a problem which had always confused her, and which was relevant to the ethical debate about her own line of work. It was the first time anyone had given her such a simple, practical reply. Yueming was not sitting on the fence, he was not avoiding thorny issues; he was willing to get straight to the heart of the matter.

'So what you're saying,' she began, picking her words carefully in the hope that she might say something suitably succinct so as not to jar with Yueming's clarity of expression, 'is that when a problem needs to be dealt with urgently, then a quick-fix policy, which seeks the greatest possible immediate gain, is justifiable, but that as soon as the problem ceases to be such a pressing one, then the pros and cons of the issue should be examined in a wider context?'

'How can I keep up with such educated talk? You

come from Beijing, you're a scientist, you have read more. You are much wiser.'

She chuckled at the irony of his words: if the events of the last couple of days had proved anything, they'd proved that she wasn't in the least bit wise.

'How do you view the resettlement programme – is it right or is it wrong?' She didn't want to miss the opportunity to ask the most difficult question.

'Every human being is to be respected,' he said.

He then explained that the primary school he worked at was going to be pulled down. This meant that he was going to lose his teaching job which was his only means of earning a living. He said he was not really an artist; he was just knocking out a few simple landscapes to pay for his stepfather's operation. He could not hope to rely on this as a means to support himself for the rest of his life. He was going to move to the resettlement area on the Tibetan plateau where the Yangtze's source is. Maybe he could find a primary school there that would employ him.

Liu was shocked. She had never heard him mention this plan before. Despite being an outsider she could still appreciate what it meant to leave one's home. 'Does your mother know about this plan?' she asked.

Yueming's face darkened. 'My mother is not at all happy about it, but people have to work, I'm no use as a son without a job. My education is not good enough to find work in the New City.'

Liu shook her head. She wanted to persuade Yueming to stay. She wanted to tell him that he was an artistic genius and that, in time, people would recognise him as such. But she thought better of it;

though he might consider himself talentless, he certainly did not consider himself in need of other people's opinions.

'My mother always says I'm not like a real son,' he smiled wryly, 'but maybe no one is ever anyone's *real* son.'

'My mother is the same – always complaining that I'm not like a real daughter,' chimed in Liu. But it was true, Liu had never been much of daughter. She'd certainly never spent half the night frantically painting landscapes for her mother. The first time she went abroad she hadn't felt any sadness at the prospect of being separated from her, and when she had wanted to see her only daughter off at the airport, Liu had told her there was 'no need', at which she had burst into tears and said: 'You're no daughter of mine!'

'Diegu is adopted, but she's much closer to my mother than I am. There is more to life than worrying about parents.'

Yueming's words sent a chill down Liu's spine. The confused sense of gratitude and resentment which she felt towards her parents had been troubling her ever since she'd arrived Liang, perhaps even before that. She felt that in some way it was binding her to the past.

Yueming put down his glass and began sorting out his paintings. It soon became clear to Liu that he was putting the most 'normal' pictures on the top of the pile while the ones which Liu thought the best were put to one side. He looked at a couple and, after pondering for a few seconds, he crumpled them up and threw them into the corner.

She wanted to tell him not to. But of course she

couldn't: what would be the point in telling him that he had so misjudged his own work? This, after all, was a man who had denied that he was an artist at all.

When he had finished he suggested that they walk down the mountain. He turned the lights off and they walked out of the door, back into the darkness of the night. Even the moon was now hidden.

The mountain path was difficult enough at the best of times but in the pitch black, after all that rain, it was treacherous; the slightest carelessness and you would slide down the hillside. The man who had entered the world at almost exactly the same time as her stretched out his hand to offer her support, just as he had when she had not wanted to jump out of the prison van. Looking at her, he bent over slightly, and she took hold of his hand. It was all so natural, no words were needed, and thus they made their way hand in hand down the mountain. It was not long before Liu had completely lost track of where they were, but it didn't matter, she felt perfectly safe with Yueming as her guide. She was even still wearing the Kasaya robe.

She lost concentration for a second and almost slipped over, but Yueming held her hand tightly enough to keep her on her feet. She raised her head and caught a glimpse of the Generals Blower and Snorter; without the moonlight or the lightening their eyes were dark and lifeless and they looked every bit as ridiculous as they had by day.

'Here is the 175m mark,' said Yueming.

'Let's stay here a while and have a look,' suggested Liu.

They sat down on the stone steps leading up to the Hall of King Yama, near the cliff edge. They were almost directly under his nose, eyed by his two devilish guards as they gazed eastward towards the city.

At that moment Liu heard something above her in the sky. The sound grew louder and louder. After a couple of seconds she realized it was a helicopter approaching at alarming speed. Suddenly a bright searchlight emerged from between the clouds and shone down onto the mountain slope. Then she saw a group of police carrying automatic rifles running up the mountain path: the search-light appeared to be guiding them.

Suddenly she recalled what Li had said about Yueming being the leader of a reactionary organisation. She hadn't thought anything of it at the time, she'd just put it down to the ravings of a jealous husband. She hadn't even mentioned it to Yueming; it would have been too embarrassing.

Now she realized how naïve she had been: these people really were capable of doing something like this. They would do anything to 'solve' the problem of the controversy over the Resettlement Fund. Li had probably ordered the whole thing in order to gain the support of the local government and, as luck would have it, turn in a personal enemy while making it look as though he were sacrificing personal interest for the sake of the greater good.

'They've come to get us,' she said calmly, but Yueming didn't seem to hear.

She turned to face him. There wasn't a trace of fear on his face, nor indeed any thought of escape. The police had almost reached them, but they ran straight past the Temple, without looking east to the slope where they were sitting.

Liu knew they would turn back from the peak and find them sooner or later, but Yueming still sat there gazing silently in front of him. Indeed, there was no point in trying to run away into the mountains; it would only have added to the humiliation.Suddenly she had a strong urge to tell him that, when coming uphill, she'd been missing him so much. She looked at him and he looked back, and finally she only gave him a smile.

A streak of pale light appeared on the horizon but the dawn offered no spectacle of bright fiery clouds. The pale dawn light slowly enfolded the whole city and beams of light began to creep up the stone steps, gingerly washing up towards their feet.

Liu knew that she would be just as vulnerable as Yueming now; without her title of 'Madam Director' there would be no obsequiously apologetic gang of cadres to rescue her this time. But, nevertheless, she began to feel a strange sense of calm; she and Yueming had, after all, died together once before.

Suddenly she asked Yueming, 'Tell me, what will this area be like in two thousand years?' She was hoping to catch him off guard.

'In two thousand years?' he replied, seemingly surprised by her question. 'Oh, you're referring to what I said back in my studio? I didn't mean anything by it. I was just thinking of that beautiful gold peacock lampholder which I was so fortunate to see. Two thousand years old and so exquisite – and to think that it was made for a practical purpose as well!'

'You mean,' began Liu, seeking deeper significance

in Yueming's straightforward response, 'You mean that we will be peacocks in two thousand years?'

'If we're lucky,' said Yueming with a smile; it was almost as though he could actually see that far-off day.

Now she could imagine what she had always believed to be impossible. Someone else's memories had become her life. Yes, she was now certain beyond all doubt: it was not fate, but something infinitely compassionate, something which transcended all suffering, that had brought them together. And thus all the humiliation and all the misery had been little more than a springboard for their rebirth.

They sat watching the early morning mist rising in front of them, drowning the city and the Gorges below. She heard the sound of policemen's footsteps gradually grow nearer while the helicopter seemed to be rising higher with its searchlight shining down on the mountain peak – on Yueming's studio. But she didn't turn her head for a better look. She knew what was going on.

The faint memories of events so many decades in the past were clear to her now. She leant her head gently on Yueming's shoulder and closed her eyes, at peace.

Afterword

Puji Bridge is at the eastern end of Puji Lane, and east of the bridge is Liu Cui Well, a place which used to be called Sword-Holding Camp. It is said that during the reign of Shaoxing (1131-162 AD), a certain Liu Xuanjiao came to the area to take up the office of prefect. On the day of the inauguration ceremony, the monk Yutong of the Water Moon Temple did not attend. Xuanjiao was displeased and dispatched the prostitute Red-Lotus Wu to trick him. She went to the Temple and asked if she could stay the night, her intention being to seduce him. Yutong had been a Buddhist monk for 52 years and was solemn in his adherence to monastic discipline. At first he adamantly refused her, but by midnight he could control himself no longer and he fornicated with her. When, after making enquiries, he found out that he had been tricked by the prefect, he committed suicide because he could not bear the shame. Just before he did so he said resentfully: 'I will without fail destroy your family's reputation!' Shortly afterwards Xuanjiao died while his wife was pregnant. The evening she gave birth she dreamt of a monk coming into the house and saying: 'I am Yutong.' They called the baby girl Liu Ciu.

Thenceforth the family's fortunes waned and they moved to the place known as Sword-Holding Camp. Liu grew up to be the most beautiful woman and best singer in the city, though penury forced her become a courtesan. Nevertheless, she was a devout Buddhist and never hesitated in giving alms; she even funded the construction of the bridge below the Peak of the Myriad Pines, and of the well in the camp, both of which were named after her. After a few years the monk Qingliao of Xianxiao Temple on Mount Gaoting said to the monk Ruhui of Jingci Temple: 'Old Yutong has fallen too low for too long, you should guide him back to leading a pure life!' Thereupon Ruhui went to Liu on the pretext of begging for alms, in order to tell her about the workings of the Law of Karma. Thinking of becoming a nun, Ruhui took her to see Qingliao who talked to her about the profound truths of Buddhist doctrine. In the end he asked her sternly: 'You have been lost in the miasma of an easy woman's life. Are you still down there?' The words caused a great awakening in Liu. She went back, washed off her rouge, sent all her patrons home, had a bath and entered into a nirvana.

She was buried on Mount Gaoting and thus her purification was completed.

From Tian Rucheng's
Tour Notes of the West Lake, ca. 1358